THE
FAMILY
ON
SMITH
STREET

BOOKS BY ELISABETH CARPENTER

99 Red Balloons

11 Missed Calls

Only a Mother

The Woman Downstairs

The Vacancy

THE
FAMILY
ON
SMITH
STREET

ELISABETH CARPENTER

bookouture

Published by Bookouture in 2023

An imprint of Storyfire Ltd.
Carmelite House
50 Victoria Embankment
London EC4Y 0DZ

www.bookouture.com

ISBN: 978-1-83790-580-5
eBook ISBN: 978-1-83790-579-9

For Dom

CHAPTER 1

JOANNA

I was with Amy tonight. Someone's leaving do. Amy wanted a kebab even though it was only ten o'clock. We went straight from the office – that new bar in town that's been kitted out like a ski lodge, serves lager in massive steins.

Or is that over the top – too many specifics?

God, it's freezing. The alcohol's long since finished its loan of a beer jacket, and of course I came out without gloves.

This street's deserted, but houses have lights on, curtains closed. There's a black cat staring at me from its perilous position on a first-floor window ledge.

I take out my mobile and scroll to James's number, get my key out, slip it between my fingers – a weapon of sorts. I should've got a taxi. Years ago, I'd have thought nothing of walking home from town.

James isn't answering.

He'll be able to tell that I lied about where I was tonight, won't he? I'll pretend to be drunker than I am so nothing I say will make sense.

Five minutes from home.

Amy wanted a kebab... straight from the office... that new ski lodge that serves lager in massive steins.

A car appears on the road next to me, matching my walking speed. It must be electric – such a safety hazard – it came out of nowhere. I pick up speed, hold my phone to my ear.

'I'm nearly home,' I say loudly to nobody because James's phone is still ringing out.

'Excuse me, love.' A man's voice from the car, but I don't look, don't engage. 'Can you tell me where Watling Street is?'

I walk with purpose to push open a gate to a house that isn't mine. My skin is prickling. It'll be nothing – just a bloke who's lost.

The car speeds to the end of the road and turns left.

Shit. That's my way home. I dial James's number again. Straight to voicemail. Typical.

I look up at the house I've wandered into, checking they haven't spotted me loitering, before walking out the gate, looking left and right.

I pull my scarf to my chin. Frost is starting to appear on low garden walls, glistening, sparkling. I turn onto our street; some houses still have their Christmas lights around their windows – it used to make me feel cosy.

A car door opens behind me. I don't turn round in time before he puts a handkerchief over my mouth.

Chemical smell.

I'm falling into...

Darkness.

CHAPTER 2
SCARLETT

I've woken up before my alarm for once, and before Mum has the chance to shout me awake. Not calmly and melodically like she used to: 'Wakey, wakey, Lettie Lou. It's time to start the day.'

Yeah, I know. Pretty cringey, but I loved it as a kid.

I check my phone – always the first thing to do, even before I'm fully awake. The glow from it acts as my sunlight – it's a brain thing, something to do with endorphins or melatonin.

Already there's a WhatsApp from Hannah: two photos of her in front of the mirror with the message:

> The blue crop top with trackies or the skull t-shirt and high-waist jeans?

She looks pretty much the same in both and she must've been up since four a.m. doing that make-up. I can never be arsed with all that. I tap out a reply – *the t-shirt and jeans* – because she'd have a meltdown if I said *whatever*.

This isn't a daily occurrence – I'm not some control freak who demands to know what my best friend wears every day. It's because it's the New Year (she always makes unrealistic resolutions) and she's heard that Jamie on her street is starting at our college today. As if he's going to care if she's showing bare midriff – about fifty per cent of the girls in my classes have their torsos on show. And lads, as a rule, don't really notice Hannah and me. We blend into the background. Nothing to see here. Which is a bit shit, but I'm used to it. I've been invisible since high school. Mum says boys aren't worth it, but I haven't had the chance to find out for myself. And it's not as though I'm an academic to make up for it, either.

I slide off my bed because I have *the apathy*, as Mum calls it. Can't be bothered with anything, she reckons, but she's only partly right.

I head for the shower and for once the bathroom's empty. Dad usually takes bloody forever in the mornings, and he leaves a trail of steam and David Beckham aftershave or whatever that stench is. But this morning there's not even a trace of moisture on the mirror, no drips in the sink or shower. But the toilet seat is up. It's always down because no one wants to deal with the passive aggressive wrath of Mother.

I flick on the shower and give myself a quick wash, but I haven't the time for the hassle that is washing my hair. I steal some of Mum's dry shampoo instead – she won't notice, she hardly ever uses it. She washes and straightens her hair every day. Ugh God, this spray's suffocating, but voilà. Hair is good as new. Jeans and an oversized stripey jumper today because it's freezing.

I head onto the landing to listen for signs of life downstairs.

Silence.

No roar from the kettle or murmurs of breakfast TV.

What the hell time is it?

I fetch my phone: seven thirty-five. Mum normally sets off at ten to eight and Dad not much later. By this time, they're normally chatting about what to have for dinner as they're eating breakfast.

I go down. In the kitchen, there's only an empty whisky glass in the sink from Dad's nightcap last night. I grab a cereal bar from the biscuit cupboard. I'm absolutely starving because Mum wasn't here for tea, and I couldn't be bothered cooking for myself. I wander into the living room to grab my bag for college, and the curtains are still shut. Are my parents even awake yet? I tug them open, turn round.

What the hell?

Dad's slumped at the table in the dining room (which is actually joined to the living room). He's still in yesterday's clothes.

I step closer. His head's resting on his arms, facing away from me as though he's looking through the window to the wilderness that is our back garden.

'Dad?' I whisper, but seriously, he should be awake – he's meant to be at work in thirty minutes.

He doesn't move.

I walk around the table. His eyes are closed.

Shit, is he breathing? I can't tell from here.

My heart starts racing. I've never seen a dead body before, and I don't want the first one to be my dad.

'Dad?' My voice cuts into the silence. 'Dad?'

His shoulders rise as he takes in a deep breath. Thank God.

I can't believe Mum has gone to work and left him asleep at the table. I didn't hear them arguing last night, but once I'm asleep there's no waking me. A bit like Dad, actually. And to be honest, he's been acting a bit weird lately. I've seen him smoking at the bottom of the garden where he thinks no one can see him.

'Dad.' I say it louder this time.

I reach over to shake his shoulder, and he opens his eyes.

It's like he doesn't recognise me at first. He blinks a few times before lifting his head.

'Scarlett?' He looks down at his clothes. 'What time is it? Is your mum back yet?'

'What? Back from where?'

'She went to the pub with Amy, remember?'

'Course I remember. But, Dad, that was last night. Didn't she come home?'

He rubs his eyes. 'I guess not, no.'

What the fuck, Dad?

I didn't say that out loud.

I get my phone out to call Mum. As I listen to its rings, I head to the living room window, looking out to see if there's any sign of her. Maybe she's fallen asleep on the doorstep, because you hear about things like that, don't you? OK – maybe not a forty-something woman who barely drinks.

'She's not answering,' I say, walking back to Dad. 'Has she texted you? Called you?'

He runs a hand through his hair, messing it up, as he scrolls through his phone.

'A few missed calls.'

'Can I have a look?' I hold out my hand for him to pass it over, but he gets up.

'For God's sake, Scarlett. I know how to work my bloody mobile.' He goes through the hallway and into the kitchen. 'I'm going to ring Amy.'

He means that I'm not to follow him and listen in because he thinks I'm still a kid. But he's talking so loudly I can hear him from here.

'Did Joanna come back with you?' he says. 'Yes, sorry. Good morning. Sorry, it's just that Jo didn't come home last night.'

I'm suddenly aware that I'm pacing the hall and Dad's standing in the kitchen doorway.

'Why aren't you more worried?' I say after he ends the call. 'Wouldn't you care if *I* didn't come home, either?'

'Don't be ridiculous, Scarlett.'

'What did Amy say?' I follow him back into the living room. 'Mum didn't stay there, did she?'

'What have I told you about eavesdropping?'

I bet he was drunk last night and that's why he didn't notice about Mum, and that's why he's in such a pissy mood. I wish he was more like Hannah's dad. He actually cares about her, and he doesn't stay up till two a.m. drinking whisky. He'd have phoned the police by now – he'd have noticed as soon as Hannah's mum didn't come home. Well, he would've done if they were still together – other parents' relationships are an enigma.

'Good morning.' Dad's talking into his phone again, and I plonk myself on the settee, even though he's just told me off for listening in. This is hardly an average situation.

Oh God. What if Mum's lying dead somewhere? I bring up Twitter on my phone – I never post on there, but it's useful to find out the news from old people with nothing better to do. I type *body, woman,* and *Preston* into the search bar, but the results are from years ago.

'Has Joanna arrived at work yet?' says Dad. 'Oh right. OK. Yeah, thanks.'

He clings on to the phone after he ends the call, and stands in the middle of the room.

'Well?' I say.

'Work haven't heard from her.'

'Call the police, Dad,' I say, standing next to him. 'If you don't then I will.'

'It's not as simple as that,' he says, not looking at me.

'Course it's simple. Mum didn't come home. What aren't you telling me?'

He throws his phone onto the settee.

'Just trust me on this one, Scarlett. Please.'

'But Dad.' I follow him back into the kitchen. He grabs a tiny cup from the cupboard and places a pod into the coffee machine. Once it's finished, Dad downs the espresso like a shot of tequila.

He grabs the edges of the kitchen counter, and looks out into the garden.

'Thing is, Scarlett,' he says, 'I think your mum is seeing someone else.'

CHAPTER 3

1985

My full name is Alexander Charles Buchanan. I'm the only ten-year-old I know called Alexander. Other people called that are grandads. Every other boy in my class is called Mark, John, or Andrew, like Jesus' disciples.

'Can someone tell me what the capital of Australia is?' Mrs Summers calls out.

Most of the other kids are slumped in their chairs because it's half an hour till home time. Mark Number Three is asleep with his head on the desk and he's drooling all over it.

One of the other Marks puts his hand up. He answers everything even when he doesn't know the answer.

'Sydney,' he says, smirking.

See?

'Alexander?' Mrs Summers holds the chalk close to the blackboard. 'I've heard you're a whizz at capital cities.'

Who the heck told her that?

My face burns as everyone turns round and looks at me – everyone who's awake at least. Why is she embarrassing me? It's probably Mum's fault – she was telling Miss Summers all sorts at parents' evening last week. Mum only knows about the capital cities because *Coronation Street* had finished and she realised I was still downstairs on Dad's Atari. I have the earliest bedtime out of everyone in my class and it's humiliating.

'What are you doing?' Mum had said. I'd heard her coming from the ice jangling in her glass like the playtime bell. She was talking in that slow way she does when she's drunk. 'You should be upstairs.'

'I programmed it in,' I said. 'It's a capital cities quiz game.'

Austria. I tapped the keys. *Vienna.*

'See?' I smiled up at her.

'Hmm.' Jingle jangle as she put the glass to her mouth. 'Bedtime, Alex. Your dad will be home soon.'

That was a lie because he's never home until after two o'clock in the morning. Mum knows that too because she never cooks us all tea any more. She doesn't laugh any more either, and her eyes don't twinkle like they used to. It's like she's a zombie.

'Alex?' Mrs Summers says again. 'Capital of Australia?'

I shrug. If I wasn't sitting at the back I'd mumble the answer, get it over and done with. Mrs Summers knows what I'm like. *Too shy*, she wrote in my latest report, even though she spends most of her energy shouting at the kids who talk *too* much in class.

'It's Canberra, Miss,' says Carrie.

Carrie's sitting at the front. She turns to look at me, and smiles a small smile as though we share a secret. She doesn't usually speak to me. No one does, really.

'Thank you, Carrie,' says Mrs Summers, looking at me.

I don't know why she hates me so much.

I'm never any trouble to her.

Life's easier when you keep quiet.

* * *

I wait on the wall outside school for thirty-five minutes before I start walking home. It's the third time in two weeks that Mum's forgotten the time or whatever her excuse is going to be today. Maybe she's fallen down the stairs or tripped over on the pavement.

But she's probably asleep on the settee.

One day I'll be kidnapped and then she'll be sorry. Maybe someone nice will be the kidnapper. Maybe they've always wanted a child of their own to look after.

I wish I'd brought my Walkman. I hate thinking about stuff.

When I get home it's nearly dark. The back door is wide open.

Crap. Have we been burgled?

Three cups and two plates are smashed into pieces on the kitchen floor.

'Mum?'

I stand still. There's no answer back.

The phone is two rooms away. I think about knocking on the neighbour's door, but their lights aren't on.

'Mum?'

Alert intruders of your presence.

They said that on *Crimewatch* the other week.

They were telling it to grown-ups, though – not puny ten-year-olds like me.

I tiptoe through the kitchen and into the hall. I picture a robber standing over my mother after tying her up. At least she'd have a good enough excuse for not picking me up from school.

I bang the living-room door open against the wall, hoping the noise will scare any burglars.

But there aren't any.

Mum's sitting in her underwear on the living room carpet, next to the telly, flipping through photo albums from when she was a teenager working as a Redcoat at Butlins. She's always looking at them.

'What are you doing, Mum?' I say, even though it's obvious what she's doing. There's a glass and a bottle of vodka next to her that's only a quarter full. 'Mum?'

I step on a pile of photos, inches from her legs.

'Hello, Alex.' She looks up slowly. 'How come you're home so early?'

'I'm not. It's nearly dark. You left me to walk home from school and it's over two miles.'

'Sorry, love.' She puts the glass to her mouth and gulps that alcoholic rubbish down. 'Time just slipped away from me.'

I grab the bottle, and she doesn't even notice. She probably doesn't realise that she hasn't any clothes on either. I stomp my way to the kitchen, uncap it and go to pour it down the sink.

'Alex.' Dad's standing at the back door. He's early for a change. He looks at the vodka bottle. 'What are you doing with that?'

He tuts and heads towards the living room.

'For fuck's sake, Gilly,' he shouts. 'Get some fucking clothes on.'

I put down the bottle and creep into the hall so I can peek through the gap in the living room door.

Dad takes off his coat and throws it on the floor next to her.

'Put it on. What if I'd come home with a colleague, eh? What if they'd seen you like this?'

Mum stands and puts on the jacket, fumbling over the zip. She gives up trying.

'So fucking what,' she says, raising her hand and pointing at him. 'What are *you* going to do about it?'

'Just go and lie down, Gillian.'

He goes to walk away but she grabs his arm.

'I'm only twenty-eight,' she says. 'I deserve a better life than being stuck in this shithole.'

'You know where the door is,' he says, closing the photo albums and putting them back in the sideboard.

'You screw everything that moves,' says Mum, swaying in the middle of the room, looking stupid in Dad's coat. 'Don't think I haven't noticed.'

'Do you fucking blame me?' Dad says, but he's gone out of view. 'Look at you.'

'Look at *you*, more like,' says Mum. 'You've barely got any hair left. And look at that belly. They only sleep with you because you've got a bit of money.'

The sound of his slap across her face shocks them both into silence.

I can see my heart beating under my school shirt.

Mum's face changes: her eyes widen before she screams and pounces on him, clawing at his hair.

I run up the stairs, lock my bedroom door, and lie on the floor.

Smashed ornaments; shouting; screeching.

How is it going to end this time?

With any luck, one of them will leave for good.

Then I'll finally get some peace.

CHAPTER 4

JOANNA

My arms feel numb, and it takes a moment for me to realise it's because they're tied behind my back and I'm lying on them. There's tape across my mouth, forcing me to breathe through my nose.

What's the last thing I remember? Come on, what is it? Accessing memories is like pushing my way through brambles.

I went with Amy for a drink. Straight from the office.

No, no. I told James I was going out with Amy.

I was meant to be meeting someone called Holly. She said she had something important to talk about, but she didn't turn up. I sat in the bar for over an hour waiting.

Where the hell am I?

It's freezing in here.

I'm lying on something soft, and I glance to my side.

A mattress, though not bare. The sheet is terry cotton with tiny rainbows. A child's sheet.

Oh God. My daughter. My baby who's not a baby any more. Seventeen, still a child but not in her own eyes. Sometimes I think I don't know her these days.

I close my eyes and she's shouting for me.

I picture her lost in the darkness.

'Mummy, where are you? I'm scared.'

And then I realise it's not Scarlett who I'm seeing, it's me and I'm calling for *my* mother, but she's not here to save me. I imagine her face when she hears that I'm dead – gone before her, a child before its mother – because I am going to die down here, wherever I am, I know it. She'll be devastated. I'm her only child. It was just her and me for years after my dad left. And now it'll be just James and Scarlett. History repeating itself.

The rambling in my mind stops.

James.

He'll be looking for me – he'll have called the police hours ago after realising I hadn't come home.

There's a tiny window opposite, high on the front wall, but there's no light behind it. I could be in a basement; it could be daylight, but the entrance is in the shade.

I'm thinking too fast about things that aren't going to help me right now.

I wiggle my feet and there's a familiar jangle: a belt buckle. If it's leather, I could prise my ankles apart, gradually loosen the strap. I stretch my feet apart, but I manage only a few seconds. I've no strength at all.

There are footsteps above.

Thuds, heavy boots.

They step down a staircase.

Oh God. This is it, isn't it?

I close my eyes again and remember holding Scarlett; James's arm is around us both. It's Christmastime – Scarlett's favourite time of year, as it always is with kids. We're watching *Miracle on 34th Street* and I wish that miracles were real so I could get up right now and run all the way home.

CHAPTER 5
SCARLETT

I'm on the bus because Dad said I still had to go to college today, even though he's skipping work to try to track Mum down. How the hell am I supposed to concentrate in class if I don't know where she is? There is no way on Earth she would be seeing someone else. The idea of it is ridiculous and I don't know why Dad's putting it into my head. If anyone was cheating, it'd be him. Mum's always here. Apart from last night, she always makes me tea, or we cook together. She's usually in bed by nine with a book, and I go to sleep well after she does. *And* she's always leaving her phone around – she doesn't even use it as an alarm clock. Cheaters are always defensive and protective over their phones, aren't they?

I'm not saying I hate Dad or anything – or that he's a horrible person – it's just that I've always been closer to Mum because Dad's always working, even when he's in the house. The only time we really talk is if we're in the car together, or on Christmas Day when we're sitting around the table together for once. Or now, when my mother has gone missing.

I haven't messaged Hannah to tell her yet. It's not something you write in a text. Not without it seeming like a joke.

Though, Hannah always writes dramatic things in a message. One time, after she sent me *'I can't do it any more. I'm done with life. Thanks for being my best friend. I love you'*, I had to ring her dad to check she hadn't harmed herself. She was really embarrassed when she came into school the morning after, and wouldn't talk to me until lunchtime, when she finally realised that it wasn't my fault for taking her words seriously. But that was three years ago and she's a tiny bit more sensible now. A tiny bit.

My phone beeps with a WhatsApp, and I dig into my bag. I shouldn't have put it in here – I should've kept it in my hand and now I can't find it. I feel something soft inside, something that isn't usually there. It's a yellow glove, one of the pair I bought for Mum last Christmas. I must've put it in here by mistake. I have been known to put my key in the fridge and my coat in the hoover cupboard, so it's not *that* unusual. She'll say I took them on purpose and now she has freezing cold hands and it'll be my fault if she dies of hypothermia.

I look round the bus before sneakily smelling the glove. Chanel N°5, definitely. Mum has worn it forever, even though it costs a fortune, because her grandmother once said that she shouldn't save precious things for best because you never know how much time you've got left.

Tears come to my eyes. My lovely mum who's so cheerful, so lovely to everyone, even me when I'm being a bitch. There's a phrase about only the good dying young, and I don't want that to happen to her.

My imagination is giving me the most horrendous scenarios and for once I wish that it was something like Mum cheating on Dad. It would mean she's still OK.

We pull into the bus station and already the bus gangway has filled up. Why are they so keen to get to college – it's not as though we're late.

'All right, Scarlett?'

I know the voice before I turn round. It's that bitch Tilly. Yeah, her name doesn't scream bitch, but that's the only thing about her that doesn't. All through high school she used to pick on me because of my red hair. I'd hoped last year, when we first started at Jameson College, that she'd have matured a little, but she hasn't. Hides it well, though. Pretends to be grown-up around her new mates.

I'm glad I put my earpods in – even without anything playing they're a good excuse to ignore people.

'Hey, Scarlett!' She's right next to me now, bending over with her big round face in mine. Her huge face doesn't match the rest of her because she's actually quite slim. Not that I'd ever give her a compliment. 'You deaf?' She says that bit quietly because she knows it's unacceptable. 'I saw your mum last night.'

'No, you didn't,' I say, taking out my earphones. 'We watched a film all night.'

'Yeah, right. I saw her in town with another man. Is she cheating on your dad?'

'As if.' I stand up and shuffle towards her, but she doesn't take the hint that she's blocking my way. 'Excuse me.'

'Why are you talking about Scarlett's dad?' says Travis, behind her. He's in my art class and went to a different high school to Tilly and me, and he's all right – not like a lot of the other loser boys from our school. 'Do you fancy him?'

Tilly's face goes bright red, and she rolls her eyes. I'm used to it. Women are always gazing at Dad in the street and he doesn't even notice. Mortifying.

Tilly finally gets moving along so the rest of us can leave. I mouth *thank you* to Travis and he gives me a small nod. This is not what I need this morning. As if she saw my mum with another man. She's a compulsive liar – always has been. Though *I* shouldn't have said we'd been watching a film. What if Tilly's telling the truth and we need her as a witness?

I need to quit overthinking.

I wait for Hannah in our usual meeting place next to the vending machine which serves the most disgusting hot chocolate you've ever tasted. How can they get hot chocolate so wrong?

I see Jamie-from-her-block walking in front of Hannah, and I know it's him because she's pointing at him, and her eyes are popping out of her head.

Yeah, OK, he's OK-looking but he's way out of our league. He's more likely to go for someone like Lucy McAvoy. She has over thirty thousand TikTok followers, long hair with natural highlights, smooth flawless skin, looks great in jeans and a T-shirt. Plus, she's really smart. I mean, come on. Who needs that much luck?

'See you later, Jamie,' says Hannah.

She beams as he turns round to look at her. His face is blank. It seems she knows who he is, and he has no idea who she is. I link her arm as we walk.

'Have you ever spoken to him before, Han?'

I'm almost holding her up – she's wearing open-toe wedges even though it's pissing down with rain.

'About seven years ago,' she says. 'At a garden party.'

'You mean that party on your street we went to when we were ten?'

'Don't spoil it for me, Scar.'

We exit the bus station and walk across the taxi rank, dodging cars as their drivers grumpily pull out.

'Something's happened,' I tell her, looking round, not that it matters if anyone is listening. 'It's about my mum.'

'Don't tell me,' says Hannah. 'She's been captured by those two weirdos who live next door to you.'

She laughs at her own joke. She's talking about our neighbours, the Shepherds. They're not how you imagine shepherds to look. They dress like they're eighty or something, in various shades of beige. They've barely any wrinkles. Mrs Shepherd has only said hello to me once since they moved in next door a few years ago.

'It's not funny.' I withdraw my arm from out of hers and stick my hands in my denim jacket pockets. 'She didn't come home last night.'

'From where?' Hannah sticks her arms out to help her balance on the ridiculous shoes. 'Your mum never goes out.'

'I know. But she went out with her friend Amy, and she didn't come home, and she didn't sleep over.'

Hannah's hand grazes mine. 'She'll be all right, Scar. She'll have just seen someone she knows. Or maybe she left extra early for work, and you and your dad didn't notice.'

'Yeah, maybe.' I glance at my phone that's been in my hand since the bus. 'But she hasn't replied to or read any of my messages.'

'She probably had an early meeting and didn't get a chance to tell you. My mum never tells me anything about her day, but then, I only see her at weekends.'

'Yeah, maybe you're right. She's done that before. But wouldn't Dad have known about that?'

Hannah shrugs. 'How would I know?'

'It was a rhetorical question. I'm thinking out loud.'

My form tutor, Mr Jackson, is standing at the big iron entrance gates, watching everyone walk in under the guise of warding off bad behaviour. He's another one Hannah fancies, but that's because she's never spoken to him. Once, Mum and I saw him in Tesco and he followed us with his eyes all the way round. He probably thought I didn't notice, but I did. Mum didn't, though. The memory makes me shiver.

Hannah notices and gives my arm a rub.

'Don't worry, Scar,' she says. 'Your mum'll turn up. Preston's hardly gangland central, is it?'

'How would *we* know?'

Hannah's attention is shifted as we turn a corner and Jamie is only a few metres in front. Which is convenient, because I don't want to tell her what Dad said about Mum having an affair. Hannah's imagination is worse than mine and, knowing her, she'd conclude that Dad has murdered Mum and buried her in the garden.

But that would never happen. My parents are normal.

Most of the time.

CHAPTER 6

JOANNA

The footsteps earlier lingered at the door, but nobody came inside. Despite my covered mouth, I tried to scream, but whoever was there wasn't my saviour. He or she was probably checking I was still alive. What could they possibly want with me?

It's so quiet here. No traffic, people, or the ambient sound of nature. I don't think I've been here long. I've not eaten or had a drink and I'm not hungry. But I'm so thirsty. Twelve hours, tops.

Has James told Scarlett that I'm gone yet? She worries about me sometimes. She says she's more streetwise than I am and she's probably right these days. Thank God it was me walking alone last night and not Scarlett. I can't imagine the thought of not knowing where she is. But then, I *don't* know where she is right now. Whoever kidnapped me might have gone into the house to get Scarlett. Wrong place, wrong time. It's not as though someone following my routine would have known that I would be out at that time. I'm usually in bed at nine to watch a box set. Boring, Scarlett calls me. 'You're forty-two, not eighty-two,' she says. But work is so hectic, I love my peaceful evenings.

Did. It's a world away now.

I shouldn't have gone out last night. It was pointless anyway. The woman I was meant to meet – Holly she said her name was – never showed up. She could have been making all that stuff up anyway.

The image of Scarlett appears in my mind again. Taller than me, beautiful curly auburn hair, a sprinkle of freckles on her nose. I know parents say it all the time about their teenagers, but she really doesn't know how lovely she is. She stoops a little when she walks because she doesn't want to stand out. She pulls her hoodie over her head because she hates making eye contact with strangers.

I can't stop myself from crying. I physically yearn for my daughter, for my husband, for my cosy little life that I took as a given.

A door slams close by. Footsteps again. The rattling of something.

The room is being unlocked. Oh Jesus.

I hope he gets it over with quickly.

The door opens.

A figure in black – trousers, jacket with the hood up. A gas mask over his face. He's carrying a tray with a plate and a bottle of water, and he pauses as the door slams shut by itself.

He's tall – just over six foot. Even if I wasn't chained up, there's no way I could make a dash for it. The self-defence classes I took three years ago haven't served me well so far. The surprise and the shock rendered me powerless. But I know now. I can think of something. I can't die here, I just can't.

He walks towards me – his breathing amplified by the mask. My heart is pounding so much he can probably see it – I hear it through my body – it echoes in my ears.

He places the tray on the floor.

'Eat this and we will give you something in return.'

What the hell?

I try to speak, but it comes out as hums.

He leans over – his face close to mine. I think he's going to say something, but he doesn't. His gloved hand grips one side of the tape covering my mouth. He rips it off slowly, but tears come to my eyes with the sting of it.

'You've got the wrong person,' I say, fresh tears flowing down my face. 'You have to let me out. My daughter will be worried.'

He puts a finger to the mouthpiece of the mask. 'Shh. Eat the sandwich.'

'I can't be here. I've nothing for you – you've got the wrong person.'

He shakes his head. 'Eat. Then you will know more.'

'How can I eat like this?'

I try to show him my tied-up hands behind my back, which is stupid because he was probably the one who did it.

He sighs. Is he angry; am I being too vocal? Will I be punished with a slap across the face for speaking out?

He gets a flick knife from his pocket and leans over to cut through the cable ties. He keeps hold of one of my wrists, strong but not overly tight. With his other hand he takes out a pair of handcuffs from one of the many pockets of his trousers and attaches my right hand to a pipe on the wall.

He says nothing else before he walks away.

'Please let me go,' I say, futile as it is. 'Please let me talk to my daughter.'

He exits the room, slams the door shut and locks it.

There is no way I'm going to eat that sandwich, but my mouth is parched. I grab the bottle, steadying it between my knees to test the lid. It's properly sealed; the serrated edges haven't been tampered with. James always says to look out for that.

I twist it open and bring it up to my lips. The water fills my mouth; there's nothing like being so dehydrated and having that feeling quenched. The relief lasts only seconds.

He said I would be rewarded if I ate, but I presume his idea of an incentive is different to mine. If I eat, I don't think he's going to take me home. But if he was going to kill me, he wouldn't feed me after being here such a short time. Or perhaps he's playing a long game.

My eyes start to close. Tiredness washes over me – even though my legs are flat, they feel like they're sinking into the mattress.

He put something in the water – must've injected it. Tricked me.

The darkness is coming again, and I don't have the energy to fight it.

CHAPTER 7

AUGUST 1989

I don't know the man – he says his name's Stan – who's driving me to the countryside. He could be a pervert for all I know. He said he's taking me to stay with my grandparents, which was news to me because I didn't know I had any. Mum said Dad's parents were dead and she never talked about hers, so I thought we were all alone in the world.

Martin and Penny, they're called, my grandparents. Their names sound made up and a bit posh, so I don't know where they went wrong bringing up my mother. Probably disowned her when she married Dad, but who knows. They're here for me now.

After Dad went to prison, people came out the woodwork. Police, social workers, snivelling neighbours who didn't used to give a damn about me. 'Poor lad,' they said. 'Do you think he saw anything?' I told them I didn't. 'He'll be traumatised for life,' they said. I told them I'd be fine, but of course no one believes a fourteen-year-old in situations like that.

'Not long now, Alex,' says Stan in the front seat.

He's like my chauffeur with me sitting in the back. There's a box of snacks and drinks on the seat next to me, but I've only had a bag of Wotsits and a Capri Sun in case they're charging per item. I don't want the grandparents I'm about to meet to think I'm greedy. They wouldn't want me staying with them then, would they? And right now, I don't have anywhere else to go.

We turn down a dirt track and I'm bouncing up and down – nearly hitting my head on the car ceiling. When I laugh, chauffeur Stan gives me a funny look in his rear-view mirror. Probably thinks I shouldn't be laughing in my circumstances, and he has a point, to be fair. I press my lips to make a straight line.

The car tyres crunch on the gravel. I undo my seatbelt and sit in the middle.

The house is massive. It looks like a working farm because it isn't that clean and there's dirt and hay all over the ground.

Stan turns the engine off, and we wait in silence.

There's an upside-down horseshoe above the black front door. It's meant to be the other way round, isn't it? The door opens slowly and an old man and woman step onto the step. They look like characters from *Last of the Summer Wine* or something.

'Come on then, lad,' says Stan, opening his door. 'Let's get your bags out the boot.'

I get out and watch as he unloads my rucksack and a big, battered, rectangular leather suitcase. He puts them on the ground.

'Not many things to show for your life, lad,' he says, which is a bit rude of him, actually.

'I've grown out of most of my clothes,' I say, the heat immediately rising to my face. I don't want him to pity me, though I'll probably never see him again.

I go to pick up my bags, but he shakes his head.

'Least I can do.' He grabs them and we walk to Martin and Penny's front door. He places them at the feet of my grandpar-

ents. 'I can carry them upstairs if they're too heavy,' he says to
them.

'That won't be necessary,' says Penny.

What am I to call her? She doesn't look like a gran or granny
or nana. Maybe she wants me to call her by her name. They
looked old from the car, but close-up they don't have many
wrinkles. Both their cheeks are red – like they've spent too
much time in the sun or the wind or the snow.

Martin has his arm around Penny; well, it's lightly resting
on her shoulder like he doesn't do it that much.

'Thanks, Stan,' I say.

He looks relieved to be going. I'm tempted to jump back in
the car and go off with him. We could have a road trip, me and
Stan.

I stand in front of my grandparents, and we all watch my
mate Stan drive away.

Penny holds the door open for me.

'You grab your rucksack and Martin will fetch your case up.
Follow me and I'll show you to your bedroom.'

She has a strong Yorkshire accent like on *Emmerdale Farm*.

I step into the hallway, which has worn-out orange floor
tiles. There are giant wooden beams across the ceiling that look
like they should have cobwebs hanging from them, but the
house is cleaner inside than it is out. I follow Penny up the
narrow creaky stairs and along a landing that has three doors
leading off it.

'We thought you might like the privacy of having a floor to
yourself,' she says as we start up another staircase.

The temperature gets colder and colder with every step,
which makes me remember watching a film that had an orphan
in it – can't remember the name – and now I can't stop worrying
that I'm going to be locked in with only porridge to eat. Like
Dad, now I think about it.

She leads me to a room at the end of a poky corridor and

pushes the door open. It's a bit old-fashioned inside – flowery wallpaper, bed covers and curtains – but it's big.

'I hope the room is all right for you.' She goes to the corner and pulls out a massive box heater, half the height of me. 'This is gas. Do you know how to work it?' She turns the dial and presses the ignitor. A nice smell of gas fills the room. 'Don't forget to turn it off, though. Don't want the place going up in smoke.'

She turns to look at me properly for the first time.

'You don't half look like your mother,' she says, looking like she's about to cry. 'Such a handsome lad – what a fresh complexion you have. Ah, here's Martin.'

I don't hear his steps until the creaky floorboard by my door. Martin walks in, carrying my case like he is carrying feathers. He flings it onto the bed.

'Well, we'll leave you to settle in, won't we, Penny.' He rubs his hands together. 'Should warm up in here, soon.' He walks up to the heater and turns the dial down. 'This thing gets hot. Make sure you don't leave it on – don't want the place going up in smoke.'

'I've already told him that,' says Penny.

'Right you are.'

'Tea'll be on the table in half an hour,' she says. 'Butter pie, tonight. You look like you need fattening up.'

Bloody hell, are they going to eat me?

Butter pie sounds disgusting.

Martin must've noticed the horror on my face.

'It's not just butter in the pie,' he says. 'It's potatoes and onions. Tastes better than it sounds. Penny here was brought up in Red Rose country, but that pie is the best thing to come out of it.' He rubs his hands again. 'Right then, lad. Make yourself at home and we'll see you in a bit.'

I expect Penny to follow him, but she's still staring at me, taking in my face like she's trying to separate my features. Some from my mum, some from my dad. Her eyes stop at the scar on my neck.

I'm ready with an answer, but she doesn't ask the question.

'We thought it'd be best if you start school when the new term begins in a few weeks. We've enrolled you at St Stephen's. Your mum went there. Small. Nice people.'

'OK.'

'Are you sure?'

'Yeah. I'll be OK.'

The tears in my eyes come from nowhere.

She tilts her head and takes me into her arms. She smells of onions and bleach.

'Oh, Alex,' she says. 'I know, I know. We'll get through this together. It'll be like having her back now you're here.' She releases me but leaves her hands on my shoulders. 'Everything will be all right.'

I nod and sniff.

She heads towards the door.

'Come down whenever you're ready,' she says. 'I can reheat your dinner if you need a nap.'

She closes the door, and I slide my suitcase off the bed so I can have a lie-down.

The ceiling has damp stains in the corner; it needs painting. Warmth from the gas heater has made its way over to me. I wriggle my shoulders into the big fluffy pillow and run my fingers over the layers of sheets and blankets that cover the bed. Old-fashioned. Comforting.

Why did my mother keep all this from me? She stole the time I could've spent here, a break from the nightmare of living with her and Dad. I reach into my pocket and take out the photograph the social worker said I should keep. In it, I'm sitting on Mum's lap and she's helping me blow out the three candles on my cake. Before everything turned bad.

I fold it into three and wedge it under the mattress. I almost feel it under me, like the princess and the pea. I can smell onions again. Onions, butter, and potatoes rising from the kitchen. My mouth waters.

I sit up and jump from the bed.

I'm bloody starving.

CHAPTER 8

SCARLETT

Now it's breaktime, I'll finally have the chance to talk to Hannah properly. As usual, we meet in the corridor near the dining room, but she's the one waiting for me for a change. She usually takes ages to walk from her lesson because it takes her a millennium to say goodbye, unlike me who dashes out. I can't stand boring small talk.

She's fidgeting with her nose ring (not actually real), but it looks like she's picking her nose. I'm about to let her know when she gets the first word in.

'He was in the same class as me, can you believe it?'

'Jamie?'

'Duh, of course Jamie, who else? The rest of the boys are so immature.'

'Really?' I say. 'Most people in my classes are all right.'

'Yeah, well. I chose Sociology, didn't I? Dad says it's not even a proper subject.' She's not looking at me now. She's bobbing her head about like a meerkat, no doubt scouring the corridor for you-know-who. I'm sick of his name already, but at least Hannah's a good distraction from what's going on at home.

'Anyway – I thought he'd be in a different class because he's older.'

'Older, is he? You've not mentioned that before.'

She ignores my snark, and we start walking towards the Lounge.

'And I said "hello" to him, and he said "hello" back.'

'Exciting.'

'But that's all we said. At the end, he went straight out but I didn't see where he went.'

We stop at the doors, and she peers through the glass.

'I haven't seen you act like this since Year 10,' I say.

'Shit, really?'

She looks properly shocked, and her eyebrows rise halfway up her forehead.

'Have you dyed them?' I say.

'Dyed what?'

'Never mind.' I push open one of the doors – there's a spare couple of seats in the corner and I head over, even though Hannah's probably huffing because we're not sitting near bloody Jamie. I sit down and dump my bag next to me and reach into my pocket for my phone. Still nothing from Mum. This is getting weird now.

'Has he texted you?' says Hannah, stroppily sitting down while gazing across the expanse of the room in search of skater boy.

'Has who texted me?'

'That guy from the other night. From, you know...'

'Are you talking about Guy from Warhammer club? The one with the nineties hair, parted by Moses.'

She sniggers, her eyes shining with the hilarity that a games geek appears to have a crush on me.

'I have no interest at all in Warhammer,' I say. 'I had to go to the first meet because he's the son of one of Dad's colleagues.

Just in case no one else turned up. He didn't have to worry, though.'

'Who knew so many people were into board games?'

'It's the geeks who get rich, you know,' I say. 'Maybe we should try it.'

'Hmm.'

I've lost her; she's looking at her face in a compact mirror.

'What's happened to you?' I say. 'Last week you couldn't have cared less about eyebrows.'

'We have to grow up some time, Scarlett.'

'There's more to adulting than grooming face hair.'

What's the point of talking to Hannah about my mum? She clearly doesn't give a shit.

She snaps the compact shut and tucks it into the pocket of her denim jacket.

'Go on,' she says. 'What's up?'

'Oh, you noticed.'

She lifts one of her perfectly shaped brows. I hold up my phone.

'What am I looking at?' she says, plucking it from my hand.

'My mum, remember? She didn't come home last night.'

'Shit, sorry, Scar,' she says. 'I've been on another planet.'

'I've sent her about fifteen messages and phoned her every hour since I woke up.' I pause to make sure I have Hannah's full attention. 'She hasn't replied, and she hasn't read her texts.'

'Who did she go out with last night?'

'She told Dad she was going out with Amy, but I think something suss is going on.'

'Like she's having an affair?'

'Not you as well.' I flop back in the chair. 'Course she isn't.'

'I know it's unlikely, but you never know with people. Like what happened with my mum. Dad was devastated when she moved in with Ken from the pub. Ken! Who's almost a hundred years old. Loaded, though.' Hannah hands me back my phone.

'Dad wouldn't have got through all of that, you know, if it wasn't for your mum.'

Hannah's dad didn't get out of bed for almost a week. Mum used to drop meals to the house every morning on her way to work. He phoned her at all times of the night, crying, after taking her up on her insistence to contact her any time of the day.

'Your house was my second home for months,' says Hannah. 'She was Dad's rock. Hey, you don't think—'

'She's not having an affair with your dad, Hannah.'

'Just thinking out loud.' She rests her chin on her hand, and her eyes flicker about as her brain goes full CSI. 'So, she hasn't replied to her one and only child. Even if she *was* having an affair, she'd pretend she wasn't. She'd reply, act normal. This is weird.'

'What should I do?'

'What did your dad say? Is he worried, too?'

'Course he is. Well, I think he is. But he said the same as you – he thinks she's having an affair. He went out looking for her.'

'Ring her again,' she says, shuffling to the edge of her seat. 'Put it on speakerphone.'

'There's no point, she won't answer it.' I glance at Mum's messages, and this time they're marked as read. 'Oh my god. Whoever has the phone has read the texts I sent.'

I select Mum's contact and press call, holding the phone in the space between us. It rings three times before it's answered. I take it off speaker.

'Mum? Are you OK?'

There's a television on in the background.

'Mum.' I say it louder, and a couple of girls near us turn round. 'Mum, it's me. Are you OK?'

The call ends with three beeps.

I stare at the phone.

'Shit,' says Hannah. 'What the hell was that?'

'I don't know.' My eyes are filling with tears. I try to blink them away. 'I'm really worried now.'

'She's probably lost her phone, or had it stolen. The person who nicked it answered and didn't want to speak. Do you have that Find a Friend thing on there?'

'No. I have it on mine, but I can't track her.'

'Shit,' she says again. 'What if they come after you next?'

'Hannah! Don't say things like that. I'm freaking out as it is.'

'Switch off your location – just to be safe.'

'I don't know. I feel safer with it on.'

She shrugs. 'If it were me I would. Though, I don't know if you can. Think you need their permission.'

I bring up Dad's contact.

'I'm going to phone my dad and ask what the hell's going on.'

I can't believe Hannah and I were talking about adulting and now I'm asking my dad for help. He answers after four rings, but there's silence.

'Hello?' I say. 'Hello? Dad?'

'Sorry, Scarlett. Was just checking. There was something weird outside the house.'

'What?'

'Just next door. Someone just knocked – thought it was ours. They never have visitors. It was a man dressed head to toe in white. So weird.'

'Have you heard from Mum?'

'No.' He sighs heavily. 'I've tried ringing her, but it keeps going to voicemail. I went to her work. No one's seen or heard from her.'

'Oh.' I frown and Hannah mouths *What?* so I turn round to stop her distracting me. 'I've been ringing her, too. It rung out for the first couple of times, but then someone answered. There was a telly on in the background.' He's pacing on the floor-boards; I can hear the echo. 'Dad?'

'There's someone at the door,' he says. 'It's Amy. I have to go, love.'

'Should I phone Gran?'

'I've already rung her. She's on her way round with Pete. Stick with Hannah for the rest of the day and I'll come and get you. Meet me by the row of shops.'

He ends the call and I'm staring at my phone.

'What is it?' says Hannah. 'What did he say?'

'He's not heard from her, either. Gran's on her way round to ours. Shit, Han. What if she's...?'

'She won't be dead. They'd have found her, wouldn't they? I mean, if someone has knocked her over or something.'

'But what if someone kidnapped her?'

I point to the tatty poster on the back wall. The one that's almost fully covered with band nights and sports event flyers. It's been here for years. Natalie Baxter, aged twenty-three, went missing thirteen years ago. Her name has always seemed familiar to me – probably because it's like she haunts the corridors with her smiling face. Her sister went to this college and plastered Natalie's missing poster all over the place. This is one of the few still visible.

When she first went missing, I bet her family didn't think they'd still be looking for answers today.

What if the same happens to Mum?

CHAPTER 9

SEPTEMBER 1989

I can hear them talking about me – they're not even trying to be quiet. I'm going to let it slide for now because it sounds like they don't know all the details. It wasn't reported much in the news and what was written was completely wrong, but I'm not going to go round saying that, am I?

'No, *you* ask him,' says the girl sitting in the row in front, three seats along. She's pretty but she's got a giant zit on the back of her neck. She mustn't know about it because her hair is in a ponytail at the top of her head. Or she does know about it and doesn't give a shit.

She must've lost the challenge because she's turning round, keeps glancing at her friend, giving her the evils.

'Hey,' she whispers, even though the teacher isn't here yet.

I stare at the blackboard, tap my pen on the desk. I'm leaning back in my seat, pretending I don't hear her. She needs to earn my attention. Calling me by my name would be a start and she should know it – I've been introduced to the whole class twice. Granted, I don't actually know *her* name.

'Alex,' she says, louder, and the two boys right in front of me turn around.

I sit forward, elbow on desk, and lean my chin on my hand. 'What?'

'Is it true about your mum and dad?'

'Which bit?'

She looks nervous now. She's gonna have to say it, isn't she?

'That your dad killed your mum and now he's in prison.'

She's gone bright red, and I don't know her well enough to know if that's what she normally does when she speaks in public.

I shrug. 'I guess.'

The lad in front of me sniggers. Right ugly get he is, too. Greasy fringe that covers most of his eyes. He'll get a stye if he's not careful.

'What are you laughing at?' I say.

'She fancies you, mate,' he says.

The girl flashes her eyes and nudges him.

'What's it got to do with you?' I say.

He's not smiling any more, and his mates are looking at him.

'Nothing,' he says. 'I've never known anyone's dad to be a murderer before. Proper dark.'

He can't even string a sentence together. Dickhead.

'Whatever,' I say.

He frowns.

'So, it's true, then?' says the girl with the neck zit – she's fully turned round now, a smile on her lips. Maybe she does fancy me after all. 'It *is* you. They didn't print your name in the papers.'

The teacher walks in, wearing a trilby. He grabs a piece of chalk and draws a hook on the blackboard, takes off his hat and places it on the hook. The rest of the class groans, but I've never seen anything like that. Impressive. And it's cool that he cares enough to do something like that. Most teachers I've had can't be arsed with anything.

'Alexis,' he shouts. 'Are you going to chat all day, or can we learn something new today?'

She turns round quickly and mumbles, 'Sorry, sir.'

I've never met an Alexis before. Bet she gets called Dynasty all the time.

* * *

Nothing else interesting happened for the remainder of the morning, so I bunked off for the rest of the afternoon, and now I'm walking along the country lanes because there's police on the streets in town. It'd be embarrassing to get sent back to school. I can't go back to the farm because I don't think Martin (it doesn't feel right calling him Grandad) would appreciate me skiving. I've been living with them for a month and already their masks are slipping. Who'd have thought old people could bicker so loudly? The first time was on Monday, when Penny didn't have tea on the table at the right time.

'I don't work my arse off all day to come back to this dried-up crap,' he said.

It had been ready for ages and Martin was late. Me and Penny had to wait for him, which was a bit awkward. Pretended I was doing homework, so I didn't have to talk about feelings and shit. The hotpot was absolutely fine, but Martin complained that the meat was too chewy.

Penny said, 'Well, I'm so sorry, lord and master. I'll try to be clairvoyant next time.'

I held my knife and fork mid-air. My heart did go a bit, I don't mind admitting. He's a big bloke.

'Hmm,' he said, shaking his head. 'Should've married Sandra Wainwright. Wouldn't have had this cheek from her.'

'You'd have died by now if you were married to Sandra Wainwright,' said Penny, winking at me. 'Of boredom.'

Which was a bit close to home if you ask me. They're

always snapping at each other, but I don't think they mean it. Who can tell?

I've reached a stream and I can see the farmhouse from here. I only have half an hour to kill, so I head over to the water's edge and find myself a flat rock to sit on. I take off my socks and shoes and stick my feet in, let the water trickle between my toes. It's bloody freezing, but it's woken me up a bit.

I open my rucksack and take out the sandwich box Penny prepared for me. Ham and mustard on thick white bread. Bloody delicious. That woman sure can cook, I'll give her that. She can talk as well, mind. Best thing to do is nod along and think of something else.

Splashing catches my eye. To my right, there's a small animal thrashing about in the water. I wipe breadcrumbs from my lap and stand, shaking drops of water off my feet.

It looks like a squirrel, but I haven't seen that many to be sure. It must've caught itself on barbed wire – two of its back legs are bleeding. It's not going to get very far on them.

We lock eyes. It looks petrified of me, but it can't move.

I look left and right. There's no one around. No cars have passed while I've been sitting here. I reach a hand out and it goes to nip it, the little shit. I grab its whole head, squeezing its skull to keep it still. It's making whimpering noises.

'There, there,' I say. 'It's for the best, you'll see. It'll make the pain go away.'

I wrap my other hand around its tiny neck. Tinier than you think under all that fur. It stares at me as I squeeze tighter and tighter. I can tell when it's dead because something changes behind the eyes. It's a look I've seen before. Consciousness leaving the body, the light inside switched off.

I wash my hands in the water, though there's no blood on them.

The little thing is lying with its four legs spread out like it's halfway through making a snow angel.

'Told you it was for the best,' I say. 'Doesn't hurt now, does it?'

I dry my hands on my trousers, pack up my stuff, put on my shoes and socks and head back onto the road.

Wonder what Penny's making for tea tonight. Hope it's butter pie.

It's becoming one of my new favourites.

CHAPTER 10

JOANNA

The faint chatter of morning television is what I hear first, like I'm back home with James as he's getting ready for work. But my reality lands on me like a weight dropped from the ceiling.

Light's streaming through my eyelids, but I feel so tired, so drowsy. My head is a woolly mess. My arms don't feel numb any more, but my right one is stretched above my head, cuffed to a bedframe. The other is free.

When I open my eyes, the sunlight hurts for a few seconds before they adjust to the light. Am I home? The same wardrobe, the same chest of drawers, same television set on top. I run my free hand across the duvet cover. Soft, cool cotton. Bright giant flowers in autumn shades. It's the same one I bought from TK Maxx last year. I pull up an edge. If it's the same one, there will be a faint red wine stain underneath from the time James fell asleep with a glass in his hand after a work's do.

No. Not there.

What the hell is going on?

I look to the window, but it's narrower than ours. The frames are silver metal – how they made them in the seventies or eighties – my grandparents used to have them.

I shuffle into a sitting position and see there's a bucket as a makeshift loo. I'll need to use it soon; a pain is growing in my lower abdomen. There's some toilet roll, and wet wipes to wash with. This might be a good sign. That he wants to keep me alive and clean. But not clean in a weird sexual way. I could be reading too much into this.

I flip myself over so I'm facing the bedframe. If I can pull the bed knob from the top, I could slide the metal cuff off.

'I wouldn't do that if I were you.'

A man's voice from above – deep, artificial-sounding. There's a speaker and a camera over the doorframe.

'Just let me go,' I shout. 'We don't have money, you know.'

The speaker crackles.

'I don't need money. As you can see, I have plenty.'

'Why have you done this?' I say, trying to keep in the tears, to stay strong. 'What do you want?'

'That's enough for now. You should relax. Keep an eye on the news and see if you notice anything.'

My skin goes cold, prickly. Who could be doing this? Has James upset someone at work? He deals with people who are worth millions of pounds, at least. It can't be someone *I* know. I work for a charity for goodness' sake.

The only thing out of the ordinary is that I was going to meet Holly that night. She said in her email that we know someone in common. That she knew what I had done. But she couldn't possibly know that. No one does. Meeting in a public place had seemed a good idea. I should've told James about it – why didn't I tell him? He would have told me not to panic and to ignore it. I suppose I wanted to protect him.

I'm such an idiot. It was probably a scam. There isn't someone called Holly, and whoever it really was had followed me home. But why? And why go to such lengths and decorate this room like mine? Our house was listed on Rightmove last year, but we didn't get the price we were asking. That's the only explanation I can think of. Unless they'd been inside. A shudder runs through me when I think of a stranger rooting through our things.

'Make sure you text me when you get there,' Amy said as we parted after work. 'Are you sure this woman is who she says she is? She might be lying about you two being at school together. It might not even be a woman when you get there. Are you sure you don't want me to come with you?'

'I'll be fine.'

If Amy tells James I was meeting a school friend and I didn't tell him, he's going to think I'm seeing someone.

Oh, the tangled web...

The television flicks to the local news: *Granada Reports*.

A flood in Ashton; a man convicted of murdering his wife; and the usual heart-warming piece at the end to counteract all the bad news: a couple celebrating their sixtieth wedding anniversary with a card from the king.

There is nothing about me.

Nobody knows I'm missing.

And if they do, they're doing nothing about it.

CHAPTER 11

1990

It's the summer holidays and as usual there's sod all to do around here. Martin and Penny don't like me having a lie-in. The one time I slept till nine, Martin banged on my door, and said, 'Come on, y' daft apeth. I've been up five hours – you're missing the best part of t' day.' So, I've been getting up at seven every morning. We're sitting around the big wooden table in the kitchen, and Martin is chomping on a breakfast of sausage and egg. He has the same thing every morning and I can't stand the greasy stench that lingers for hours.

It was his sixtieth birthday yesterday – I thought he was at least eighty. He said he didn't want any fuss, but I saw him sneak a smile in when Penny presented him with a cake (just the one candle, didn't want to push the boat out). Martin's brother was here, too. Dexie, they call him, but I don't know why. His name's probably something boring like Derek and he's given himself a nickname to sound more interesting. He's nothing like Martin. He was wearing clean clothes and after-shave. He couldn't convince Martin to go to the pub with him, so the whole 'party' was done by eight. A late night for Martin.

Now, in the kitchen, where she always seems to be, Penny

has finished her tiny corner of bread and jam for breakfast and is staring into space while holding a fancy porcelain cup of tea.

'It's half seven, lad,' Martin says without looking at me. He grabs a chunk of buttered bread and sweeps it across his plate to mop up the egg yolk. 'Those pigs won't feed themselves.'

I'm so tired, even after seven hours' sleep.

Pigs, hay, sweeping, shovelling shit. Every single day.

'I was thinking I could have the afternoon off,' I say. 'Wanted to head into town.'

'If you get all your jobs done, I don't see why not.' Martin wipes his mouth with a napkin. 'You can take the bike, but make sure it doesn't get nicked.'

That was easier than I thought. I expected him to freak out, chain me up in the cellar or something.

'What did your dad say in his letter?' asks Penny.

I thought she hadn't seen it. It came last week, and this is the first time she's mentioned it. Over the thirteen months my dad's been in prison, this is the first letter he's ever sent me. Was it the first time he thought about me, too?

'Asked how I was,' I say. 'Nothing much, really.'

'Hmm.' Martin gets up and places his plate in the sink. 'That was lovely, thank you, Penny.'

'Did he mention your mum?'

'Enough, Penny!' Martin's leaning against the sink, his back to us. 'There'll be no talk of that man in this house.'

He fills a glass with water and downs it in one before walking out the door.

Penny places a hand on mine, and it feels weird, her touching me. Her skin's warm, dry, cracked, but I don't want to offend her by swiping it away.

'Did he mention anything about his release? I read in the library that when people are sentenced, they only serve half. And what with him using self-defence because' – she points to the scar on my neck – 'he did it with what your mum used to...' She takes her hand away from mine and places it over her mouth. 'I'm sorry, Alex. I shouldn't be talking to you about this. I'm so sorry. You've been through so much. It's just that I can't talk about it to Martin, and I don't know what he'd do if...' She pats the table. 'Never mind.' She gets up and turns the hot tap to fill the sink. 'I'll do your favourite for lunch: a nice cheese and pickle sandwich.'

I stand and place my crumby plate on the side.

'Thanks, Penny.'

I pull on my wellies in the hall, and as I go to open the back door, she shouts, 'You can call me Gran, you know.'

I step outside.

'Bye, Gran.'

And a part of me feels good about that but I don't think it'll stick.

* * *

I finish my jobs by twelve, so after I wash and change, I head out on the bike. I have about seven quid saved up, but I'm not going to splash out all at once. All I need is batteries for my Walkman. I've already used six of Martin's. 'That bloody thing guzzles juice.'

I've reached town now. It's pretty small, but it has a Woolies and a McDonald's. There's a group of five or six kids that I recognise from school, hanging round a bench near a couple of bins. A few of them are smoking cigarettes like they're well hard. Idiots.

'All right, Al,' shouts one of them, a lad. 'Grandad lend you his bike, did he?'

The rest of them laugh like the lemmings they are.

'Yeah, he did actually,' I shout over because there's no denying it. The bike is painted in thick black paint that's chipped all over. I rest it against the giant glass window of

Woolworths, stick my hands in my pockets and stroll in without looking at them.

Four quid for a ten-pack of batteries! What a bloody rip-off! Yeah, they have the cheapies, but they'd only last five minutes. I hand a fiver over to a girl not much older than me, who looks like she doesn't want to be working at all.

'Are there any jobs going here?' I say.

She looks at me for the first time as she gives me my one pound change.

'You have to be at least sixteen to work here,' she says.

'I am sixteen.'

'Yeah, right,' she says, snarling her top lip like Elvis.

'I am,' I say. 'I'm only shorter than you because you're standing on a platform.'

I peek over and I'm right.

She shrugs and glances at her nails that are painted neon yellow and as chipped as Martin's bike.

'We don't need any more staff.'

'But you're the only one on the tills, and there are five people waiting.'

'Which is why you should clear off and let me get on.'

'I'm going to complain to the manager,' I say, pushing my shoulders back.

'Yeah, sure you are.'

She beckons the next customer with her hand, not looking at *them* either and I stand there, looking at her, but she doesn't care.

When I get outside, the bike's gone.

Shit. I didn't lock it. Martin's gonna go mad.

The group has gone from the bench, but I see them up the road in the distance, so I pelt it to catch up with them. The one in front is wheeling the bike.

'Oi!' I shout. 'Give us that back.'

I run up alongside him – Mark his name is. He's wearing a parka, greasy hair.

'I said, give us that back.'

He stops, and they all do. Of course.

'Sorry.' He takes a toke on his cig. 'What's that you were saying?'

I yank one of the handles towards me.

'You heard.'

I reach to grab the other handle, but he tilts the bike away from me. His groupies snigger. Ha bloody ha. I glance over at the loudest. It's Sarah-Jane, the one who sits behind me in Maths. Cow.

Mark shoulders me out of his way as he climbs onto the bike, his feet on tiptoes when he sits. I push his arm with both hands, but he barely budges.

'What are you gonna do?' he says, throwing his burning ciggie towards me. It misses by an inch. 'Murder me?'

He pushes on the pedals and the rest of the group follow, except for Sarah-Jane. She stares at me – chewing gum with a gaping mouth. I turn to run after them, but she gives me a shove. My foot catches on the other. My hands flap in the air as I feel myself falling backwards in slow motion. The pain of the cobbles on my backside makes my eyes water.

She stops chewing. She seems as shocked as I am, but she just stands there.

'Dickhead,' she mutters before running to catch up with the rest of them.

She's going to pay for this. She really is.

* * *

I've still got blood on my hands when I reach the farm. Penny must've seen me coming because she opens the front door, wiping her hands on her pinny.

'Whatever happened?' she says. She runs towards me and stops a few feet away. 'You've got blood all over your face and you've been gone for hours.'

'It was a group of lads,' I say. Some part of me must believe it because hot tears run down my cold face. 'They fought the bike off me.'

Penny puts her hands to her face, like how Wilma looks shocked in *The Flintstones*.

'What's all the fuss?'

Martin's walking from the side of the house, an axe resting on his shoulder.

'Alex's been attacked,' says Penny and she's tearing up too. 'A group of them in town. They stole the bike.'

'I'm so sorry, Grandad,' I say, wiping the tears with the back of my hand. I've probably made my face look worse. 'I tried to fight back, but there were ten of them.'

'Ten?'

I nod quickly.

'Do you know them?'

I shake my head.

'They were older than me. About nineteen.'

'Nineteen? What would they want with my shitty old bike?' He mutters something I can't make out as he heads towards the door. 'I'm calling the police. You can't have children being beaten up on the streets.'

'No,' I shout. 'What if they come back for me? It's their word against mine.'

'Well, we'll have to deal with that if it happens.'

Shit. I've told the wrong story. Should've said it was a hit and run. It's too late to change my story. But I've learned for next time. Every day's a school day.

'They went after this girl when they were done with me,' I say to Penny. 'A girl from my class. I hope to God she's all right.'

'What's she called?' says Penny, pressing a hand against her chest. She calls after Martin. 'Wait, love,' she says, rushing into the house. 'Tell them they might need an ambulance.'

I linger, watching the commotion.

'Sarah-Jane Crosswell,' I say quietly. 'But I doubt an ambulance is any good to her now.'

CHAPTER 12

SCARLETT

Amy's still here when I get back from college. She's sitting next to the seat Mum usually sits on, her hands wrapped around a mug of tea. She stands, placing her drink on the floor, and rushes over to give me a hug.

'Oh, Scarlett,' she says. 'Are you OK? No, of course you're not. I haven't been able to do a thing today – left work early. Everyone's worried about her.'

'I'm OK,' I say. 'I keep thinking about where Mum could be.'

She releases me and wipes the tears off my face.

'I know, I know.'

'She'll be OK, Amy,' snaps Dad, with a slight edge to his voice. 'I'm staying positive in front of...' He's lingering at the living room door, gripping his phone. 'Did Jo give you a name,' he says to Amy, 'of who she was meeting last night?'

'Holly,' she says. 'She said the woman was called Holly. I checked my texts again this morning.'

Dad looks as though he's been shaken. He rests his arm against the doorframe.

'What is it, Dad?' I say. 'Do you know someone called Holly?'

He leaves the room, climbs slowly up the stairs.

'Why was she meeting someone called Holly?' I say. 'Why wouldn't she tell us?' I lower my voice. 'Do you think it was something to do with Dad? That he was seeing this Holly and Mum found out and that's why she's not come home?'

Amy shakes her head.

'I've no idea, Scarlett,' she says. 'Your mum said it was a school friend, but I heard nothing from her after she was in the pub, waiting. I should've gone with her – made sure she was safe.'

'Maybe it *was* a school friend,' I say. 'Maybe they got drunk and Mum stayed over and she feels too ill to come home. Mum hates hangovers – they last her half a week, these days.'

'Yeah,' says Amy. 'Maybe.'

But I don't think she believes it, either.

* * *

Before Amy left, Dad called the police, but there's no sign of them so far. He jumps up when the doorbell goes.

'That'll be them.'

'I didn't hear a car pull up,' I say, going to the window.

And I'm right. Standing on our doorstep is Mr and Mrs Shepherd from next door. She's standing in front of him, carrying a dish wrapped in a tea towel; he's standing with his hands in his pockets. We don't see them much, but their bedroom is on the other side of my back wall. I hear their lamp switch off at eight thirty every night, yet I've heard them talking after midnight, listening to some weird music. Though they might've been chanting. I've no clue what they get up to at night and I try not to think about it.

I can't tell what age they are, but they're at least ten years older than Mum and Dad. He's wearing dark-rimmed glasses and his thick black hair is combed into a rigid side parting. She has a halo of curly hair, and she's wearing pastel blue eyeshadow and bright pink lipstick.

'We heard about what happened,' she says, her voice piercing through the windows. 'I'm so sorry. I hope Joanna's all right. We noticed all the police cars, so we put two and two together.'

'The police haven't been round yet,' says Dad, and I can't make out the tone of his voice.

'Really?' She glances back at her husband. 'Oh... so Joanna's all right?'

'I don't know,' says Dad. 'We haven't seen her since yesterday.'

She pushes the dish into Dad's hands.

'I thought there was something wrong. We usually see her in the mornings, don't we, Jerry?'

He nods, hands still shoved in his pockets.

'We didn't think you'd be up to cooking. It's vegetarian. I didn't know if you young people ate meat, so I made a macaroni cheese. I hope that's OK for you both.'

'Er. Yes,' says Dad. I don't think he's ever said more than a few words to them before. 'Thank you. That's very kind of you.'

Mrs Shepherd notices me at the window. Before I have a chance to duck, she comes closer. She has the most intense stare, unblinking. The blacks of her eyes are huge.

'Thinking of you, Scarlett,' she says, then makes the shape of a heart with her hands. What the fuck? 'Just give me a tinkle if you need to talk.'

Her husband tilts his head, smiling. When Mrs Shepherd's attention is back to Dad, I feel his – *Jerry's* – eyes turn towards me. His smile fades and when I meet his gaze for the briefest of moments, a jolt of adrenaline runs through me. The life behind his eyes is empty. It's something I can't describe. Hatred, perhaps. Or ambivalence. It's hard to tell, but it makes me move away from the window.

Maybe he doesn't get out much and has forgotten what's socially acceptable. I dive back onto the settee and cover myself with a blanket.

'Well, thanks very much,' says Dad. 'I'd better be getting back inside. We're expecting the police any minute.'

When the door closes, I get up and follow Dad into the kitchen.

'Well, that's going straight in the bin,' he says, dumping the dish on the side.

'Shh,' I say. 'They might hear you through the walls.'

'What?'

'How else do they know Mum's missing? They must be listening in.'

'Don't be silly, Scarlett. They probably saw Amy's post – she put it on Facebook an hour ago.'

'Wouldn't put it past them,' I say, peeling off the tea towel and examining the contents. I cover it back up. 'How do they know I'm vegetarian?'

'Lots of people are vegetarian.' Dad starts to fill the kettle. 'Make yourself useful and get out some cups. And milk, sugar. Put it on a tray – there's one on top of the fridge, I think.'

'You think the police actually drink in people's houses?'

Dad shrugs. '*I* wouldn't, but maybe they do it to be polite. Keep the peace and all that.'

I grab the stuff out the cupboards and place it on a tray. As I'm taking it through, my phone beeps with a text.

It's just Hannah wondering if there's any news. I tap out '*Nothing*', and go to look out the window, half-expecting Mr and Mrs MI5 to still be on our step. They're not.

A police car pulls up and two women in uniform get out, put on their hats.

'Dad.' I run into the kitchen, trying to be stealthy so they don't see me – even though I've done nothing wrong. 'It's uniforms. They put on hats. Isn't that a bad sign? Why didn't they send detectives? They always send out detectives when someone's disappeared.'

'Calm down, Scarlett. They take *off* their hats if someone's died.' He smooths his hair in his reflection on the oven door. 'Do you want to go upstairs while I deal with them?'

'No,' I say, but I'm nervous. I've only spoken to a police officer once and that was when Hannah was having a panic attack after we nicked some pick 'n' mix from the cinema. She'd thought they were there to arrest us, but she'd just drawn attention to us. They were there for some drunk person who'd fallen asleep through two showings of *The Greatest Showman*. She's the worst accomplice ever. Plus, we ended up throwing the sweets in the river out of guilt anyway.

'Mr Sawyer,' says one of them when Dad opens the door.

They're coming inside. Oh my god, my heart's racing and my legs are trembling as I walk into the living room. I go back to my place on the settee and under the blanket as they stand in the middle of the room.

'I'm PC Stern,' says the one with her hair in a messy ponytail. 'And this' – she sticks her thumb towards her colleague, who looks only a few years older, and nearly a foot shorter, than me – 'is PC Waterhouse.'

PC Waterhouse is looking at me with her eyes wide, like she's more nervous than I am.

'We had a report,' says Stern, 'that your wife, Joanna, has been missing from home since last night. Is there any reason why you waited until this evening to report your wife missing? You know you don't have to wait twenty-four hours.'

'Yes, I know,' says Dad. 'I thought she stayed somewhere else.'

Waterhouse's focus is now on Dad. She's looking at him as though he's a murderer – not even trying to hide her hatred.

They always focus on the husbands, don't they? That's what Gran said. She loves reading about true crime. Used to write to prisoners on death row in America, after watching a documentary years ago about a young man wrongfully convicted of murder in the 1980s. She was in tears when they showed his release thirty years later – he said he'd lost the best part of life. No kids, no wife. She took it upon herself to *spread a little joy* in the letters she wrote to those behind bars awaiting execution – just in case it turned out they were innocent.

'Where did you think she stayed?' says Stern.

'Initially, at her friend Amy's house. Then I received something in the post. Anonymously.'

What?

'In the post?' Waterhouse has found her voice. 'Like through the letterbox?'

Stern gives her a look of contempt that silences her. Waterhouse is definitely a noob.

Dad goes to the sideboard and gets out a poly pocket.

'I put it in this in case there were fingerprints.'

I want to stand but I haven't the courage.

'Why didn't you tell me about this?' I've found my voice, too. 'What does it say? Is it a ransom note?'

After she's read the note, that's written on light blue notepaper, Waterhouse presses her lips together, tilts her head as she looks at me. The police academy probably told her it looks sympathetic, but it doesn't. It looks condescending. I want to stand up and tell her I'll be eighteen in six months, but that would make me look even more immature than I already do.

'Can you go upstairs for a bit, Scarlett?' says Dad, and I narrow my eyes at him.

But it's only then that I look at him properly for the first time in ages. He hasn't shaved; his eyes are red with shadows underneath. Sometimes I forget he's a real person with feelings because he usually does a good job of hiding them.

I take off the blanket, in the least belligerent way I can, and walk out the room. I don't linger in the hall like I'm tempted to do because Dad will be listening for my footsteps up the stairs. I close my bedroom door calmly but loudly. Then I lie down with my ear to the floor.

All I hear is muffled sniffs. God, I think Dad's crying. I've never heard or seen him cry in my life. Not even at my nana's funeral.

I pull my phone out of my pocket and text Hannah.

> Police are here. Dad's really upset.

She reads it straight away. There are three dots as she starts her reply. *Shit*, she replies.

> Have they found your mum?

> No. They're just taking some info. Dad said he got an anonymous letter. Dunno what it says. Told me to go to my room.

> Letter? Like through the post?

> Yeh.

> How weird. Did your dad take a copy before he gave it to them?

> No clue. Didn't even know about the letter.

> Maybe someone said your mum was having an affair. Maybe that's why he said that this morning.

> Yeah. And the neighbours were a bit odd earlier. Was probably them. They seem like the letter type.

> Shall I come round?

> Maybe later, if that's OK?

Course.

I fling my phone onto my bed and lie there until I remember I haven't rung my mum in nearly an hour. This time it goes straight to voicemail like it's been doing for Dad.

'Mum? It's me, Scarlett. Can you please ring me back and tell me you're OK? The police are here. Everyone's worried about you, Dad's really upset.' I pause to wipe the tears from my face. Her going missing is now becoming very real. She might never get this voicemail. 'I love you, Mum. Please come home. I'm sorry if I was horrible to you yesterday. It's my fault, isn't it? I won't be like that ever again, I promise. I love you.'

I end the call before it asks me if I want to re-record.

I haven't wanted to think about yesterday morning, before she left for work, because I was so horrible to her. And if she does come home, I'm not even sure she'll forgive me.

CHAPTER 13

1991

If you'd told me, when I was ten years old, that I'd be at college studying A levels, then I'd have said you were off your head. But here I am, sitting in a Sociology class next to Rachel, the fittest girl in the class.

The teacher, tutor, whatever they call them, is sashaying at the front of the class. She's pretty fit for a fifty-year-old and she keeps giving me the eye. Probably cos the rest of the lads in this class look about thirteen.

I'm wearing glasses, even though I don't need them. I want to avoid being recognised by the five or so kids from my old school. Not that I give a shit, really, but I'm a new person here. Don't want all that messy shit to come out when I'm trying to make a good impression.

'Anyone?' says Ms McGiveron (Mc-give-her-one). 'Anyone?'

I raise my hand.

'Hegemony, Miss.'

She points her pen at me.

'Excellent, Alex! Nice to see one of you has been listening.'

I know. It sounds like I'm a kiss-ass now, doesn't it?

Someone polish my halo. But Rachel next to me is the proper studious type.

She passes me a note.

Don't forget to polish your apple for the next lesson

Great minds.
I write my reply.

Fuck off

She passes the note back.

:-)

*   *   *

In the common room, later, I'm sitting in a circle with some of the lads from Business Studies, waiting for my cheese and tomato toastie to be called from the nice lady behind the kiosk.

'Party tonight at Simon's,' says Phil, dishing out the cards for blackjack. 'Bring your own booze as per.'

'Nice one,' I say.

'You going, too, Alex?' says a voice behind me.

It's Sociology Rachel.

I turn round. She's looking at the hand of cards I've been dealt and raises her eyebrows when she sees the jack of spades. Maybe she thinks I'm lucky.

'You know Simon, then?' I say.

'Everyone knows Simon,' she says. 'What Simon says, everyone does. Isn't that how it goes?'

'Not always.' I think about giving her a wink but that'd be a step too far.

'Cheese and tomato toastie!' shouts Maureen at the counter.

I stand quickly. Bloody starving, *as per*.

'Cheese and tomato,' says Rachel. 'Very sophisticated.'

'Ha.'

I don't know what else to say because I don't know if she's joking or not. I find it hard to tell with most people. And by the time I get back to the group she's gone anyway. I place the toastie on the table – it'll take forever to cool. I learned that the hard way after being scalded on the first week. Who knew that cheese turns into molten lava in a Breville?

'She's going out with Simon,' says Phil. 'I think.'

'You think,' I say, 'or she is?'

'They were last week. But apparently, they're not going out out. Just seeing each other. According to Simon, anyway. But you know what he's like. Keeps things to himself.'

'Yeah.' I chance a bite of a corner of compacted toasted bread. 'That's Simon for you.'

I barely know Simon. None of us really know each other yet because we only started two months ago and we're all from different high schools. I'm one of the few who rides the bus here – it takes almost half an hour, but it's worth it to get away from that town and that bunch of losers.

'I thought she was going out with some meathead who's studying PE,' says another lad, can't remember his name. He pushes his glasses to the bridge of his nose. 'What kind of idiot takes PE as an A level?'

'Right.'

I'm eating with one hand and holding my cards in the other.

He places a three of spades and I take that as my cue.

'Oh, you bastard!' he says, picking up seven cards from the side deck.

Bastard sums me up pretty well.

'I hate this game,' he says, arranging his fourteen cards.

He has a shit hand as well; I can see it from here in his glasses.

* * *

This party's crap. Everyone's standing round in separate groups eating pizza and drinking weak bottled beer. Eating's cheating, isn't it? Mum used to say that.

I've been thinking about her a lot recently. I don't feel as bad about it these days because I was a different person when I was a kid.

Rachel's not here yet so I'm stuck talking to Phil and he's going on and on about Warhammer. I take out a SodaStream bottle and pour a large measure of vodka into a plastic cup and down most of it neat.

'Yeah,' I say, agreeing to whatever he's just said about some weird medieval shit. 'What's the deal with this party? Are they always like this?'

He shrugs and cradles his bottle of Newkie Brown Ale.

'I dunno. This is the first party I've been to.'

'Ever?'

'Yeah.'

'Not even a kid's party?'

'They weren't really my thing. We had a ZX Spectrum at home.'

'Oh,' I say. 'That explains a lot.'

There's some commotion at the door, but it's only Simon. Late to his own party (though technically, it's his parents' house). The walls are cladded with wood; the floor and most of the furniture is pine. It's like one of those ski lodges you see in American films.

'All right, lads,' he says, walking towards us in the open kitchen diner. He's carrying a Netto carrier bag full of bottles. 'This should make it interesting. Help yourselves.' He places the bag on the counter and takes out a bottle of Cinzano, two large bottles of Diamond White and a bottle of what looks like 10p lemonade. 'It's like a bloody wake in here.' He glances at his watch. 'Though it is only nine. What say we go to the pub – catch people at closing time?'

'Sounds good to me,' I say, offering him my SodaStream bottle. 'It's vodka.'

'Nice one, fella.'

Simon takes a swig. Phil's starting to look really uncomfortable, cuddling his warm ale bottle even tighter.

'What's your name again?' Simon says to me.

I'll let this one drop because we haven't really spoken much before.

'Alex,' I say.

'There are so many Alexes in our year. What's your surname?'

I'm the only Alex in our year.

'Buchanan.'

'Ah OK. Not really a nickname in there.'

'Alex is fine.'

He takes a quick sip of the vodka.

'Finish it if you like,' I say. 'There's not much left.'

'Cheers, Alex.' He winces after finishing it and puts the SodaStream bottle in the bin. I don't want to make a show of getting it out. Penny will notice it's missing if I don't bring it back.

I plant a smile on my face. 'Pub is a great idea.' I turn my back on him. 'This party's shit.'

* * *

The pub's blaring out 'Move Any Mountain' by The Shamen and the place is packed full of underage students. The bouncers didn't give a shit about Phil walking inside, even though he looks about twelve.

'Pint of Kronenbourg, please, mate,' Simon says to the barman, taking out a tenner.

I don't wait for him to offer me a drink – everyone else has a fiver for the night. I get my pint of cheap lager that I can't stand the taste of and follow Simon through the crowd. We get to a table as a bunch of uni students are readying to leave.

One of them – dyed black hair and a nose ring – shakes her head at me, a smug grin on her face.

'They're letting anyone in these days,' she says.

The fucking bitch.

'You what?' I say, stepping closer to her.

She puts a hand on my chest and shoves me, even though I'm at least a foot taller than she is. I'd be impressed if she wasn't showing me up.

'Fuck off, pretty boy,' she says, laughing.

The rest of her poncy gang are waiting behind her.

'Leave him alone, Megs,' says a lad behind her, but I know he finds it funny, too.

My left fist is clenched, as though all my hatred towards her is pooling in my hand. I want to drag her outside and strangle the life out of her.

'Sit down, mate,' shouts Simon.

I remain standing, watching as the wankers snake through the crowd. I look out the window as Megs slips an arm through another's.

There's a static in my ears, a pulsing as though my heart is in my head. *Bitch, bitch, bitch.* Adrenaline circles through my bloodstream.

'They're not worth it, Alex,' says Simon, as though reading something in my demeanour. 'They're jumped-up twats – probably studying Philosophy or some shite.'

He's looking at me, not unkindly, his lips in a straight line.

And I sit, just like he told me to. Simon says, and all that.

I think he gets his way a lot.

But the rage is still burning inside me, and I mask it by replying to useless wanky small talk.

'Yeah, she's well fit,' and, 'Nah. Can't be arsed with *Top Gear*,' and, 'Kylie's always going to be Charlene for me.'

We patter along for another two hours until I've had three pints and been for three pisses and now it's time to leave.

* * *

We're back at Simon's house and I've just spotted Sociology Rachel standing outside on her own. She must be seeing that fitness thicko and doesn't want him to see her smoking. He's in the kitchen, talking to another girl with big tits and a skirt that barely covers her arse, but it's OK because she's wearing thick black tights with DMs.

I take my chance and head outside, casual like. I swipe a packet of cigarettes from the arm of a chair on the way.

'Got a light?' And when she turns round, I say, 'Oh, it's you.'

It takes a while for her eyes to focus on my face.

'Alex.' She puts her arms around my neck, and I smell her sickly sweet cheap perfume. 'I thought you might be here.'

'Oh yeah?'

'Not like that.' She laughs, as though the idea of fancying me is ridiculous. 'I've got a boyfriend, you know.'

'Yeah. I saw.' I wave the unlit cigarette around, but I've no intention of smoking it and she doesn't seem to notice. 'Doesn't like you smoking, though, does he?'

'Eh?' She looks at her hands and the cigarette. 'He's not arsed about that. He takes E and everything. Smokes weed, too, but don't tell his mum.'

'I don't know his mum.'

She bends over double, pissing herself laughing.

She stands and sighs loudly.

Yeah, hilarious. She's pissed as a fart.

She turns to face me fully and points her cigarette at me like she's holding a dart that's about to pierce my heart.

'I know about you,' she says.

For a moment, she looks into my eyes, and it feels as though she can read my soul: what I did to Sarah-Jane Crosswell, and the pathetic animal I helped.

But she can't possibly know about that.

'What do you know?' I say.

'About your dad.'

'How do you know?'

'My cousin went to your high school. I mentioned you the other day and she told me all about it.' She rests a hand on my arm, and I want to rip it off. 'I'm so sorry to hear about your mum.'

'I came here to get away from all that shit,' I say, wishing I really did smoke. 'I want to forget what happened in the past.'

'I won't tell anyone,' she says.

But I don't believe her.

If she were to tell only one person, they could tell two and before I know it the whole college will know and everyone will look at me in that way again: like I'm scum, the son of a murderer, someone not to be trusted. And then I'll have to move away and start all over again. Somewhere so far away that no one knows me.

A vision of that bitch Megs from the pub forms in my mind and for a moment she and Rachel are one. I feel the adrenaline circling again. The anticipation of something I don't know, pulsing all over my body. I want to fuck Rachel right now but that wouldn't be enough.

A flash of my dying mum's face as my dad stood over her – the way the light in her eyes faded in an instant. Death so visible on her face, from one place to the next. My heart races and I feel the electricity between me and Rachel, like sparks of static in a thunderstorm. Like the whole universe is just her and me and everything else has disappeared. But there's only enough energy for one of us here and she's taking all of mine.

'I'm freezing,' says Rachel. 'Gonna head back inside.'

'What's that?' I shift my gaze to the distance, towards the darkness at the side of the house. There's nothing but brambles, spiky hedges. 'I think a cat's stuck in there. I can see its eyes.'

'Oh no,' she says, because she's nicer than me.

She walks slowly towards the hedge.

I look around and the street is empty, and the people inside Simon's house are either off their faces or not interested. At the back of the house is a field, empty, with just one lamppost about half a mile away and a kids' playground that's falling to pieces.

I pick up a stick so thick it's almost a log.

Don't think about it. Just do it.

She's crouching, hissing, 'Puss, puss, puss,' to an invisible cat.

I bring the stick as high as I can and thump the top of her head.

One is enough. She slumps to the side, a solitary domino. Two, three would've been too much – that's when the blood spatter starts.

I drag her through the hedge, through a hole – man-made, probably kid-made – that leads to the field. When I'm sure there's no one here, I straddle her. A part of me wishes she were conscious to witness this, but that would run the risk of her screaming.

I can almost see the energy between us now, almost hear the crackles.

I circle my hands around her neck and squeeze as hard as I can.

It takes longer than I thought.

I remove my hands, check her pulse. Put my cheek near her mouth and nose. No breath.

I get up quickly, and drag her into a small coppice, full of dense fern.

Music blares from the house – they've turned up the

volume. It's 'Move Any Mountain' again. Think it's my new favourite song.

I start walking back, looking at my hands to check for dirt but they're clean. There's only a couple of damp patches on my jeans, but no one's going to notice them.

I walk back into the house and go straight upstairs to the bathroom to throw water on my face. Dry it with a towel. A towel that loads of people will have used – it's crammed downstairs now. I wait a few moments for my breath to return to normal, holding the sink and staring into the mirror. It's like all the light from Rachel's life has lit up my eyes. They're shining like tiny torches. My cheeks are bright red, but other than that, there's nothing. No sweat on my forehead or on the top of my lip.

I head back down. Simon's in the hall.

'Where've you been, mate?' he says.

'Sorry, mate,' I say. 'Been the loo. I'd steer clear for another ten if I were you.'

'Ha,' he says. 'Cheers for the warning. I'm nipping out for a smoke. Do you want to partake?'

'I'm all right for now. I'll have to head home soon – got to get a taxi. I live miles away.'

'Kip on the couch,' he says. 'Parents won't be back till eleven in the morning.'

'That'd be great, ta.'

He heads outside into the cool, sweet fresh air, and I head to the kitchen. Brandy, I reckon. A sort of celebration. That's what proper blokes drink, isn't it?

Oh, bloody hell. It's her boyfriend, Mr Motivator.

'Have you seen Rachel?' he says to me. 'No one's seen her.'

'Sorry, mate.' I down a small measure of Courvoisier – obviously from the parents' drinks cabinet. I open my mouth to release the fumes, a dragon that's used all its fire. 'I don't know anyone called Rachel.'

CHAPTER 14

JOANNA

It's getting dark outside. It must be almost six o'clock, but with what he put in the drinking water I can't be sure how long I've been unconscious for. The television is off so I've no way of telling.

There are no sounds from outside. I could be in the middle of nowhere. He must've been in here while I was under because there's another sandwich and a bottle of water on the floor next to me. It feels like a violation that someone I don't know has control of me when I'm at my most vulnerable.

There's something different about this room. Tacked to the wall, to the right of the television, is a newspaper cutting. The paper is faded, yellow, old. I sit up to take a closer look, but I can't read the small print from over two metres away. The headline reads:

MISSING, NOW MURDERED

There's a picture of a girl around the same age as Scarlett. Her smile is beaming into the camera.

'I don't know who that is!' I shout, even though he's probably not even listening. 'I'm telling you: you have the wrong person.'

Is this a threat? That I'm missing soon to be murdered. Did he kidnap her, too?

The television comes back to life and my photo appears on the screen. It's the one of me at Christmas after two glasses of wine, wearing a wonky cracker hat.

'*A local man is helping police with this missing person enquiry.*'

I'm a missing person. Not deemed at risk. But who is assisting with their investigation? Does that mean they've arrested someone? It can't be the man who's keeping me here – the television has just switched on.

Oh God. What if the police think James has harmed me? Who'll look after Scarlett?

The TV switches off.

'Please let me talk to my daughter.' I can't stop the tears again. 'Please let me hear if she's all right.'

The speaker in the corner crackles.

'Drink the water.'

I'm sobbing pathetically; I can't help it.

'I don't want to go to sleep again. Please, just let me go.'

'You know the rules. Drink the water and you will be rewarded.'

The thought of being carried, unconscious, like last time, makes me feel sick. I haven't eaten so it's bile that rises to the back of my throat: hot, burning liquid. If I don't do as he says, I'm going to stay like this in this room. Stalemate. He's hardly going to just come in, if I stay awake, and let me out, is he?

I bend to reach the water, unscrew the already broken cap. I'm parched but the comfort is only fleeting, again. It doesn't take long before my eyes begin to close. But this time I just want to be in the darkness; it's my only way of escaping right now.

CHAPTER 15

1996

It's only a two-hour car journey away, but it might as well be a thousand miles. I hate coming here, I hate the routine of it, and I get an ominous feeling every time I round that bend. HMP Kirkham. An open prison and another step closer to my father's freedom.

I'm patted down, and this time there's a sniffer dog. I'm not a fan of dogs. Why do people enjoy having animals in their homes – animals that shit and piss everywhere? This one's not so bad, though.

The visiting room is pretty modern and there's only one guard standing at the door. Not like the last place he was in. That was proper full on – they pounced on you if you dared to touch each other let alone hug.

It's busy today – the air is grey with cigarette smoke – but Dad's bagged a seat by the window. He likes a window seat, but it's not as if he doesn't see daylight. They let them do all sorts here: work in the public on-site veg shop; handle knives in the kitchen. Some are even allowed out on weekends. It's like a reverse holiday camp.

'Looking sharp, son,' he says. 'Chip off the old block, eh?'

I don't know what he sees when he looks in the mirror, but I was not created in *his* image.

He's still sitting, even though hugging *is* allowed here. Probably for the best.

'Didn't you get my last letter?' he says.

'I'm fine thanks,' I say. 'How are you?'

His mouth falls open; he pulls his index finger with his other hand, so it clicks. A habit he's developed in here.

'What's got into you?' he says.

'Nothing.' I rub my face. 'End of year exams.'

'Ah right. I never went to university.'

I've heard that a thousand times, self-made man that he is.

'How's that car running?' he says. 'I hope Ronnie didn't set you up with a shitter.'

'It's fine. Thanks.'

'Not long now and I'll be able to get back to it all. I've missed it. The smell of petrol, the thrill of a sale.'

He's romanticising it. All he did was sit in his cramped office hollering orders at Ronnie while smoking, and drinking endless tea.

'You said you'd send some of your grant over,' he says.

'I thought you got a wage here.'

'I know, but smokes have gone up – have you seen the price of them?'

'I don't smoke, Dad.'

The tops and nails of his index and middle finger are tinged dark yellow.

'Right. You don't. Sensible that, lad.' He shifts about a bit, glances out the window. He's itching for a cigarette, but he doesn't touch his packet of Lambert & Butler, sitting under a five-for-a-pound lighter. Must be torturing him, that. But he wants something from me, and he doesn't want to spoil it by blowing smoke in my face. 'And phone cards. I need some of them, too.'

'Who are you ringing?'

His knees are moving up and down. He's smiling and I've only just noticed that he's had a shave and a haircut. Seems to have turned a corner.

'I met someone,' he says.

'A woman?'

'Of course a woman.'

'Well, you never know,' I say. 'Does she know where you currently reside?'

'Aye, yeah, she does.' He straightens a pretend tie around his neck, looks really pleased with himself. 'Some women like the danger of it all.'

'Really? They like it?'

'Ah, I dunno. But I read the other day about the number of women writing to cons on death row in America. I suppose there's the other side of it. Write to a bloke a thousand miles away. A relationship with someone you never have to see. So really, there's no danger there at all.'

'Jesus, Dad,' I say. 'Thought about it much?'

'Well, you know. Days are long.'

I should say I'm sorry, but sorry's not enough. It's just a word.

'So, what's her name?' I say, instead.

'Iris,' he says. 'A lovely name, don't you think?'

'If you're about a hundred years old.'

Dad laughs. 'She's only thirty-one. And she's beautiful.'

'Already has kids, then?'

He's tapping his cigarette packet, playing with his lighter.

'A little girl.'

'Cool,' I say, but the news seems disconnected from me. It's like hearing about someone's dreams, something unreal that will never happen. 'Pleased for you. You deserve a bit of good news.'

'She's been visiting,' he says, ignoring my superficial sentiments.

'Local?'

Tap, tap, tap on the packet. God, it's almost as annoying as him smoking.

'Yeah.'

'Where did you meet?' His feet are starting to go now – he's like a bloody one-man band. 'Just light one up, Dad. Please.'

He dives on the packet, which has only one missing. Not as broke as he makes out, then. He drags on it then leans back as though he's taken heroin or something. We've only been here five minutes. He really needs to sort that shit out.

'That's better.' He sits up straight again. 'In the prison mag. There's a personal ads section.'

'Right. A whole other world, eh?'

There's a light in his eyes that hasn't been there for years – even before Mum died.

'Yeah, son.' He pulls on his cigarette, blows the smoke towards the ceiling. 'Do you still see much of Penny and Martin?'

'You've not asked about them before.'

'Didn't want to upset you.'

'Why would that upset me?'

He shrugs, presses his lips together.

'You don't like talking about your mum.'

'I don't like thinking about her either.'

'Alex!'

'Well. She was a waste of space.'

'You can't say that about her. She loved you so much.'

'She was a raging alcoholic with a violent temper.'

'She was never the same after she had you,' he says. 'I've read about it. Postnatal depression.'

I push my chair back a bit, look out the window.

'You really don't think about her, do you?' he says quietly. 'You were only fourteen.'

A robin lands on a branch outside. I've heard that robins are signs from dead people, but that's a load of superstitious crap.

'Maybe you should get some counselling,' he says. 'I've had some in here and I thought it was going to be a load of wanky bollocks, but it was actually helpful.'

'I don't want to talk about stuff to a stranger. What would be the point? It won't change who I am.'

'Do you ever think about that night?'

I'm still looking out the window as the bird flies away. I wish it would take me with it.

'Try not to.'

'I've had to talk about it a lot recently. Remorse is a condition of my release. But...'

'What are you trying to say?'

'I'm not trying to say anything. Sometimes it's as though you've blocked everything out – as though it happened to another person.'

'I haven't blocked anything out.'

'So, you remember what happened?'

'Of course.'

'That it wasn't me, it was...'

'Yes, I know.' I say the last bit through gritted teeth and my fists are balls again. 'Why are you saying this now? You've never talked about it before.'

'I just wanted to make sure you were OK. The look in your eyes that night.'

I glance around the room. The security guard at the door – a right fat bastard – is staring at us.

'I don't want to talk about that night. I was a kid.'

He leans closer and whispers, 'But kids don't just stab their mother to death, do they?'

There, he said it.

Out loud.

Anyone could've heard. My eyes fill with hot tears of fury.

Tears I haven't shed since I was a kid. I wipe them as they drip down my face; and his expression softens because he thinks the reason I'm crying is that I'm sorry.

'It's OK, son.' He looks at the scar on my neck. 'I know you put up with a lot from her. I'm sorry. I'll never mention it again.'

I take my time to regain composure, to practise the words before I say them. Years and years of practice because I knew I would finally have to say it.

'I appreciate what you did for me, Dad,' I say, not quite making eye contact. 'I'll never forget it. And I'll make sure I look after you when you come out.'

'I know you will, son,' he says. 'But I'll be OK. I'd do anything for you, you know.'

'Thanks, Dad. And I'll sort the cash and the phone cards. Get you double the usual.'

'Thanks, Alex.'

'I'd better go,' I say. 'Got to revise. The last exam's tomorrow.'

'Good, good. Glad to see you're taking it seriously.'

* * *

I lied about the exam – I've already finished them, but I needed to get out of there. Why the hell did he bring up Mum? Her name hasn't passed his lips in years.

I pull up outside the house, which isn't actually a house because it's been divided into two flats. The kitchen window is steamed up because Simon's cooking tonight. Spaghetti bolognese, probably, because that's all he can cook.

I let myself in and head upstairs. It doesn't smell like spag bol to be fair.

'All right, mate,' he says when he sees me. 'The guys'll be here in half an hour.'

'OK.'

The kitchen is also the living room and the dining room, but we haven't much furniture – just the basics of what the place was furnished with when we moved in at the start of term. From Halls to sharing a flat. Not bad for a couple of twenty-one-year-olds, but I got the maximum grant. Simon didn't. His parents still pay for most of what he has. Not a part-time job for our Simon. I have to work part-time at the Union, but it's not so bad. Serving pissed students a pound-a-pint saves me from getting pissed myself.

I head into the bathroom but I've no time for a bath. I need to get the stink of prison off me, but this flat hasn't reached the modern era of having a shower. I wash my hands and face in the basin, change into a fresh T-shirt, and coat myself in Lynx like a fifteen-year-old. One day, I'll have designer *fragrances* like Simon.

'How was it today?' he says when I come back into the kitchen area and grab myself one of those stubby continental lagers from the fridge. 'Was your dad OK?'

Simon's the only one who knows where my dad is and why.

Well, not the full story, obviously.

The official story.

He pities me, I think. And it was such a coincidence that we chose the same university. One might say I've landed on my feet. Simon can be extremely generous with his parents' money and his own compassion. In short, he's not a bad bloke compared to some.

'Yeah,' I say, leaning against a set of drawers. 'He's met someone. A woman called Iris.'

'Really?' Simon's stirring the stir fry. It's about time that wok got some use. 'Lining himself up for when he gets out, is he?'

'Something like that,' I say. 'He won't be used to being alone.'

'And the routine of it all.' Simon's studying Psychology. 'Bet he won't know what to do with himself.'

'He's got his own business,' I say, watching as he cracks a couple of eggs into what looks like beef and onions. 'What are you making?'

'It's a mix-up of two different recipes. Not sure if it'll taste good. Thought I'd make it now and reheat once everyone's had too much to drink... alcohol dulls the tastebuds.'

'How very domesticated.'

He ignores the comment. It's a bit silly, the way we're pretending to be grown-ups.

The buzzer on the intercom sounds.

'Get that, will you, mate?' says Simon.

I'm already on my way. I grab the handset.

'Hey, Simon,' says Greg, a guy from one of Simon's classes.

'It's Alex.'

'Ah right. Hi, Alex.'

I press the buzzer. God, why did Simon have to invite Greg? He's such a dick.

There's more than one set of footsteps coming up the stairs – sounds like a mob. I open the door and Greg gives me a slight nod of a greeting as he walks in.

'All right, Si?' he bellows – loves the sound of his own voice, you know the type. 'How's the happy couple?'

Very fucking funny, Greg.

Two girls file in, carrying plastic bags of booze. The three of them head to the seating area and take over the settee.

One of the girls – the one with short hair and big earrings – shouts over, 'Have you got any wine glasses, Simon?'

'Wine, Nicole?' says Simon. 'Since when have you drunk wine?'

I can see her blush from here.

I swipe my beer off the counter and sit in the armchair – battered and no doubt sat on by hundreds.

'I'm Alex.' I look to Nicole and her friend. 'I don't think we've met.'

'I'm Greg,' he says, reaching out a hand. 'Nice to meet you, mate.'

'We've already met, but...' I shake his hand anyway because there are witnesses to this awkward exchange. I should've just pretended I'd never seen him before.

'This is my girlfriend, Chloe,' he says, putting his arm around the other one, AKA marking his territory, even though she can hardly take her eyes off me. 'She's from your neck of the woods. Went to high school with Simon, didn't you?'

'Uh huh,' she says. 'Thought I'd follow him round the country.'

Greg doesn't look best pleased with this comment.

Chloe's wearing a flowery dress, fishnets, and clumpy DMs. Such a strange combination that girls have taken to wearing. Nicole's unscrewing her Lambrini.

'That's not wine,' I say. 'Isn't it sparkling perry – like Babycham?'

'Shh,' she says, smirking. 'I'm trying to look sophisticated here.' She turns the bottle around to hide the label.

'Do you want me to put it in the fridge?' I ask. 'Bet it tastes rank when it's lukewarm.'

She grabs the bottle and hands it to me as I stand.

'Is it Simon you're trying to impress?' I say, not too loud.

She goes bright red again.

'Yeah,' says Chloe, talking for her friend. 'She's had a crush on him since the start of first year.'

Nicole gives her friend the evils. I take the bottle to the fridge, sliding it next to the milk. I spin it so the label faces the back. She doesn't seem a bad lass, does Nicole.

* * *

We tried the food. Simon was right when he said egg fried rice and beef chow mein weren't a good combination. We're sitting on the floor now, like teenagers about to play Spin the Bottle.

Nicole's wasted, which is surprising because Lambrini has as much alcohol as a thimble of vodka. Chloe's sitting cross-legged in front of Greg – he's got his arms circled around her as though he's scared she'll escape. Simon's puffing on a giant spliff – he offers it to me, but as always, I shake my head. Weed's for losers. I read once that continued use can lead to mental health issues, but Simon would probably argue that it *helps* one's mental health. Terrible things don't happen to people like Simon.

'Anyone want in on a pizza?' he says, standing up and wandering over to the telephone. 'I fancy a meat feast. Chicken, pepperoni, chilli beef, peppers.'

'God, that sounds disgusting,' says Nicole, looking pallid, holding a hand against her mouth. 'I think I need to go soon.' She glances at Chloe but Chloe's oblivious. There's no chance she's leaving right now – plus it's only ten o'clock. Nicole rolls her eyes and takes little sips from the glass of water I put next to her.

Simon returns to his place on the beanbag, sits cross-legged.

'Twenty minutes,' he says to himself because no one else is listening.

I choose a CD single. The Shamen, 'Move Any Mountain'. Haven't heard that song in years.

I slide it into the hi-fi and turn up the volume.

Thud, thud, thud, thud.

I close my eyes and see Sociology Rachel standing outside Simon's parents' house. She's smoking a cigarette, the smoke mingling with the cloud of her breath in the cold, which may or may not have happened, but I like it better this way. The look of terror on her face as I sat astride her.

No. That didn't happen. The narrative keeps changing in my mind. Her eyes were closed. She wasn't there, not really.

'Hey,' says Chloe, rudely interrupting my internal video. 'Does anyone remember Rachel Beckwith?'

What the fuck?

'Did you go to Runsdale College, too?' I say.

'No,' she says.

My eyes bore into hers, but she's not looking at me. How did she do that – can she read my mind? I send Rachel away and replace her with pictures of balloons, cake, pizza. The song ends and the room fills with silence.

'Yeah,' says Nicole, resting her head on the seat of the settee. 'I remember the name. What happened to her?'

I learned far more about Rachel in the days, weeks, and months she was missing. Tearful appeals told me how loving she was and how much other people loved her. I don't know if it was serendipity, but no one else remembers seeing Rachel at that party. Everyone was wasted, including her meathead of a boyfriend, but all of that doesn't matter any more. I can't get myself worked up about it. The irony is that I've taken up running to get rid of that energy, to clear my head.

'She was found dead,' says Simon.

'She never was.' Greg lights up a cigarette. 'Shit.'

'He never watches the news,' says Chloe.

'Not if I can help it.' He sends a cloud of blue smoke towards me, and I wince, trying not to splutter. 'Sorry, mate,' he says, so I let it lie. 'How did she die?'

This is always my favourite bit when Rachel is brought up in conversation, but it doesn't happen often these days. I didn't realise these people even knew her. I keep my mouth straight, trying to kill the light I can feel blazing out of my eyes.

'Body was too decomposed to tell, from what I remember,' says Simon.

'She was at your party,' says Chloe, her eyes fixed on him.

'Everyone said they hadn't seen her there, but *I* saw her.'

'Bollocks was she at my party,' says Simon, straightening his shoulders, narrowing his eyes. 'Everyone knows she was last seen at the bus stop – she didn't make it as far as my house.'

'I wasn't imagining it,' says Chloe quietly, fiddling with the buttons on her burgundy cardigan.

'Did you tell the police?' I say, my voice coming out croakier than I'd have liked.

'Course I did,' she says. 'But no one else saw her and they asked me how much I'd had to drink. I said I'd only had a few Bacardis, which was partly true, but I could tell when they looked at me that they thought I was just another pisshead.' She folds her arms as though she's freezing. 'She was my best friend. I would've spotted her anywhere.'

'I didn't know she was your best friend,' says Nicole. 'You don't mention her that much.'

'It's too painful.'

She covers her hand with her sleeve and dabs her face, but there aren't any tears. I wouldn't be surprised if Chloe here is exaggerating her connection to Rachel. Some people do that, to make themselves feel more important, more involved with something out of the ordinary.

I want to ask something, but it can't come from me.

'Where in the house did you see her?' says Simon.

Who was she with?

'Outside,' says Chloe, and my heart begins pounding. The static sounds in my ears. I watch as her lips move again. 'She was standing outside waiting for her boyfriend, Richard, or whatever his name was.'

'You said you were her best friend,' I say, 'but you don't remember her boyfriend's name?'

All their eyes are on me. Silence for a few tense moments. Simon takes a drag on his joint. I feel the tension as he inhales and holds his breath. He exhales with a hiss.

'That's a good point, mate,' he says, finally. 'She wasn't found anywhere near my house. She was found in the cemetery. I'd hate to think that anything bad happened to her at my house. It wasn't a wild night or anything.'

No one saw me kill Rachel and no one saw me move her.

Luck, rather than design, no doubt.

'Her boyfriend's name was Rick,' pipes up Nicole.

'How would you know that?' says Chloe, slighted by her friend knowing more than she does.

'Just one of those random things I remember.'

'Did anyone go to the reconstruction?' asks Chloe.

'No,' I say. 'That's a bit morbid, isn't it?'

'It was shown on *Crimewatch*. Before they knew she was dead.'

Of course I went to the reconstruction. And of course they filmed her last whereabouts in the completely wrong place. It was laughable. Her parents and sister stood just off-camera as a girl – who was a surprisingly good likeness, actually – was filmed walking to the bus stop from her house on Calderdale Street. Headphones on, hands in her denim jacket pockets, long dark hair flowing behind her in the wind.

'Did he kill her, then?' says Greg, interrupting my thoughts. 'Her boyfriend?'

'Probably,' says Nicole. 'More often than not it's someone the victim knows.'

'How do you know that?' I say.

She shrugs. 'Did a module on criminal psychology. Pretty interesting actually.'

'What else did you learn?'

'Lots.'

'Sounds interesting.'

I'm mocking, but I'm dying to know what secrets she uncovered between the pages of her coursebooks.

'What if it was a serial killer?' says Chloe.

'Doubt it,' says Nicole. 'They're really rare.'

'Really rare?' I can't help it. 'Do you think?'

'Yeah.'

I turn to smirk at Simon, but he's not smiling. He seems to be examining my face. Either that or he's completely stoned.

'It probably *was* her boyfriend,' says Greg. 'Or Chloe here. You say you were the last one to see her. How would you know that?' He tickles her sides. 'Only the killer knows they're the last person to see their victim.'

'That's not something to be joking about,' she says, getting up. 'I need to take Nicole home. She's wasted.'

It's like Chloe can feel the static in the air and she wants to get away. That I'm the devil, and an angel on her shoulder is whispering in her ear to leave.

Shit. I'm more pissed than I thought.

'I can hear you, you know.' Nicole's legs almost collapse as she stands. 'I need to go now.'

'I know, Nic.' Chloe links her friend's arm. 'Are you walking us back, Greg?'

'Do I have to?' he says huffily. Love's young dream. 'It's well early.'

'I'll walk you,' I say, getting to my feet. 'I need to collect something anyway.'

'Collect what?' Simon's still staring at me.

'I fancy a bag of chips,' I say. 'I'm starving.'

'I could do with some chips,' says Nicole. 'Starving.'

'Oh God,' says Chloe, pulling her friend towards the door. 'Come on, then. Let's get some food down you.'

'There's pizza coming,' says Simon and everyone groans. He stands as I put on my jacket. 'Make sure you walk them home safely.' He's deadly serious.

What does he think I'm going to do? Murder the pair of them at the same time?

'Course,' I say, shutting the door behind us.

Nicole is surprisingly spritely down the stairs; Chloe opens the main door for her.

'We'll be OK,' she says. 'You don't have to walk us. I only accepted to piss Greg off.'

'Oh, right,' I say. 'Aren't you a bit old for immature games?'

She's slightly stunned. Perhaps she assumed I was a nice person because I don't constantly spout meaningless bollocks.

'Fuck off,' she says, hoisting Nicole's arm again, pulling her away. 'Leave us alone.'

'I said I'd walk you back,' I shout after them. 'Don't blame *me* if anything happens to you.'

I'm tempted to follow from a distance, but that bitch isn't worth it. Let her live a long sad life. Fat cow. Who does she think she is? Greg's the only ugly idiot prepared to be seen next to her.

Shame about Nicole, though. She's beautiful. Just my type.

I head over to the chippy – it's open till one in the morning most days.

There's a girl, woman, can't tell, standing outside. Fishnet tights, again. What is it with them?

'I don't suppose you've got some change?' she says, making a beeline for me because there's no one else around and the chip shop's empty. 'Only I've missed the last bus and I don't have enough for a taxi.'

'You can share mine,' I say to her. She's pretty. Very pretty. Her eyes are lined with thick black liner and her lips are sparkly red like Dorothy's ruby slippers. There's no place like home. 'Just round the corner.'

'Really?' she says, her eyes trusting, grateful. She's had too much to drink. 'That's really kind, thanks.'

'That's no problem,' I say, guiding her towards the back of the shops. It's quiet round here, dark. Only bins and rubbish and dog shit. 'No problem at all.'

CHAPTER 16

SCARLETT

Gran and Pete have come round – they missed the police by five minutes. Dad's upstairs taking a shower and he's been extra-long because he's still upset about the letter. I'm not sure if Gran knows about it yet – I doubt Dad's told her.

I'm sitting next to her, under my blanket, which is also where I'm clinging to my mobile. I have it on silent so Gran doesn't hear when it vibrates.

'What does that mean?' says Gran, turning off the telly. *Granada Reports* said a local man is helping with their enquiries. 'What local man?'

'I don't know, love,' says Pete.

Pete's my grandmother's third husband. I've never met my biological grandad but from several hints he was – is – a bit of a bastard. Lives on the Costa del Sol or Tenerife or something. Mum never talks about him any more, but sometimes he sends her a postcard that she throws straight in the bin.

Gran's been married to Pete for about five years. He has a uniform of jeans, white T-shirt and leather jacket that probably looked all right in the eighties. Hard to imagine him in the eighties, though – his hair's been grey since I met him. He's probably about sixty, I guess, but no one mentions it. His last birthday cake only had one candle. He's always been kind to me, though. Bit of a talker. Knows a lot about weird stuff that he's learned on YouTube. Gran used to write to him when he was in prison. It was after one of her death rowers in Texas died. Devastated, she was. She decided, then, that losing *dear friends across the pond* was too distressing, and signed up to the more local (and less precarious) Prisoners Penfriends. *It must've been fate* that they gave her Pete's contact details so soon after her second divorce. Romantic, huh? I don't know if she tells that story at dinner parties. It definitely wasn't mentioned at the wedding.

She's about ten years older than Pete, but she looks good for her age. She still wears jeans, not like Hannah's nana Lilian, who wears flowery dresses whatever the weather. Except for when she came to ours last Christmas, with Hannah and Hannah's dad, and she wore a burgundy tracksuit with reflective stripes down the sides. Must've been a gift.

Pete's sitting at the dining table, scrolling through footage from our front-door camera on his laptop, from the night Mum went missing.

Everyone keeps saying no news is good news, which is what I'm clinging on to. You get people turning up years after being kidnapped. But I can't think about it – I can't think about where Mum is now. If she's safe. Or if she's being tortured. Or if she's been run over and lying in some undergrowth somewhere.

I get up, trying to stay casual, and head to the downstairs toilet. I close the door behind me, run the tap on full and cry into the hand towel.

Where are you, Mum? It's not the same without you.

I splash freezing cold water on my face and pat it dry.

Maybe I could speak at an appeal. Let whoever has taken her know that she's a mother, a kind person who doesn't deserve any of this.

'I think I've found something,' says Pete as I walk back into the living room. 'A car drove past two nights in a row.'

Gran leaps off the settee and sits next to him. She narrows her eyes as she concentrates on the screen. I want to go and look but I'm scared I'll see Mum. See her before, when she didn't know what was going to happen.

'Did the camera pick up anything suspicious?' I say.

'No,' says Pete. 'I've sent over a copy to the police, but I thought I'd go through it anyway.'

Pete was the one who set up our cameras. One at the front and one at the back because Dad is always worried about security. He owns a security company – Pete, that is. Maybe that's why he was in prison: blackmail, hacking, disabling security cameras for a robbery. No one talks about why he was inside. I asked Mum once and she said it was a misunderstanding. They all say that, though, don't they? There's not one guilty person in prison, apparently. And Mum said that no one who actually hurts people ended up in HMP Kirkham, but she's hardly the expert on ex-cons. Unlike Gran...

Pete presses play on one of the paused captures: next door's cat saunters across the end of our path. Seconds later, strobes from car headlights pass by.

'This is at ten thirty-four on Saturday night.' He clicks on another tab. 'And this is from Sunday night.'

A silver Prius drives past our house, then three more times, as slowly as the first time.

'But why?' I say.

Gran and Pete both turn around.

'Why what?' says Pete. 'Why are we looking at this?'

'No,' I say. 'Why would this car be casing our house? Mum never goes out after nine p.m. Well, almost never. She hadn't been on a night out for months before last night. So, it's not as though she has a routine where she goes out every night.'

'They probably weren't just checking out *this* house,' says

Pete. 'Prowling. Hunting. Taking any opportunity to take what he can. Bastard.'

Pete would know, I guess.

'So Mum wasn't targeted?'

'It doesn't seem likely,' he says.

'That's not true.' Dad's standing at the doorway. 'Maybe they were following her.'

'What would anyone want with Joanna?' says Gran. 'She hasn't done anything to anyone.'

Dad walks towards the table.

'To get to me.'

'Have you upset someone at work?' says Pete. 'It's a lot of money you're dealing with at your place.'

To be honest, I've never understood what Dad does for work. It's for an investment company, but he's not a stockbroker.

'Last week,' he says, pulling out a seat and sitting, 'a client – let's call him Bob—'

'Why don't you just call him by his real name?' says Gran. 'It's not as if we're going to hunt him down.'

Dad glances at Pete, who looks away quickly. Dad *definitely* knows what Pete did to get into prison.

'I send a lot of business Bob's way. Start-up companies, small businesses who need capital to get up and running or to get to that next level.'

'So, Bob's like a dragon?' I say.

'What?' Gran's looking perplexed.

'Like on *Dragons' Den*,' I say.

'Exactly, Scarlett.' Dad keeps looking at the drinks cabinet; he always has a quick shot when he's had a bad day at work. Not that he's obvious about it, I just notice things. 'Anyway, last week, Bob signed with Audio Tech – a company that's been trading for nearly two years but had a big project they wanted to take forwards. Home communication systems to be implemented into all new-builds as standard.'

'Like on *Big Brother*?' says Gran.

'Sort of.'

Dad gets up and lingers by the whisky. Pete gets up and pours shots into four glasses.

'Scarlett shouldn't be drinking whisky,' says Gran.

'I'm nearly eighteen,' I say. 'I've been drinking for years.' Her head jolts back. 'I mean at parties and stuff,' I add. 'Not, like, every day.'

'But with what's going on right now,' she says, 'I don't think it's wise to start down this path... what if...'

Dad swipes one of the glasses and almost slams it down in front of me.

'If Scarlett's going through what I'm going through then it'll take the edge off. I'm not saying she has to down the bloody bottle.'

'So, what happened with Bob?' says Pete, sensing the verge of World War Three.

Dad downs the whisky then pours another before sitting back down opposite me.

'It was a sham. There was no Audio Tech. It was an elaborate scam.'

'But that's not your fault,' I say, but he's frowning; his jaw's clenched.

'I should've been more thorough. I've had a lot on my plate recently. Should've done my due diligence. But the VAT and company registration certificates came back fine. I visited their offices, checked their passports.'

'How much did *Bob* lose?' asks Pete.

'Just under half a million.' He finishes his second whisky, goes to stand, but Gran gives him a look. 'OK. OK.' He gets out his phone. 'I'll order some pizza. Scarlett must be starving.'

'Thanks, Dad.'

I doubt I'll be able to eat, though. It's been hard to find my appetite. I feel guilty every time I think about food, and every moment I'm not focused completely on Mum.

'Would he drive a Prius, though?' I say. 'If he's a millionaire, wouldn't he have a Porsche or a Bentley?'

'He wouldn't do anything himself,' says Pete. 'People with money don't like to get their hands dirty.'

Gran gives Pete a withering look.

'That's enough with the criminal talk,' she says. 'We're just coming up with stories here and they're getting more and more outlandish. Has anyone checked Joanna's wardrobe to see if any of her things are missing?'

'I think the police did,' I say. 'Didn't they, Dad?'

He puts his phone on the table. 'No. They didn't look round the house at all. I had a quick look – everything seems to be there. Her going-away bag is still at the bottom of her wardrobe.'

Gran stands and heads towards the hall.

'I'll have a better look. Make myself useful.' She lingers at the doorway. 'Do you think we should be out there looking? It's getting dark outside. I hate to think of my little girl out there on her own.'

The feeling catches me at the back of my throat so strongly that I almost burst out crying. I dig my nails into my palms. I need to stay strong for Gran, for Dad. They don't need to be looking after me; I'm not a kid any more.

But even so. I just need my mum right now.

CHAPTER 17
2002

It's not going to be a big glitzy affair, as Penny would call it. Just a few of us at the registry office.

I met Angela at a charity masquerade ball at the Hilton in Liverpool just over a year ago. Although, technically, it had taken me far longer to catch her attention. I first saw her in an article in the *Chester Chronicle* – her father's business was handing a huge cheque to Alder Hey Children's Hospital. They're a very generous family.

The car will be here soon. Penny stayed at my flat last night, and she got tiddly on half a glass of Chardonnay and reminisced about Martin. She only briefly mentioned Mum, which was understandable. She was her daughter after all, and I could tell she wanted to say more, but I pretended I was choked with the emotion of both my parents missing my wedding day, so she changed the subject.

Penny's sticking a flower in my lapel.

'Yellow rose,' she says. 'For friendship. Because when all the romance fades in years to come, a friendship is all that's left. And that's more important than a roll in the hay.'

'I've missed your country sayings, Penny,' I say. 'People are far too crude in these parts.'

She brushes my jacket with a lint roller then stands back to admire her handiwork.

'You never did take to calling me Gran, did you?' she says. 'All those years we missed while you were growing up. I'll never forgive myself.'

Ever since Martin died two years ago, Penny's allowed herself to get more sentimental. It's like she was hiding pieces of herself.

'It's not your fault, Pen,' I say. 'You know that.'

'I should've put my foot down. Maybe even come to see you when you were little, when your father was out the house.' She shakes herself out of melancholy and dabs at her hair in the mirror. 'There's no point in what ifs now.' She glides the roller over the sleeve of her pale green suit. 'Are you sure this isn't too showy?' she says because she's not used to wearing anything brighter than beige. 'It's a lot more out there than I'm used to.'

'You look perfect.'

A car horn sounds from outside, which is our cue to leave. Waiting outside is Harry. I've only known him a year or so but he's proving to be a good friend. Goes above and beyond. Like today, for example. He's borrowed one of his dad's motors – a nice Porsche Carrera. He's got the roof down and he's puffing on a cigarette. Luckily, he flings it before Penny clocks it.

'It's so lovely of you to drive us,' she says. She probably can't remember his name. She has trouble keeping up with the names of my friends. She'd only just got Simon's right the week before I left town. 'And such lovely weather for it.'

'Right you are, Penny,' says Harry, revving the engine. 'Let's see what this baby can do. Hold on to your hair.'

Poor Penny. Her head jerks back as Harry floors the accelerator, but we don't get far because we're in a thirty-miles-an-hour zone and the traffic light's on red.

I should be nervous, shouldn't I? I feel more excited than nervous. I picture Angela's lovely round face, big blue eyes, and white-blonde hair – even better looking than Gwen Stefani. She's like no one I've ever met before. It helps that her family is minted and I've been given a nice cushy position as Director of Operations as a wedding present. I'm not averse, though I am a stranger, to a bit of nepotism.

Harry screeches to a halt outside the registry office.

'I'd better park this round the back,' he says as Penny and I get out. 'Dad would kill me if this got towed.'

'Thanks, mate,' I say. 'See you in there.'

There's confetti all over the pavement from the last three or four weddings before us. The town's busy with people on their way home from work. A Thursday, perhaps, is an unconventional day to get married, but there were slim pickings if we wanted to do it this year.

It doesn't take long for Harry to reappear, and we file into the council building. Angela wanted to do the whole me-wait-at-the-altar bit, so we go in first. It's no grand altar, though. Just a table with two chairs at the front. I wait near the officiator; something by Céline Dion is playing, but I don't know what it's called because I'm not her biggest fan. Bit screechy for my liking.

The door opens and that's my signal to turn around.

She looks breathtaking – like the angel she was named after.

She walks slowly towards me, her little sister walking in front. Angela wanted her included in the ceremony, and I didn't mind at all. She's only ten years old and it's been hard for them both after their mother died four years ago. It's something that bonded us: bereavement.

'Hi,' whispers Angela as she faces me.

'Hi.'

The vows are exchanged in minutes and there are tears in her eyes by the end. It's something I've never been able to do a lot, cry. Twice, I remember. The day I came to live with Penny and Martin, and that time I saw Dad at HMP Kirkham. I can't even summon the tears to fake it right now, even though I've been trying all week. I went as far as pinching myself to conjure them, to no avail.

Angela's dad, Mike, comes over to shake my hand.

'Well done, son.' He's always wanted a son. He tells me all the time, especially because he's finally got someone to go with him down the pub to watch Liverpool play. It means a lot, to be wanted. It actually makes pretending to like football worth it. 'Welcome to the family.'

He grabs me in a bear hug, which I'm used to when Liverpool score, but Penny is taken aback. She's not used to public displays of affection after decades of being with Martin. Mike sees the panic in her eyes when he turns his attention to her. He shakes her hand. 'Welcome to the family, Penny. Sandra would've loved you.'

Sandra, Angela's mum, died in a car accident. There was another person in the car, but no one really talks about it. Whoever it was fled the scene, leaving poor Sandra bleeding and dying alone on an empty A483 at four in the morning.

I didn't question where she was going at that time because she's dead now and none of that matters, because they only remember what they want about her. Re-write history to make it all better.

Perhaps I should take a leaf out of their history book. Tell people that Mummy dearest would have done anything for anyone – that it's a tragedy she passed at such a young age. She had so much more to give. But those kinds of lies wouldn't make it past my lips. I'm not going to do her any favours.

It's just a quick walk to the reception. It's in an impressive Victorian building and the room is laid out with white linen and white roses. Nothing but the best for Angela. Well, Mike paid for it all. Couldn't insult the man by refusing.

Angela's auntie Mo guides us to our places at the front. We're to face the whole room while we eat, which is a novelty. Mike, little Daisy, and Mo are on Angela's side, and Penny and Harry are on mine.

The rest of the room is filled with mostly friends of Angela's. School friends, university friends, work friends. Clusters of people who keep themselves to themselves and have nothing in common with other groups. In a way, I'm glad Simon couldn't make it. Things haven't been the same between us since I left York. That whole Chloe bitch-face thing came back to bite me. I thought he'd have stuck up for me no matter what, what with my mum being dead and everything, but it seemed he had reached his limit. Especially after Chloe gave me a 'second chance' when we hosted a poker night, but I ended up calling her a cheap ugly whore. So *she* says. I probably didn't. I have no recollection of it whatsoever.

After we've eaten, Harry gets up to say a few words. He's got them printed on cards and everything. I have no idea what he's going to say because he doesn't really know me. He taps his glass with a fork to silence the room. His cheeks are flushed – I saw him downing a few brandies for courage.

'Welcome, ladies and gentlemen. It is a great honour that I have been asked to be Alex's best man. We met at work – like most grown-ups do. I hope he doesn't mind, but I had to do a bit of digging.'

Oh God. I hope he doesn't mean literally.

I loosen my tie. Bloody hell it's hot in here.

'I managed to contact some of his school friends' – he glances at Penny – 'thanks to Alex's grandma.'

Oh shit, Penny. What have you done?

'A practical joker, it seems, was our Alex. One schoolfriend recalls him ordering pizza for the whole class during Biology.'

What the fuck is he on about?

Penny leans towards me and whispers in my ear.

'I gave you a different surname – said you changed it when you came to live with us. God knows who *he's* talking about.'

She leans back and sips her champagne.

I give her a conspiratorial grin.

So *that's* who I get it from.

* * *

At last, the formalities are over. People are drifting away until there are only a handful left. Harry's looking worse for wear and talking to an empty chair.

'You all right, mate?' I say, sitting opposite him.

'Drowning my sorrows,' he says, staring into his glass while swirling the amber liquid.

'What are you sorry about?' I say.

He places his glass down and raises his head, shakily, to meet my eyes.

'Are you being deliberately obtuse?' is what I think he says.

'You've lost me.'

He looks around the room but doesn't appear to focus on anyone.

'Angela,' he says, clearer this time. 'She was the love of my life. We were going to travel round the world together.'

'What?'

'You heard me.'

'Are you talking about my Angela? She's scared of flying.'

Harry's head sways slowly down till he rests it on the table.

'No,' he says. 'I don't know what you're talking about.'

Jesus, the guy is absolutely wasted. I catch Angie's dad's eye and beckon him over.

'What do we have here, then?' he says, jolly as ever.

'Can you sort Harry out for me,' I say, getting up quickly to head over to my newly wedded wife.

'Come on, Ang,' I say. 'Let's head up to the honeymoon suite.'

Her cheeks are flushed. She doesn't usually drink but she's let her hair down tonight.

'OK,' she says, skimming past me, grazing her lips against mine. 'I'll just say goodbye to Dad.'

'OK. Good luck with that.'

I head to the men's while I wait. There's a figure standing at the bar that I recognise. Tall, short greying hair. He turns round when he sees me in the bar mirror.

Oh God. Angela doesn't know anything about it. She thinks my mum died in a car accident, too.

Shit. I need to get him out of here.

I stride up to him.

'Hello, Dad.'

* * *

We're standing outside the venue and the street is busy; it's still reasonably early.

'How did you find out where I was?' I say, searching round for anyone who might be watching.

'I thought you'd be pleased to see me. I'm a free man.'

'Yes, yes,' I say. 'I am pleased to see you. It's just that... I haven't...'

'You haven't told her about me, have you?'

'Not the details.'

'Not anything.' He lights a cigarette. 'Where did you say I've been for all these years? Hasn't she wondered why I haven't met her?'

'I haven't known her that long,' I say. 'I told you last time I came to see you. We've only been together a year. So, it hasn't been that hard. I said you lived in Australia, couldn't get over in time – what with the business and all.'

'What business would that be?'

'Telecommunications.'

'Fuck me,' he says. 'She must think I'm a right boring bastard.' Another drag of his ciggie. 'Why are you rushing into this? Why do you feel the need to get married?'

'Bit late to be the doting daddy, isn't it?'

'Now that's not fair. After what I did for you.'

I take him by the elbow and lead him down a side street.

'But why did I do what I did?' I say. 'It was because I was trying to get you two to stop arguing.' I'm still holding him, pushing him against the wall. I release him, take a deep breath. 'I don't want to be talking about this, not today.'

'Have you ever told anyone what you did?'

'This conversation is over, Dad.' I go to walk back inside, but the ball of fire in my chest wants to explode out of me. I turn back around. 'I was just a kid.'

He grabs the tops of my arms. 'I know. Look, I'm sorry for bringing it up. I just came to say congratulations. I didn't want to make you feel bad on the most important day of your life.'

'I know.'

He's lost weight, his jawline is more defined, and I think he's wearing fake tan.

'Are you still seeing that Iris?' I say.

'Going to meet her tonight. Her daughter's out for the night. A teenager now.'

There's a fleeting moment between us – a glimpse into what might've been. But he didn't know me as a teenager, not really. And now he's in another child's life. The time he should've spent with me.

'I'd invite you inside but...'

'It's OK, son,' he says.

I feel as though I'm rejecting him, like we're breaking up. But if he comes back into my life there's always a risk of... What? I don't know.

He puts his hand on my shoulder.

'I'm proud of you, son,' he says. 'You've really turned your life around.'

'Thanks, Dad.'

I sigh. If only he knew.

CHAPTER 18

JOANNA

I woke briefly in the darkness, but nothing seemed to have changed. I was in the same clothes, and in the same room. Now it's morning – I assume it's the morning. Monday night I was taken and there have been two nights, so it must be Wednesday. Or Thursday. God, I don't know.

There is something else peeking out from underneath the bed.

One arm is still attached to the bedpost, and I stretch over so widely it feels as though my chest might rip in two. I crawl my fingers towards it.

Yes. I've got it.

It's a small tape recorder with a tiny Post-it note that says, *Play me.*

I press the button.

'You have five new messages.'

It sounds like it's from my mobile phone.

I'm not prepared for this. He's trying to torture me.

'Hi, love.' It's James. *'We need to talk when you get in. I think you know what it's about.'*

I have no idea what it's about. What the heck does he

mean? We didn't part on an argument. He doesn't get angry. Merry from a glass of wine, perhaps.

Next message.

'*Me again. It's now two in the morning.*' He's been drinking – a lot. His voice is deep, his words merging into one another. He probably won't remember leaving it. '*Look, I know you're with him. Got a letter – someone's spilt your secret. Just call me back.*'

The third message is just background noise. Then comes the fourth.

'*Joanna, it's me. Where are you? Scarlett's really worried about you, but I said she should still go to college. She'll be home soon. Please call me back. If I don't hear from you in the next hour or so, I'm calling the police.*'

Does he still think I'm missing? Did no one see me being taken? Who the hell is keeping me here? Why haven't the police found me? He must've called them on Tuesday afternoon. If they can trace my mobile, they'll find me. Though I don't know if that works in real life. I doubt my kidnapper's careless enough to switch my phone on in this place. Not with a set-up like this.

I wish the television would come back on so I could find out what day it actually is.

'*Next new message.*'

'*Mum? It's me, Scarlett. Can you please ring me back and tell me you're OK? The police are here. Everyone's worried about you, Dad's really upset.*' My darling girl pauses, sniffing. '*I love you, Mum. Please come home. I'm sorry if I was horrible to you yesterday. It's my fault, isn't it? I won't be like that ever again, I promise. I love you.*'

Oh, Scarlett. What must be going on in her head if she thinks all of this is her fault? It was only a silly argument we had, because I wouldn't let her go out at nine on a school night. She said she was going to her friend Kai's house to study, but that was a lie. I'm not proud of myself, but I checked her phone. Kai's mum was going out and leaving them with alcohol. Just so irresponsible. And when I asked Scarlett about it – basically calling her out on her lying to me, and me admitting that I snooped on her phone – she shut down. She said everyone parties at college and that I was boring because I didn't have a life. I hate arguing with her and I'm always the first to make up, but I had to leave for work.

From the sound of her voice on the message, she's truly sorry. It's such a small issue compared to what is happening now.

I need a strategy. I cannot keep allowing this man to control me. I have to get back to my daughter.

Next time he offers me a drink, I'll pretend to comply.

But I'll stay awake.

CHAPTER 19

2004

I never thought I'd be a bloke who had a den but here I am. Stuck in the converted attic with a PlayStation and a bed settee because she has her best friend over ('Wednesday Girls' Night'). The best friend who is going through a break-up. It's better when it's just the two of us, when we watch films together, or go to the seaside because she likes to do things I want to do and vice versa. Sometimes. But I think the mask is slipping, for both of us. Marry in haste and all that.

We're meant to be trying for a baby, but my heart's not in it and it's becoming increasingly difficult to find excuses not to have sex with her.

'Two years, Alex,' she said earlier. 'Two years we've been married, and you said you wanted three children. I'm not getting any younger.'

Stating the bloody obvious.

If she wants kids that much, then she'd probably be best looking elsewhere. But separation doesn't fit in my timeline right now. Angela's dad is due to retire soon. If we split up now, my promotion will go tits-up. And I need that to open doors to new companies.

I down another beer and open my mini fridge but it only contains Diet Coke.

Fuck it. This is my house too.

It's only Jess. It's not as though she'll confess to Angela, is it?

I throw my controller across the settee and stand, smoothing my hair in my reflection in the full-length mirror in the corner. I hate getting fucking old. I'm cultivating the same belly as my father, but it's not as bad. It's only an inch, tops, above my belt.

No more beers. Vodka is what's called for.

I'm quiet down the stairs in just socks, and I know where the creaks are. I hear Angela's soft laugh. Jess on the other hand, well, her cackles resonate throughout the house.

I listen at the door. They're so drunk because it's almost ten thirty and Jess has been here since seven.

'So.' Jess is topping up wine, glug, glug, glug. 'What's he like in bed?'

Oh my fucking god. Why would she ask Angela that?

'Ha!' says my wife. 'Wouldn't you like to know.'

Jess already knows. She knows from a week ago, three weeks ago, and two months ago. If she comments or suggests anything, I'll barge in. Fucking kill the pair of them.

I won't really.

Cameras everywhere outside this house because Angela's daddy protects his precious princess.

'Actually,' says Jess, 'I don't want to know.'

The actual cheek of it. Who does she think she is?

My phone buzzes in my pocket and I pause my breath in case they heard it.

'What was that?' says the sly bitch, Jess. 'Did you hear that?'

'Hear what?' says Angela as I retrace my steps and clomp down the stairs.

'Nothing.' The tone of Jess's voice has changed. Is that shame I detect?

'Hello, ladies,' I say, swanning into the kitchen and grabbing a beer from the fridge. Vodka will have to do for another time. 'You weren't talking about me, were you?'

'Always.' Angela gets up and puts her arms around my waist, snuggles her face into my neck. She's not like this when we're alone. She's putting on a show to camouflage the distance between us. 'Do you want to join us?'

Jess's eyes briefly flash. She was wasted last week. After Angela had fallen asleep on the couch, she came and sat on my knee. It was two in the morning, and I'd come downstairs wondering where my wife was.

Does Jess remember the whole of it, or did she get a flashback when I walked into the room? She's avoiding eye contact, which suggests she recalls something.

'You're not going to fall asleep on the sofa again?' I say to Angela but I'm looking at Jess. She's made an effort tonight. She's usually in jeans, but she's wearing a low-cut tight dress. 'You off out somewhere, Jess?'

She places an arm across her chest where the skin has flushed.

'You do look more glam than usual, Jess,' says Angela.

'I had a date before I came here,' she says.

'What?' Angela removes her arms and stands in the middle of the kitchen with her arms out. 'Why are you only telling me now?'

Because it's not true, that's why.

'I want *all* the details.'

And as much as I'd like to stay here and watch Jess squirm, I'm bored and my mobile buzzes with a reminder that I've got a text.

'See you later, ladies,' I say, but I've lost them.

I take out my mobile.

Well, that's a blast from the past.

> I'm up in your area in a few days. It would be great to catch up – it's been too long!

Well, well, well, Simon Kennedy. I wondered when he'd come crawling back.

CHAPTER 20
SCARLETT

I slept on the settee last night, and Dad's still passed out in the armchair after finishing the last of the whisky. I should be in Art right now. I don't know if Dad rang college yesterday to tell them what's going on, but I guess everyone's seen the news or at least heard about it.

My phone vibrates on the wooden floor, but Dad doesn't react.

I'm standing outside your door.

It's Hannah.

I tiptoe around Dad's long legs – he's halfway down the chair and he'll probably be aching when he wakes up.

'Hi,' I whisper, beckoning Hannah inside. 'Let's go upstairs. Dad's asleep in the living room.'

'Shit,' she hisses. 'So, your mum's not back yet? I've been checking Twitter for news but they're just repeating the same story.'

'Why didn't you message me to ask?' I close my bedroom door. 'I could've given you an update.'

'I didn't want to... intrude.' She sits on my bed, her legs dangling like an eight-year-old's. 'Didn't know if the police would still be here.'

'They only stayed for half an hour.' I sit next to her. 'Is that why you didn't come round last night?'

She nods, taking a used tissue out of her jacket pocket.

'I'm so sorry, Scar,' she says. 'I feel like I shouldn't be crying. It's just that I love your mum. She's been so good to me since...'

I put my arm around her.

'And now I'm being a grief thief.' She slumps, sobbing into her hands. 'I'm so selfish.'

'Oh, Han.' I pull her closer. 'You're not. You're here, aren't you?' She nods, and I suppress a smile. 'Does your dad know you're not in college.'

'He wasn't at home when I left this morning.'

'What?'

'He had to start work early this morning. He's been going in early for days. Said there are rumours of redundancy, so he has to be seen to be keen. I sent him a text, so he knows I'm here.'

'Did he reply?'

'Yeah. Why?'

'Nothing.'

'You think there's someone out there targeting our parents? Shit, sorry. I didn't mean to make a joke of it.'

'It's OK.'

But I'm lying because it's not OK. None of this is OK.

I lower my head onto Hannah's shoulders, and I can't stop the tears. Trying to be strong in front of Dad and Gran has been so hard.

Hannah strokes my hair, which makes me cry even more. We've seen each other cry so many times, but over silly things like boys or breaking friends with other kids at high school.

My phone beeps with a message. I sit up and wipe my face.

Hannah looks at the screen as she passes me my phone.

'What party is Kai on about?' she says.

Kai and Hannah fell out last week, so it was lucky I didn't go to his party. She'd have killed me if I went without her. It was a bit embarrassing telling Kai that my mum said no to drinking alcohol on a school night, though. But he's cool, not a nasty bone in him.

'Monday night,' I say, not looking at her. 'Told him I didn't want to go if you weren't going.'

'I should hope not,' she says. 'He still hasn't said sorry for standing me up.'

'It was a misunderstanding,' I say. 'You had your phone on silent.'

'He prefers you to me anyway.'

She's deep in thought and looks as though she's about to say something but changes her mind.

'What does he say after the party bit?'

I open the message.

'It says, "Sorry to hear about your mum. If you need a chat, I'm here for you." That's nice of him, isn't it?'

'I guess.'

'What is it?'

She's picking at the tear in her jeans. She shrugs, arms floppy.

'Nothing.'

I stand and look out the window. Dad's having a coffee and a cigarette at the wooden table and chairs outside. He's not even hiding it.

'What are you looking at?' says Hannah.

'It's just my dad. Smoking outside.'

'I didn't know he smoked.' She gets up and joins me at the window. Dad's still wearing the same clothes as yesterday and his hair's all over the place. 'God, he looks like shit,' she says. 'Sorry.'

'Stop saying sorry. He does look like shit.'

We watch as Dad heads back to the house and we listen as he locks the back door, and pulls across the top and bottom bolts. Now he's coming up the stairs.

It's a habit that we both rush to the bed to sit down as though we were doing nothing, but he doesn't come to check in or say hello. He probably doesn't realise Hannah's here.

He's lingering on the landing, on one of the creaky floorboards. Through the crack of the door, I see him open the loft hatch with the metal pole and drag down the ladder.

'What's he doing?' Hannah whispers.

'Going into the loft. Don't know what for, though.'

I'm not whispering, and Dad doesn't hear me. Sometimes, when he's been up drinking as much as he did last night, he's still pissed in the morning. This might be the case right now – maybe he doesn't know what he's doing.

'What's up there?' says Hannah.

Dad's climbing up the stairs and into the hatch. The one light bulb lights up the wooden slats on the roof.

'Christmas decorations, old photos, I think.'

'Maybe he's missing your mum so much he's getting out their wedding album.'

'Doubt that. I've never seen a wedding album. They're not the type of people to have a wedding album.'

'My mum and dad had a wedding album,' says Hannah. 'And they can't stand the sight of each other these days.'

Hannah's fiddling with her jeans again. There's definitely something she wants to tell me.

'Did you speak to Jamie yesterday?' I say.

'How do you know?'

I shrug. 'You're almost bursting, but I knew you were holding it in because you didn't want to talk about it with what's going on with my mum.'

'It's trivial in comparison.'

'It's not, Han. It's your life and it's important to you.' I turn to face her, bring up my legs and sit cross-legged on the bed. 'So, did he ask you out?'

She matches my position.

'Yeah,' she squeals. 'But not the when and where. He said "sometime".'

'Well, that's OK.'

'And... I hope you don't mind, but I told him about what you're going through.'

'Course I don't mind. It's been on the news. He probably already knew.'

'Nah, he didn't know.'

'Oh.'

'We're teenagers. All we care about is other teenagers.' She gives a shy smile to let me know she's kidding. 'Your dad's coming back down.'

He's climbing down the ladder with a large box under his right arm.

'It looks like a box full of papers,' I whisper.

Hannah puts her hand on mine.

'Why are you whispering?' she says. 'Why don't you just ask him?'

'Good point.'

I slide down from the bed and open the door loudly.

'Hi, Dad.'

His shoulders tense like I've given him the fright of his life.

'Scarlett.' He places the box on the floor and pushes the ladder back up. 'I didn't think you were up yet. I thought you'd gone back to sleep in your room. You weren't there when I woke up downstairs.'

'No, Hannah's here.'

'Oh.' He runs a hand through his hair. 'This early?'

'It's nearly half ten,' I say.

'Yes, yes.' He looks past me, into my room. 'Morning, Hannah!'

'Morning!' says Hannah.

'What's in the box?' I say. 'Must be important if you're getting it this morning.'

'Just some papers, certificates. Old photos, things like that.'

'What do you need them for?'

'Erm.' He turns and grabs the metal pole to close and lock the hatch. 'Amy's coming round in a bit. Asked me to get out the album of her and your mum from their college days.'

'Really? She asked you to do that... after all that's going on?'

'Gives me something to do. Keep busy.' He picks up the box. 'Right, I'll head downstairs with this.' He lingers at his and Mum's bedroom door. He's waiting for me to leave him to it. 'Say hi to Hannah for me.'

'But you already...' I step back into my room. 'OK. See you later. Let me know if you hear anything.'

I close my bedroom door. Dad's going into their bedroom – he's not taking the box downstairs.

'That was a bit strange,' says Hannah. 'What the hell is in that box?'

'I've no idea.' I open my laptop and select a random YouTube video to play to mask what we're saying. 'But I'm going to find out.'

CHAPTER 21

2005

Simon hasn't been in touch since we left university nine years ago. I thought we were proper friends – the only friend I've ever had, if I'm honest. But when there was radio silence, I had to come to the realisation that no, he wasn't. I was useful to him because he wanted company in that student flat of his. Saying that, it was useful to me, too. And, you know me. I don't like to play the victim.

I've been looking at his profile on this Myspace shit. Trust Simon to be one of the first ones to get on there. It's been all over the news, but like hell am I going to sign up for it. According to this, he's living near London. Course he is. Always lands on his feet. His profile picture is of him in a sharp suit standing on the bank of the Thames with the Houses of Parliament in the background. He looks happy, healthy and I feel a stab of envy.

There are several posts on his profile that other people can see. I don't think some of them realise it.

Hey, Si. Great to connect with you this afternoon. Any chance of a meeting tomorrow? Dexter

Hey, mate. Out of town the next few days on business.
Let's take a rain check. Maybe next week? Sx

Going to miss you so much, ring me every day you're
away xxx

Course. Sx

The woman Simon's seeing seems a bit soppy. God knows why she didn't just text him that message. Unless she wants everyone to know they're an item. He's still a good-looking guy with no imminent middle-age spread like the one I'm cultivating.

So, he's some big shot in the city. And I work at Angela's bloody father's company. I'm going to try to think of something sexier to tell him. I could be vague and hint at the security services, but that's too naff. Plus, Simon would see right through it. Best thing is to stick as close to the truth as possible. Not that I have a need to impress him or anything.

There's a knock on the door, which is weird as Angela doesn't usually bother me up here.

'Come in.'

She's in her pyjamas already and it's only seven in the evening. She's really letting herself get loose now, isn't she? Doesn't care about impressing me any more. She shuffles towards me in her granny slipper boots. They seriously need to be in the bin.

'I've got something to tell you,' she says, perching on the arm of the settee next to my desk.

'Go on.'

I give her a smile that I hope comes across as though I actually give a shit.

She takes something out of her pocket and hands it to me.

Fuck.

It's a pregnancy test.

She's literally handing me something that she's pissed on. I glance down and already know it's positive. She wouldn't have bothered otherwise.

'We're going to be parents.' She stands and reaches out a hand. 'Isn't it wonderful? After all these years of trying.'

I stand and open my arms out to her, and she sinks into me.

'It's wonderful, darling,' I say into her hair. 'Honestly. The greatest news.'

A million thoughts race through my head. Yesterday, I was having doubts that I even wanted to be married. But there's no way I'm letting her raise my child alone. Milking me for money while her parents hire shit-hot lawyers to make sure I get little to no access to my own flesh and blood. And it doesn't matter now that I don't want to have sex with her – she probably won't notice. I can say that I want to protect the baby.

I stroke Angela's hair and kiss the top of her head.

'Really, my love,' I say. 'This is the best news.'

CHAPTER 22

SCARLETT

Hannah left when we started getting visitors. First Amy, then Gran and Pete, who I think will be coming over every day until we find Mum. At least it'll make the house seem less empty. I'm still in my room and I keep thinking about the woman in the missing poster at college. It was dated 2010 – thirteen years ago. I can't imagine waiting that long to find out what's happened to Mum.

I bring up the photo I took on my phone.

Natalie Baxter, aged 23, has been missing since 10th July 2010. Natalie is 5' 6'', dark hair, slim build and has a mole on her right cheek under her eye. She was last seen at approximately 18:15 on the B6265. If you have information regarding the whereabouts of Natalie, please contact Crimestoppers.

How could she have gone missing in daylight?

It's such an old poster. She might've been found by now. I tap her name into Safari and loads of results come up. The most recent is:

Family Issue Appeal on Ten-Year Anniversary.

Shit. She hasn't been found. They've not even recovered her body.

Natalie was last seen by a passing motorist who stopped to ask if Natalie needed assistance after her car broke down. Natalie declined and said help was on its way. An hour later, when roadside assistance arrived, her car was there, but there was no sign of Natalie. Natalie's sister, Catherine, stated: 'We *will not stop looking for our Natalie. She's a wonderful person who's greatly missed by so many people'*.

Her sister still talked about her in the first person. She hopes Natalie is still alive, but how realistic is that? If someone goes missing of their own accord, would they really stage a breakdown on a busy road, leave their passport behind and not withdraw cash from an ATM?

A girl around my age – Serena Johnson – has posted an age progression of Natalie on the timeline of the 'Find Natalie Baxter' Facebook page.

I was only six years old when my auntie went missing, but all of our lives have been affected by it. Please share.

Clicking on Serena's profile, I think about messaging her. There's not much on it – several hundred friends, but the only public posts are about her aunt. That's not unusual. People our age rarely have Facebook profiles let alone post on them. What would I say? Just the facts, I guess – say my mum's missing. She probably won't read it – she probably gets loads of messages from weirdos.

After signing up, adding the picture from my TikTok account, with links to that in case she thinks I'm another one of those weirdos, I tap out a message.

I exit Facebook, trying to not cringe about what I wrote.

I navigate back to Safari.

Missing found years later.

A mother in the nineties who started a new life; a man whose wife claimed his life insurance to clear his debts as a scam; three women, kidnapped separately in different locations by different perps when they were girls, who managed to escape years later. Most missing cases ended with no conclusion, or their remains were found.

I swipe up to close the app and throw my phone across the room. It's probably caused another crack on the screen, but I don't give a shit. Mum needs to be found in the next day or week or month. Or we're going to be living this nightmare for years.

Amy's still crying downstairs and it's stressing me out. Her and Mum are like sisters – or so Mum keeps saying – because they've known each other for over twenty years.

I head downstairs. Gran will be stressed with all the sobbing, too, because she hates people crying in public. I've never seen her cry, because she doesn't want anyone to feel sorry for her. Proper stoic. Think she grew up as a Catholic.

No one looks up as I walk in. Amy's got my blanket round her shoulders, but I don't say anything. I sit on the floor by the window. I forgot to bring my phone down so now I've no idea where to look.

'There you are, Scarlett,' says Gran, bringing in a tray of tea and biscuits. 'Do you want me to make you a hot chocolate?'

'I'm OK, thanks, Gran,' I say. 'But thank you.'

She busies herself making everyone's tea, asking if they want sugar and milk. I can see from her eyes that she's trying hard to keep it together. She hands Amy her tea – three sugars instead of her usual one because she hasn't eaten in twenty-four hours.

'You need to keep your strength up,' says Gran.

Amy smiles through her tears. I think she likes being looked after.

'How are you doing, Scarlett?' she says.

'I'm all right,' I say. 'Just trying to keep busy.'

Amy nods, even though I'm obviously sitting here doing nothing.

'You ring me whenever you like, day or night,' she says. 'I'm not sleeping anyway.'

'Thanks, Amy.'

Dad's at the dining table on his laptop. He's not showing any of the photos he said he was bringing down for Amy to look at. I knew he was lying about that. The box is probably still upstairs.

I get up and head over to him.

'What are you doing, Dad?'

He's actually changed out of yesterday's clothes and his hair's wet from the shower.

'I'm going over the CCTV from the past few days. It hasn't picked up anything suspicious so far, except for that car Pete spotted.'

Gran joins us. 'He'll be round soon with some more cameras,' she says. 'He thought you could put one in your car – see if it can pick up any activity on the street.'

'Good idea,' says Dad.

'I left my phone in my room,' I say, which nobody takes any notice of.

I take the stairs two at a time. Dad's really engrossed in that footage so I'll have at least five minutes to search for that box.

I avoid the creaky floorboard at the entrance to their room.

Mum's make-up and perfume are scattered across her bedside table, and I feel another pang of sadness. I keep forgetting and remembering and it's horrible. Chanel N°5. I pick up the bottle and breathe in the scent. Although I'm tempted, I don't spray it on me. It'll hurt too much to smell of her all day.

I open her wardrobe door. Dad's right – all her things are there: no empty spaces and her suitcase and holdall are still at the bottom. I run my fingers along all her clothes. Clothes she might never wear again. I step back and close the door. There are no cardboard boxes in here.

Dad's wardrobe is on the other side of the room. Even though I tiptoe I catch a noisy floorboard. I freeze on it. If I lift my foot gently, it might not make another sound. It doesn't work, but I'm over the kitchen. They shouldn't have heard it downstairs unless they're all completely silent. Even so, I wait a minute to see if anyone comes up, but I think I've got away with it.

Dad's shirts are in colour order, from white to black, and his trousers are categorised from casual to smart. Everything in order. Except for the cardboard box at the bottom. I take it out, close the wardrobe door and place it on the bed. It's slightly damp and cold from being in the loft. Old, grey cobwebs cover the top, but I leave them as they are in case Dad remembers they're there.

Inside are papers, envelopes, and cardboard folders. Bills, mainly. Bank and credit card statements. One of the folders has an asterisk drawn in red marker.

I flip it open and inside is a birth certificate and passport.

The name on the certificate is *Simon Kennedy*.

What the hell? Why would Dad have someone else's documents?

I open the passport, my heart racing as I look at the man in the picture.

It's my dad.

CHAPTER 23

JOANNA

I feel as though I've been awake for days and haven't risked closing my eyes for more than a second, but I must have slept at some point. I'm physically exhausted even though I've barely moved. I haven't eaten today and it's getting dark outside. It's like he knows what I'm planning to do. But what *could* I do? I'm tied to the bedpost and no amount of jiggling and wrestling with the handcuff has even loosened it.

'You need to sleep.' His voice doesn't make me jump any more because it feels as though it's inside my head. 'If you go to sleep, I will unchain your hand.'

'Of course you will.'

Crackling on the speaker.

'I told you your daughter is OK, didn't I? Kept my end of the deal.'

'Why are you doing this? Where am I?'

'Let's not get ahead of ourselves. You'll find out soon. What would be the point of keeping you for only a few days? That'll do nothing.'

'Are you going to kill me?'

His laugh booms into the room. I cover my ears when he doesn't stop.

'You're insane.'

The laughter stops. An intake of breath.

'Now, now,' he says. 'There's no need to get personal.'

A high-pitched sound floods the room. It pierces my ears, makes my brain feel as though it's being fried.

'Stop it, please.'

Louder and louder, but covering my ears does nothing to blank it out. I put my fingers in them but it's still there. I cover my head with a pillow, but this makes him increase the volume. I hate to cry in front of him, but I can't help it – I bury my face into the covers, but he'll know because I can't stop my shoulders from shaking.

It stops.

'Drink the water. Go to sleep. We could all do with a break.'

All?

Either that was a turn of phrase or there is more than one person doing this.

I take a deep breath as I bend to pick up the water. I know what my face will look like: skin blotchy and lips trembling as I fight the tears. I unscrew the lid and with shaking hands put it slightly to the right of my mouth. I tip it up and let the lukewarm water flow down the side of my face, down my neck. I exaggerat-edly wipe my face with my chained-up hand and replace the cap. It took around eight seconds last time. I count them in my head.

Eight. Place the water on the floor. *Seven. Six.* Lie down, facing the wall.

Five. Four. Three. Two. One.

I slow my breathing, but nothing can lower my heart rate.

Deep breath in for five. Out for seven.

I'm trying to still myself with such concentration that I'm praying my body doesn't betray me and twitch. My eyes don't want to stay shut. Scarlett used to scrunch her eyes and little frown lines appeared between her eyebrows. 'I am asleep, Mummy,' she used to say and my heart aches for her right now.

It must be my fault I'm here. What I did has come back and it's time for me to pay for it. I knew the day would come – I've been waiting for it. But I thought it would be a knock at the door, or a tap on the shoulder. But this is it. It's almost a relief.

There's been no sound from upstairs, or downstairs. He might not actually be in this building. Every communication might have been transmitted remotely, and it could take him hours to get here to replace my water. I don't believe he's going to unchain me. Unless he's confident I won't try to escape.

My arm is going numb; I should've chosen a better position. Sedated people don't shift in their chemically induced sleep.

'Why aren't you sleeping, Joanna?'

Shit.

I stay in position. It might be something he says every time as a test.

'Joanna.' He almost sings my name. 'I know you're awake, Joanna.'

I remain still. Breathe in for five. Out for seven.

'Your heart rate is a hundred and ten,' he says. 'Stop messing me around.'

How the hell—

My Fitbit. He's reading my stats. This means my phone is ten metres away from me, max. My brief moment of hope dissipates when I remember police can't track a phone using Bluetooth alone.

'I'm bored now,' he says. 'Drink the rest of the fucking water or I'll get Scarlett. She's going to college tomorrow. You really should've warned her about talking to strangers online. Easy target.'

The bastard. He's probably bluffing. James won't let her out of his sight.

I drag my numb hand from underneath me and wiggle my fingers to get the blood flowing. I reach behind, feeling my way to the bottle, and bring it in front of me – I don't want him to see me crying.

I down what water's left.

Eight, seven, six.

There's no way he's going to unchain me now.

But I'll find a way to beat him.

Five, four, three, two, one.

CHAPTER 24

2005

I'm sitting in a sprawling beer garden inhabited by only a few people because it's bloody freezing. I'm twenty minutes early so I can see him coming. It's a quiet Tuesday night, and it's between terms so there aren't many university students hogging the decent seating.

It's been nearly ten years since I've seen Simon. We didn't part on bad terms, but it turned out that the woman from the chippy was a student in one of Simon's classes. They were quite close, apparently. What were the chances of that? It hit him really hard, and I felt pretty bad about it, but how was I supposed to know?

She was called Siobhan O'Hara and this time, unlike poor Rachel Beckwith, she was found pretty much straight away, which was a shame. I thought bin day was Thursday.

I make a note of the two cars that pull into the car park, but neither are Simon's. A woman slams the pub door open and stroppily sits at the wooden table next to me; her hands are shaking as she plucks a cigarette from her packet. A man comes out after her and they sit next to each other in silence, and she begrudgingly lets him light her cigarette with his Zippo lighter.

They almost distract me from noticing the next car to pull in. A silver Lexus. Now *that* would be a typical Simon Kennedy car. His parents' wealth always overspilled into his pockets. Though I have no idea what Simon does for a living these days. *Business* is such a broad term; it could mean anything.

Yes, it's his car. I can't make out the last three letters of his number plate, but that doesn't matter. It's only a precaution. I get up quickly before he spots me and take a seat in the middle of the pub, near a few old blokes playing dominoes, each with a tankard of what looks like brown ale.

I stand when I see him, though it takes him a few moments of searching before his eyes land on mine. His eyebrows rise, and he smiles as he walks towards me.

I hold out my hand.

'Good to see you, mate,' I say as he shakes my hand. 'All's well with you and yours?'

Yeah, I know I'm talking like a bit of a wanker, but it's what blokes are meant to do sometimes.

'Not too bad, not too bad.' He takes off his jacket, unwinds his scarf, and places both on a stool. 'Can I get you a drink?'

'I'll have the same again, please, mate.' I hold my pint up. 'Carling.'

He heads to the bar. I don't know why I feel so strange about this. Is he here to talk about something specific, or is he really passing through? I feel unprepared, and slightly uncomfortable, but try to bury it and put on another smile as he places a drink in front of me.

'Cheers, mate.' I down what's left of my now-warm lager and put the empty to the side. 'You not drinking, then?' I say, pointing to his half-pint glass of Coke.

'Driving back tonight,' he says. 'Stayed over in Scotland last night. Thought I'd look up my old friend, see if you're still in the area.'

He holds up his glass, and I clink it with my fresh cold one. I take a small sip and decide I'm not going to drink much more. I don't want to make a dick of myself. Simon was always the one with a drink in his hand or a spliff between his fingers.

'It's good to hear from you. We haven't seen each other for so long.' I'm beginning to sound like a desperado. 'What is it? Eleven years?' I say, trying to reclaim some dignity.

He looks up to the ceiling, counting in his mind.

'Nine years,' he says. 'Can you believe it?'

'What is it you do now?' I take another sip. Luckily, I've chosen one of the weakest of lagers. 'Must pay a lot if you're travelling round the country.'

Every bloke I've come into contact with in the past nine years is in some sort of salary competition. We're judged on our car and our job, and I've done exactly the same with Simon.

'I'm in aerospace,' he says. 'Not as glamourous as it sounds, though. Mainly project management.'

'Really?' I say, though I can't admit to snooping on his profile. Being a project manager is hardly someone in 'business'. 'That's so different. I mean, your degree was in Psychology.'

'Yeah.' He swirls the ice in his drink. 'Didn't fancy interpreting people's minds. It was all a bit intense.'

'I suppose.' My knees are going up and down. I need to relax, but I didn't expect to feel so awkward and I can't pinpoint why. 'Are you married?'

'No,' he says. 'Been seeing someone a while, though. What about you? So sorry I couldn't come to the wedding.'

I feel a flash of adrenaline across my chest. I try to maintain a neutral expression.

'Oh,' I say. 'I didn't think you'd got the invitation. When I didn't get your RSVP, I thought—'

'We were travelling at the time. Six months across Europe. Couldn't wait to get home, to be honest. We got the invite when we went back to visit Mum. Sorry, mate.'

'I didn't have your new address.'

'We'll make up for it,' he says. 'We could all get together some time.'

'We're expecting a baby.' I blurt it out. 'Though I'm not supposed to be telling anyone yet. We only found out a few days ago.'

His jaw slackens before he quickly corrects it, but his eyes are still wide.

'Jesus, Alex!' He finally smiles. 'That's brilliant news. Congratulations.'

'Can't believe I'm going to be a father.'

'No.'

He's blinking too fast. What the fuck is wrong with him? I narrow my eyes as I try to read him. Perhaps he can't have children and I'm rubbing his face in it.

'That's really great,' he says.

His shoulders relax when I say I'm nipping to the men's.

I take a piss, wash and dry my hands, and stand at the mirror to smooth down a rogue clump of hair that always sticks up.

Poor Simon. So what if he's had it easy in the past. He deserves success – he's a good guy. Maybe some of that luck could rub off on me. We could start a business together – a side hustle for him. It's the perfect time to get back on track with our friendship. This is what it's like to have a normal life: a good friend, a loyal wife, and a child on the way. I could be happy with that, couldn't I?

Simon's eyes are on me as soon as I exit the gents. I sit back down, take a big glug of my drink.

'I should be going soon,' he says, picking up his scarf that's fallen to the floor. 'Don't want to be falling asleep at the wheel.'

'Already? But you've only been here ten minutes.'

'I know,' he says. 'But we'll arrange a proper catch up.' He swipes his phone off the table. 'I'll just nip to the loo before I go.'

Did he think I'd steal his mobile?

Why the hell is he—

And then I see it. Just peeking out of one of his deep pockets. A glass wrapped inside a clear plastic bag. My empty has gone. He must've taken it.

A hundred thoughts and pictures run through my mind. The last time I saw him, all he talked about was where I was the night Siobhan was killed. He kept talking about Chloe – how she said she'd seen someone wearing a hoodie talking to Rachel on the night she died. Is he still in contact with Chloe? I take out my mobile phone as a way to focus, to steady my hands. I could just take the glass and run. He wouldn't know where to find me. I'll change my number, move away.

'You all right, mate?' he says, standing over me as he puts on his coat.

'Yeah.' *Don't look at his pocket, don't look at his pocket.* 'Well, no, not really. I've just got a text from Angela. She's not feeling too well.' I look up to him, a worried expression on my face: raised eyebrows, corners of the lips down. 'I don't suppose you could give me a lift home, could you? She was meant to be picking me up; morning sickness has turned into all-day sickness for Ang.'

'Well... I...'

I stand. Put on my jacket.

'It's OK, it's OK,' I say, not looking at him. 'There'll be a black cab outside, or I can ring a taxi. It's no bother. We're only five minutes away.'

He glances at his watch; the scarf in his other hand is covering the pocket where the glass is calling to me like a beacon. His mobile phone lights up with a text message, but I don't allow myself to look. Instead, I press a button on my phone, hold it to my ear.

'Hi, love,' I say to no one. 'I won't be long... It's all right... Just lie down, I'll be there to look after you soon... I love you, too.' I take the phone away from my ear, put it in my pocket. 'It's been great to see you, mate. I'll have to go. She's really suffering, I need to be there for her.'

Come on, Simon. Say it.

'I'll drive you home,' he says. 'Five minutes away, you say?'

'Really? Oh God, thanks. It's on the way to the motorway. Not too much out of your way. Thanks, mate. You're a life saver.'

* * *

We pull up on a drive of a house that isn't mine. The lights are off, curtains closed. He's talking but I can't hear what he's saying because I can't think of him as my friend any more. Nothing he can say will change my mind.

I get out first and go round to him in the driving seat. He goes to open the door and I drop my phone on the ground. He does what I predicted he would do because Simon's a nice person.

When he bends to pick it up, I slam the car door against his head so hard that he slumps in half. He didn't make a sound. I slam it again, and a trickle of blood flows from his right ear.

I push him back into the car and walk calmly round to the other side.

It takes three heaves to get him onto the passenger seat. I take the glass out of his pocket, along with his phone and wallet. I look closely at his face – there isn't a flicker of life – before scrolling through his messages. The most recent thread is from Chloe.

> 17:25 Chloe: Good luck. You can do it. All we need is that DNA and the police will take us seriously. Finally, justice for Rachel and Siobhan!

> 18:01 Simon: Shitting it tbh. What if he susses me?

18:05 Chloe: No way will he suss you. The man's in love with you!

18:10 Chloe: Seriously, though. If you think he's onto you, just get out of there.

18:11 Chloe: Good luck.

19:05 Chloe: If I don't hear from you by 8 p.m., I'm calling the police.

> 20:01 Simon: Got it. Heading home.

20:02 Chloe: I knew you would do it! Well done. Now get the hell out of there. Stay safe. Text me when you can. I'll call you if I don't hear from you by 10 p.m.

The scheming bastards. Who the fuck do they think they are? Of course the police wouldn't take them seriously because they've got nothing on me. Well, they don't *now*. Is this what they've been planning for nine years?

I tap out a message.

> 21:10 Simon: At petrol station. Just about to get onto motorway. All safe. Heading home. Will drop it at the police station tomorrow morning.

I slip his phone and wallet into my pockets, close the passenger door, and get into the driving seat.

* * *

It took fifteen minutes to get here. The reservoir looks inky dark, with only the light from the moon shimmering on the still water. I've driven past this place hundreds of times on the way to work.

The ground is dry, so there are minimal tyre tracks. They're only here if you know to look for them, and every time I've been past, there's been no one in sight. There are warning signs for no swimming. Not even kids come here to swim because we've all heard those horror stories of people drowning in reservoirs.

Simon is still out for the count. He didn't move on the way here. He's still breathing, though that won't be for long.

I drag him back onto the driving seat and reach over to open the glove compartment. There's an A4 envelope. Inside is his passport and a cardboard Thomas Cook wallet. An all-inclusive to Mexico, no less.

'Ah bless,' I say, folding it and slipping it inside my jacket. 'Looks like a holiday of a lifetime. Bad luck, mate.'

I release the handbrake and flick off the lights. The engine is still ticking over, but there's no way I can press the accelerator without hurting myself, and there are no heavy rocks to place on the pedal, so I shut the door and try to push from the back.

There's a loud bang in the distance. Is it someone shouting? Is that a torch?

Need to carry on. This has to happen now.

I take a huge breath in and push with every inch of my body until the car finally budges. It crawls slowly down the embankment. There's not even a splash.

For a few heart-stopping moments, the car hovers at the water line. Is it going to stay like that?

No, of course it won't. A ton of metal doesn't float.

It starts to sink, the water flooding the engine first. Seeping through to the cabin. And still Simon doesn't make a sound.

I watch until the car is fully submerged before turning and running like hell.

Poor Simon.

CHAPTER 25

SCARLETT

I took pictures of the birth certificate and passport before someone came upstairs. I closed the box and shoved it under Mum and Dad's bed, and made the excuse that I was looking at Mum's things to make sure there was nothing missing.

Everyone else has gone home and the silence is deafening. I'm staring at Dad as we sit opposite each other at the dining table. It's on the edge of my tongue: *Is your real name Simon Kennedy?* but I can't say it. It's too big a thing to ask when we're sitting here, me pushing now-cold chips around on my plate.

Simon Kennedy. Dad doesn't suit that name. And it's not rare – there are hundreds, possibly thousands of people with the same name. The passport was issued September 2006: the year I was born.

'Dad?'

He shifts his gaze from his meal, still in the chip wrapper.

'What?'

I need to blurt it out before I change my mind.

'Where's my birth certificate?'

He frowns. 'What do you need that for?'

Now really isn't the right time to be talking about this, but it might be connected to what's happening.

'Just something for college.'

'I don't know,' he says. 'Your mum knows where everything like that is. Is it urgent? I didn't think you were going in until...'

'I need to keep busy,' I say. 'It's hard being here. The days are just...'

'Unbearable.'

'And Gran coming round here every day is...'

'Exhausting.'

He gives me a small smile and folds the wrapper over his barely eaten tea.

'I wasn't going to say exhausting,' I say. 'But I feel as though I have to put on a brave face, so I don't upset her even more. I don't want to be at college either. It's just... I don't know what to do. The waiting, the not knowing. It's horrible.'

A tear runs down my face and I brush it away before Dad sees. I have to be strong for him, too.

'OK. I'll take you there and pick you up,' he says. 'And I'll have a word with the principal – let him have your phone switched on during class in case there's any news. I need to see where you are at all times, so please keep it with you.'

'Course.'

'I needn't worry about that, eh?'

Another smile. He stands and takes both of our plates into the kitchen. It's only six o'clock but I'm exhausted, especially after sleeping on the settee last night. I head into the hall and linger at the kitchen door.

Dad's standing in front of the open dishwasher, head in his hands. Before I move to comfort him in some way – place a hand on his back, touch his arm? I don't know, I've never had to do it before – he turns around.

'Sorry, Scar,' he says. 'Sorry you have to see me like this.'

'Don't say sorry, Dad.'

It's like he's five inches smaller, shoulders hunched, head hanging.

'Are you going to be OK if I head up to bed?' I say.

He walks towards me and takes me in his arms and kisses the top of my head.

'Don't worry about me,' he says. 'You need your rest. Especially if you're going back to college tomorrow.'

'I don't have to go,' I say. 'It's a bad idea. I'll stay here with you.'

'We're only going to be waiting for news. It's best you keep busy, like you say. Do you want me to make you a hot chocolate?'

'I'm OK, thanks, Dad.' I linger at the door. 'Shall I make you one?'

He ruffles my hair.

'What would I do without you, eh? You get yourself to bed.'

'Will you wake me if there's any news?'

'Of course.'

I go upstairs. We're both pretending that I'm going to sleep soundly enough that I'll not hear his phone ringing. And we both know that he'll drink just enough whisky for him to get a couple of hours' rest from this waking nightmare.

I get into my PJs and climb into bed. I pull the covers over me and go onto YouTube and play the randomest vid: sounds of rain on a tin roof. I close my eyes and listen and imagine that I'm hundreds of miles away and everything is fine, and Mum is safe.

Simon Kennedy will have to wait.

* * *

My alarm sounds at seven and for a few seconds I forget what day it is and that Mum's not here. Two hours' sleep, tops, but I get up anyway and shuffle straight to the bathroom with some clean clothes.

Mum and Dad's bedroom door is still open – the box is still under the bed. Dad must've stayed downstairs again last night. I know *I* couldn't sleep in Mum's bed, the pillow still smelling of her. At least downstairs he can pretend he's waiting up for her.

The sound of the hairdryer is such an everyday noise that it sounds strange in this house. When it's dry, I gather my hair into a loose bun. It'll have to do because I can't look at myself in the mirror.

Hannah's calling my phone.

'Hey, Han,' I say. 'What's wrong?'

'Eh?'

'You're ringing instead of messaging.'

'I wanted to check you're OK. And to see if you're still coming in.'

'Yeah. Dad's taking me, if he's fit to drive.'

I feel a pang of guilt. Disloyalty.

'Do you want us to pick you up? Dad said he doesn't want me wandering the streets when there's a weirdo on the loose.'

'Uhm.'

'Shit, sorry, Scar,' she says. 'I can't say anything right.'

'Don't say sorry,' I say. 'At least you rang – at least you're here for me.'

'Thanks. So?'

'I think it'll be OK. My dad probably hasn't slept much.'

'K. See you in an hour.'

I say goodbye and head downstairs.

Dad's not in the living room. Or the kitchen. And he's not smoking at the end of the garden. I check the kitchen sink. There are no whisky tumblers, and the plates from last night and the past few days have been cleaned in the dishwasher.

'Dad?' I shout, to a seemingly empty house. 'Dad, are you here?'

Panic shoots through me as I run back up the stairs, afraid that someone's taken him, too. The bathroom is empty; so is his bedroom. Wardrobes still have his clothes inside. The loft ladder hatch is closed but I bang it with the metal pole. He might've got stuck.

'Dad, are you up there?' I shout, banging another three times. 'Dad?'

I take the phone out of my jeans pocket and select his number. It's ringing.

But so is his phone – somewhere in the house. Downstairs.

Living room.

It's coming from the settee. Between the cushions.

Shit. Where the hell is he?

The front door opens and shuts; I run into the hall.

'Dad!' I run towards him and hug him tight. 'Where were you?'

He holds the tops of my arms and pushes me gently away.

'I was outside for literally five minutes, defrosting the car.' He rubs his hands together – his fingertips are almost glowing red. 'Making sure it's thawed out by the time you need to get to college. It's not been used in days.'

'Hannah's dad offered to pick me up,' I say, clocking the wave of disappointment on his face. I hold up my phone. 'I'll ring her – tell her you're taking me.'

'It's OK,' says Dad. 'You go with your friend. It'll be nice for you to catch up on the way. I've made you some sandwiches. They're in the fridge.'

'Thanks,' I say. 'You're like a different person this morning.'

'I took a night off the whisky. Made all the difference.' I follow him to the kitchen. 'There are some bottles of water in there, too,' he says as I take the foil package off the shelf. 'It's cheese salad. Hope that's OK.'

'It's great. Thanks, Dad.'

He opens a bottom cupboard and places a canvas lunch bag onto the counter.

'I haven't used that since primary school,' I say, trying not to laugh.

'Really?' He opens it and has a sniff. 'Smells OK.'

I put the sandwiches and water inside the Harry Potter bag, knowing I can hide it in my rucksack once I've left the house.

'Thanks, Dad.'

'It's OK, kidder. Come through to the living room with me. We'll watch out for Graham.'

We don't have to wait long. At eight thirty on the dot, Hannah and her dad pull up outside.

'I'll walk you to the car,' says Dad and I don't argue.

* * *

It's absolutely freezing out here. The passenger door takes me a few pulls to open.

'Sorry about that,' says Hannah. 'Dad doesn't see the point of getting a new car if there's nothing wrong with this one.'

I look to her dad to see if he's offended, but he's making small talk with my dad. Things like, 'So sorry,' and, 'If there's anything I can do.'

'It'll be the ice,' I say. 'Our car does that, too.'

Hannah undoes her seatbelt and climbs over into the back. Neither dad notices.

'We can talk better with me here,' she says, belting up again. 'Are you going to be OK today?'

'Anything's better than just waiting around for news.' I move my head close to hers. 'It's awful staying inside. Felt like a prisoner. Everything's so unfamiliar. I need routine. Something normal to take my mind off things.'

Dad opens the passenger door.

'Remember, Scarlett,' he says, leaning in, 'if you notice

anything strange, call me straight away. If you feel someone is following you, go to the nearest trusted adult.'

'Will do, Dad.'

'Thanks, Graham.'

Dad shuts the door and watches until we turn the corner.

'You all right, Scarlett, love?' says Graham (though I never actually call him Graham to his face). 'You must be beside yourselves.'

'Dad!' Hannah tuts. 'Talk about stating the obvious.'

'Hannah!' I say.

'It's OK,' says Graham. 'I'm used to her.' He winks at me in the rear-view mirror. 'Brought her up to be an independent woman and she's taken it too far.'

'Hey!' Hannah sticks out her bottom lip, but quickly turns it into a smile. 'Can you turn up the radio, please, Dad.'

Graham does as he's told.

'How would I go about finding out if someone's changed their name?' I say.

Hannah turns to face me. 'You what?'

'If someone has changed their name. Would it be public?'

'God knows.' She narrows her eyes. 'Do you think your mum's changed her identity and gone on the run? That she's robbed a bank and had plastic surgery?'

'What the hell have you been watching, Han?'

'Dad's got me into true crime on Netflix. He's addicted.'

'Really?'

She shrugs. It's really sweet they can sit down and watch a series together. Everyone in our house sits in separate rooms in the evenings. Me in my room on my laptop or phone, Mum upstairs on the bed reading, and Dad downstairs, either on the Xbox or watching some kind of sport. Well, that's how it used to be. Maybe Mum got bored with her life, and that's why she left. Especially after our argument about me lying to her.

That wave of shame covers me again. It stirs up my stomach, the nausea rising up to the back of my throat. I reach inside my rucksack for my water and take a few cautious sips in case I throw it back up again.

'Is that Harry Potter?'

'Yeah.' I replace the water and zip up my bag. 'What you got first?'

'Sociology,' she says. 'So not that bad. You?'

'English Lit.'

We pull up outside the gates, and Mr Jackson is standing outside again. Shit, I hope he's not waiting for me. He makes eye contact as I get out the car. God.

'Your tutor is so hot,' Hannah says in my ear just metres from him.

My face feels flushed, even though it's so cold I can see my breath in front of my face.

'Morning, Scarlett,' he says, solemnly, as Hannah's dad beeps in goodbye. 'Thought we could have a chat before everyone else arrives. If that's OK with you?'

I nod. 'OK.'

***

People are staring at us as we walk towards Edgerton Building, but that's probably because, like Hannah says, of Mr Jackson's appearance more than what's happening with my mum. When I pointed him out to Mum in the supermarket, she said he looked like Colin Farrell, but taller and tidier. So, Mr Jackson is obviously old enough to be my dad. Just. Who knows what his deal is?

He holds the door open to the red-brick building and leads the way through two corridors until we come to our form room. Already there's a bottle of water on the table in front of my chair.

'This won't take long,' he says, sitting at the front and

gesturing for me to sit. 'I just wanted to run a few things past you. That water's for you, if you need it.'

I dump my bag on the floor, pull out my chair and sit.

'I'm OK thanks.'

He leans back and folds his arms, which is a bit casual if you ask me.

'I spoke to your dad this morning,' he says. 'I hadn't realised it was one of my students that was affected by Joanna's disappearance. I've seen it on the news and on these forums and...'

Joanna?

He clears his throat, stands, and walks towards me. He sits on the chair next to me.

There are shadows under his eyes, and the irises are almost black. He looks haunted. I've never been this close to him before and my body is screaming at me to shift back, but I don't want to offend him.

'I'm here for you,' he says. He reaches for my hand, but I swipe it away, scratching an imaginary itch on my nose. 'Any time of day.' He places a folded Post-it note in front of me. 'Here's my number in case you're in another part of the school and you feel unsafe.'

I feel unsafe now; he's far too close. I don't want his number, but I take the note anyway. He's probably not used to people giving his number back.

'Thanks.'

I'm probably imagining this. He's probably just trying to be nice. How many times will he have dealt with a student whose mum has gone missing? Probably never.

My body sags with relief as the bell goes, and I resolve from now to never find myself alone with him again. I didn't have him down as a creep, but a nice face doesn't mean anything.

He stands and quickly gets behind his desk as other students file in.

'Oh my god, Scarlett.' Kai pulls out his chair next to me. His hair is in a topknot and he's wearing jeans and a white T-shirt despite the weather. To show off his flawless fake tan, probably. 'How are you feeling, lovely? I can't believe what's happening with your mum, hun.' He opens his arms and I lean towards him and relax as he hugs me. 'I'm so glad you came back to college.'

'Being at home's too hard, just sitting around waiting for news.' I feel my bottom lip wobbling, and the two lads opposite are whispering and looking at me. 'Too much time to think about where she is and how she is. I needed to come in for the distraction.'

He strokes my hair as he releases me. 'I've been checking online all night,' he says. 'My mum's constantly checking Twitter, too. She's obsessed.'

He doesn't mean any harm, I guess. And it's good that he's not treating me as though Mum is dead.

'Do you want me to start a Go Fund Me?' he says, still scrolling on his phone. 'To help with the search etc?'

'It's OK. The police are doing it at the moment.'

He places the phone on the table.

'Let me know if you change your mind, Scar.' He rubs the top of my arm. 'Here for you.' He glances at the front of the room then locks his eyes onto mine. 'Don't look now,' he says, lips together, 'but Jackson is looking right at you. Like, really staring. OMG. I'm so jealous of you right now.'

'He's creeping me out,' I say, not moving my lips, even though Jackson can't see my face.

'What?'

'Got weird vibes from him before everyone came in.'

'You think he's a paedo?'

'No clue. Can't tell. But you never know.'

'Fuck me,' he says.

'Don't say anything to anyone, Kai,' I say, grabbing his hands. 'I'm just being sensitive. Picking up on things that aren't there. Don't want to ruin someone's career or rep. Remember what happened when you started that rumour about Gina McPherson?'

'I didn't start that!' He looks pained, though I don't believe his sincerity. 'And it was totally true, so technically not a rumour.'

The bell goes again.

'Can I walk next to you out the door,' I say, 'so you're nearest Jackson?'

'Hell, yeah.'

But even as I hide beside Kai, I catch a gap and Jackson is still staring.

But I'm looking right back.

CHAPTER 26

2005

It's been three days since I met up with Simon and there's been nothing on the news. It's not like the girls. Perhaps people think blokes going AWOL of their own accord is much more acceptable. But Simon's phone has been beeping and ringing. I keep it charged in case there's something I need to know. I've been replying to some of his girlfriend's messages, trying to mimic Simon's style. I texted Chloe as well:

> I dropped the glass off but the police said it could take months, so I have to lie low for a while in case he suspects anything. Let's not contact each other for a while.

I don't know how long I can put off doing something drastic. For the time being he's been 'stuck in Leicester' for some work stuff, but I'll have to think of something a little more permanent.

I have a child on the way – that's if it *is* my kid. We last had sex six weeks ago and she couldn't have been less interested. She's been banging on about having kids since our wedding night because she's probably getting it in the ear from her auntie.

My mother's face flashes in my mind. The look of panic in her eyes as I took the smashed vodka bottle out of her hand – the same one that caught my neck when she smashed it on the wall. The way she closed them and braced herself in a brief moment of calm before I pushed it into her stomach.

Simon's phone beeps again with a message from his girlfriend.

> You're sounding really weird. If you don't answer your phone by the end of the day, I'm going to the police.

Fuck.

I obviously didn't get Simon's tone right. I need to change the direction this is going in. I scan the letter that came with the tickets to Mexico, Photoshop a few details and print it out. I tap out a few texts from his phone to mine, then go onto his Myspace page – it's becoming more useful than I thought – and click onto her profile. Her workplace is listed for everyone to see. I go onto MapQuest and print out the directions. Three hours from here. Trust Simon to have lived in Milton Keynes. So sensible.

I don't know if they had lived together. I'll just have to wing it.

I grab a change of clothes and place them in an overnight bag.

Angela's hairdryer is blaring from the dining room. I don't know why she doesn't get herself ready upstairs like normal people.

'Morning,' I say, kissing her cheek.

She switches off the dryer.

'What's wrong?' she says.

'Nothing. Why?'

'You don't normally kiss me in the mornings.'

'It's not just you,' I say. 'It's my baby.'

'Our baby.'

'That's what I meant.'

She looks at my bag.

'Going somewhere?'

'I was just about to say. Work messaged this morning. Meeting a new client in Milton Keynes.'

It's a good job she's never in the office these days, though her dad tends to avoid business talk with his daughter. She won't know I've told a little white lie.

'I've never been to Milton Keynes,' she says, still holding the dryer, her hair half dry.

'Nothing to write home about. Do you want to come?'

I've never asked her to come on a trip with me before. She's actually thinking about it. Fuck. What if she's gone all clingy with her pregnancy hormones?

'Nah,' she says, and I can't stop a flicker of a smile. 'I'm having lunch with Gabby today. So excited to tell her.'

'Thought we weren't telling anyone before the twelve-week scan.'

'But she's my best friend.' Jess seems to have gone off the radar. She takes me into her arms. 'Please say you don't mind, please, please, Alex.'

She smells of coconut and berries. Just like Rachel. A wave of nostalgia floods over me. The feeling that I had her life in my hands, and I can feel my heart racing again. Stirring in my cock. I back away from her, trying to plaster a smile on my face.

'OK, OK,' I say. 'If it means that much to you.'

I can't think of Angela like that. She's going to be the mother of my child. She's carrying precious cargo.

'Thank you, Alex!'

She goes back to drying her hair, smiling to herself in the mirror. She'll be a good mother, I think. She's been desperate for years and it's not as though she has a career any more. And she doesn't drink herself into a coma, like Gilly often did. I'm finding it easier calling my mother by her first name. Takes away any sentimentality that comes with the word *mum*.

'Shall I ring you when I get there?' I say, grabbing my jacket.

'It's OK,' she shouts over the noise of the hairdryer. 'Don't worry about me, I'll be fine. I might invite Auntie Mo over tonight to keep me company. We can look through the Mamas & Papas catalogue.'

'Right, yeah. Excellent. Make sure you stay out of trouble.'

I take my keys out the bowl, and she laughs.

I head to the front door as she wraps the cord around the dryer.

'Alex, wait!' She almost skips to the door and puts her arms around my neck. 'I think this is going to be the making of us,' she says. The whites of her eyes are so bright, glistening, healthy. 'I really do.'

I kiss her on the lips, tasting the chemically fruity taste of her lip gloss.

'I do, too,' I say. 'Take care of yourself.' I rub her tummy. 'And this little one, too.'

She beams at me, like the day we got married. The expression I haven't seen for years because we've slowly been making each other's lives miserable. But now we have a distraction. For a few years, at least.

I head out the front door and towards my car as I replay our brief conversation in my head. Jesus, I'm getting soft in my old age. Didn't even think I'd make it to thirty-five, let alone be a father. She waves at me from the living room window.

Finally. I think I can play the part of a family man. I really can.

* * *

I've been waiting outside her office for three hours now. It's almost five o'clock and there's been no sign of her, but there are sixteen cars in this car park. It's in the middle of nowhere on an industrial estate, which is my summation of Milton Keynes from what I've seen. Identikit houses, buildings, and streets. Soulless.

She works for a printing company. I can see the unit from here and the lights are still on inside. A gaggle of blokes in suits pile out of the main door, linger for a bit, chatting and blocking the path of two women who shake their heads as they walk round them.

At last, she comes out. Sleek dark hair in a sharp bob, heavy fringe. There are so many photos of her on her Myspace page. She must've had the same hairstyle for years. She's wearing a blue winter coat, with a belt around the middle. She doesn't talk to the blokes lingering at the door; she barely registers them.

She gets into a red 1999 Renault Clio. I turn on my engine and follow as she heads out the car park. I flick on the radio to see if there's any local news about the missing Simon Kennedy. There isn't. I need to make sure it stays that way.

Roundabout after roundabout and finally she turns off into a bland housing estate. It's like a rabbit warren has mated with a maze. She parks on the drive of a semi-detached that's red brick, like the rest, neat front garden with roses in pots under the windowsill.

I turn around a little way up and park about thirty metres away. I take a map out of the glove compartment and fold it out over the steering wheel, so I don't look too dubious. They're probably used to it around here because it's hard to tell one house from another.

I rehearse in my head what I'm about to say to her, and all her possible responses.

It'll be fine. If she's anything like Simon, she'll be pretty gullible, but easy-going. Pleasant. I get out the car and stride towards her house, trying to look as though I've been here a hundred times. I'm wearing a suit in the hope she'll believe what I say. I toyed with the idea of playing detective and saying her beloved was missing presumed dead, but that would be traceable. It's not as if she'd take my word for that – after a day or so anyway. She's not an island. Simon's family live here too, now. Lost their money, though. Read it on the internet yesterday. Shame, that. And now their son's dead. Bad things happen to good people all the time.

I give three strong knocks on the door, even though there's a doorbell. I see her through the frosted glass, still has her coat on. When she opens the door, I see that her eyes are red, her nose is glistening. She dabs her cheeks with a tissue.

'Now's not a good time,' she says, going to close the door. 'I'm not interested.'

I hold up a hand.

'Wait. I'm not selling anything. I'm here about Simon.'

She eyes me suspiciously. 'What about Simon?'

'I've known Simon for years,' I say. 'I met with him last week and there's something I need to tell you.'

'Are you Alex?'

Fuck. Shit. What has he told her about me?

'No,' I say. 'My name's Johnny. I'm one of Simon's colleagues.'

'Oh, yes,' she says. 'He's mentioned you.' She opens the door wider and steps aside. 'Come in.'

She guides me into the kitchen. It's modern – shiny white cabinets, pristine. But the dining room is another story. Stippled terracotta paint effect complete with an arched entrance.

'We're still doing it up,' she says, rubbing her back. 'Room by room.'

'Ah.'

'So?'

She takes off her coat and drapes it on the work surface. Bit leftfield.

'He told me he's going away,' I say. 'That he needs a break from it all. After what happened with his parents.'

'What?'

'The money disappearing from their business account. He told you about that?'

'Yes, yes, of course.'

Really? Bloody hell.

'The stress of it all made him look at his life,' I say. 'Said he wanted to get out of the nine to five. Said he felt constricted. He couldn't face telling you himself. Asked me to do it.'

Her eyes are narrow; she's staring into mine. Her mouth has formed a small O.

Is she in shock – should I give her a shake, a slap across the face?

'What the actual hell?' she says, finally.

'I'm sorry.'

She almost knocks me over as she walks out the kitchen. She opens the front door.

'Is he here?' she shouts to the street. 'Is this some kind of joke? Is that your car?'

I run to catch up with her as she's striding up to my hire car.

'Simon! Simon!' Her voice is so loud I sense curtains twitching in suburban Milton Keynes. 'I know you're in there.' She cups her hands as she looks inside. Finding no Simon, she bangs on the boot. 'Come on. Get out.' They must've been into some weird shit on the quiet. Why the hell would he be in the boot of a car? These MK people aren't what they seem behind these identikit exteriors.

'He's not in there,' I say, opening the boot so she can see for herself.

'Jesus Christ! Where the hell is he?'

I follow, trying not to break into a run, as she heads back to her house and into the living room. I take out my phone and show her the texts from Simon's phone to mine.

'You should see these,' I say.

> Mate, she keeps calling me.

> What should I do?

> Any chance you could do me a favour? Tell her
> it's over. I can't face doing it myself.

'You've spoken to him about me?' she says.

I nod solemnly and take out the piece of paper. An all-expenses-paid trip for Simon and his new girlfriend. In fact, they should be there right now. The mobile reception over there's terrible.

'This can't be happening.' She goes to the sideboard and opens a drawer, throwing papers onto the floor. She takes out a large leather wallet, unzips it. She takes out a passport, flicks it open. 'No.'

'What?'

'No, he wouldn't do that to me. He wouldn't.'

'What is it?'

'He's taken his passport. Oh.' She collapses to the floor, on top of bank statements, brown envelopes. One, I notice, has a red *overdue* stamp on it.

'Oh my god,' she says. 'He was seeing someone else. I knew he was hiding something from me. He was texting and ringing some other woman – he thought I hadn't noticed.'

That would be Chloe. It bodes well for me that they haven't met.

'What am I going to do?' she says.

I crouch down in front of her.

'If it's money you need,' I say. 'I could help out.'

She covers her face and cries into her hands.

Jesus. I'm not great with crying women, which won't surprise anyone. Her shoulders shake with great big sobs. Shit.

I place a hand on her arm, but she bats it away.

I let it slide. She needs to get it out of her system. Probably hates all men right now. Don't blame her, really.

I need to make my exit. 'I'll leave you to—'

'What am I going to do?' She's brilliant at bawling. 'I can't do this.'

'Is there someone I can call for you?'

No answer. She starts a fresh bout of crying. Fuck.

I could sneak out. Run out the door.

I take the car keys out of my pocket.

She wipes her face with the sleeves of her cardigan. Now her make-up's smeared across her face like a clown in a nightmare. She's even making *me* feel sorry for her.

'Shall I get you a drink?' I say, standing up quickly. 'Maybe a brandy?'

She's worn herself out with the crying and now she's got her arms wrapped around herself.

'I haven't got any brandy,' she says. 'Simon doesn't like alcohol in the house.'

'Really?' I say. 'Shall I pop to the shop for you?'

'What for?'

'Brandy.'

'I can't drink.' More tears flood down her face. It seems she has an endless supply of them. 'I'm pregnant.'

I grip my keys so tightly that I think my hand might bleed.

'What?'

'Pregnant.'

'Is it Simon's?'

'Of course it's Simon's.'

'Oh.'

'I was going to tell him when he got back from his business trip. It's a surprise. We'd given up trying.'

Fuck, shit. Think, think.

'Are you sure he didn't know?'

'What do you mean?'

I stand and pace the floor. 'Well, he did say to me that he wasn't ready for responsibility – that he couldn't face being tied down when he wasn't even sure he loved you.'

I know. I'm a total bastard. But this will help her in the long run.

'What?' she says, looking to the ceiling. 'Oh God. This is getting worse.'

I crouch down. Smooth down her hair that's all over the place.

'Maybe you've had a lucky escape,' I say. 'What kind of man runs away when his girlfriend's pregnant?'

'Fiancée. We're getting married next month. Well, we *were* getting married.'

She's a gift that keeps on giving.

'Are you sure there's no one I can ring for you?'

'Just because I'm pregnant doesn't mean I can't work a phone.'

'Right you are. Well, I'd better get going.'

She's staring at the beige carpet. 'Right.'

'If I hear from him, I'll let you know.'

'Yeah. Course you will.'

'Take care, now.'

I'm almost running out the door, which slams shut accidentally. I turn the ignition on before I put on the seatbelt.

Jesus Christ.

No amount of planning could have prepared me for *that*. I pull out slowly, calmly, even though adrenaline wants me to floor the accelerator. I'm going to have to keep an eye on her.

CHAPTER 27

SCARLETT

Hannah's standing next to me outside the college gates when my phone pings with a message.

'Was that Facebook Messenger?' she says, scrolling through her own phone. 'Have we time travelled back to 1999?'

'Facebook wasn't even invented in 1999. I don't think they even had mobile phones in 1999.'

'True,' she says. 'Everything was in black and white in 1999.' She giggles.

The message is a reply from Serena Jackson – Natalie Baxter's niece.

Hi Scarlett,

Thanks for your message. I'm so sorry you're going through a bad time with your mum. I don't remember what it was like when my auntie went missing as I was only six. But everyone talks about her as though she's going to walk through the door any minute. My grandad puts a present under the tree for her every Christmas. He feels it the most, I think. I'm here if you want to chat. Whereabouts do you live? We're in Black-

*pool now, but Grandad still lives in Lytham. Says he can
never move in case Natalie comes back and doesn't know
where to find him.*

Serena x

'What's wrong?' says Hannah. 'Why are you crying – what
does the message say?'

It was the bit about Serena's grandad that got to me. It was
just all so sad. I hand my phone to Hannah.

'Bloody hell,' she says. 'That's not want you want to hear,
is it?'

'It's not her fault. I messaged her last night.'

'Why?'

'No idea. Spontaneous decision. Not thinking straight.'

She hands me back my phone. 'Don't blame you.'

'I guess I wanted to talk to someone who knew what it was
like. It's like something out of a movie.'

'Your dad's here.'

He manages to sneak into a space as another car leaves. The
passenger window opens.

'Do you want a lift home, Hannah?' Dad shouts.

'That'd be great, thanks.'

She gets in next to him, calling shotgun without actually
calling it. She knows I always sit in the back anyway. Even if the
front passenger seat's empty.

'Any news?' I say, doing up my seatbelt.

'Afraid not,' he says, setting off slowly to avoid the swarm.
Ten points for a student, he used to say, when things hadn't
turned to shit. 'The police came round again, though. I've
packed you a bag. Thought we'd stay the night at a hotel.'

'What?' I grab the headrest of Hannah's seat and lean
forward. 'Why?'

'Are they searching your house?' says Hannah. 'Dad said

they might do that. He said they search homes of missing kids, too, in case the parents have harmed them.'

Dad grips the steering wheel tighter. I give Hannah a shove in the back through the seat.

'Sorry,' she says. 'I didn't mean to say...'

'It's OK, Hannah,' says Dad. 'I know you were trying to make us feel better.'

'Sorry.'

She slides down a little; I can tell she's sulking. She hates offending people. She's really good at it, but she never means to be so thoughtless. Most of the time.

'Will they go in my room?' I say.

'Don't think about it, love,' he says. 'I'll go in tomorrow and tidy it up while you're at college.'

'OK.'

God. I've got empty crisp packets under my bed, and chewed-up gum and used blackhead strips in my bedside cabinet. My face goes hot with the shame. I try not to think of anything else that's in my room. Like the diary I started in high school at the bottom of my wardrobe that's full of shit about the boys and girls I had crushes on. Mortifying. Most of them were complete arseholes.

I scroll through TikTok and stick in my ear buds. Watching people walk into glass doors and windows will take my mind off it. Idiots.

Hannah doesn't say anything for the rest of the journey, but luckily Dad caught the vibe and turned on Radio 1. We're stopping outside her house and her dad is standing at the front door. Hannah must've been texting him on the way here. He's walking down the path.

'Everything all right?' he says, leaning into the car after Hannah gets out. 'Heard they were searching the house.'

There's no denying where Hannah gets her tact.

'Yeah,' says Dad. I can't make out his tone. Trying to sound breezy and serious at the same time. 'I hope they find something to help find Jo.'

'Me too, mate.' He turns to Hannah, who's waiting at their gate. 'You go in, love. I won't be a sec.' He waits till she's out of range. 'Do you two want to kip at ours? Till the coppers have left?'

'That's kind of you, Graham,' says Dad. 'But we're already checked into a hotel. Really appreciate the offer, though.'

'It stands for as long as you need it.' He leans further in and shouts over like I'm at the end of the street: 'Bet it'll be an adventure, staying at a hotel on a school night.'

'Yeah,' I say, tight smile. 'Sure will.'

He pats the roof of the car.

'Right, then. You two take care.'

He closes the door just the right amount, so it doesn't shatter our eardrums. He bends and sticks his thumbs up.

'Oh, God,' Dad says without moving his mouth.

We set off and I give Graham a wave.

'Aren't they both quite the characters?' says Dad. 'One digs a hole and the other sticks their foot in it.'

'You get used to her.'

'I suppose.'

Even though Mum and I are close to Hannah and her family, Dad has only tasted them in small doses. He always seems to busy himself in company.

'What hotel are we staying at?'

I'm getting used to the idea, now. A change of scene is just what I need.

'A Premier Inn, but it's in town so not far from college.'

'Nice. Do I get my own room?'

He smiles at me, and I catch his eye in the mirror.

'Yeah, but we have joining rooms. And you need to make sure to lock your door at all times. Not just at night. And no wandering about the corridors.'

'As if.'

'You're not like I was as a k... teenager. Always up to something.'

'Like what?'

'I'm not going to give you tips.'

We park up on a side street and Dad gets some change for the meter.

'Are you all right?' I say. 'You seem a lot better than yesterday.'

'No more alcohol for me, Scar. It's not productive. Not good for the mood. There's a tip for you.'

'Cheers, Dad. I'll pass on the whisky tonight, then.'

We get out and I wait as he gets a ticket and places it on the dash.

'The bags are in the room,' he says as we start walking to the entrance. 'I wasn't actually lying to Hannah's dad about checking in.'

* * *

We had a takeaway but ate in separate rooms because we wanted to watch different things.

I've a double bed and I can starfish in it and still not reach the edges. I've had a shower and used the toiletries and now my skin is itchy and tight. Dad never thought to pack shower gel and shampoo, but it doesn't matter.

Mum could be in a hotel. She might be in hiding. What if she's a spy and we're not her real family. Would it matter? That she was alive, but her whole life was a lie?

I turn to face the window that's surrounded by heavy curtains – thick, dark to keep out the light. I picture Mum in a box, still, sleeping. Or dead. I can't tell.

My phone pings next to me. It's a message from Serena again. Shit, I haven't replied to her message.

Hi Scarlett,

I hope I didn't offend you with my last message. If you want to chat, I'm coming into Preston tomorrow – around lunchtime. Do you want to meet for a coffee?

Serena x

I've never met anyone online for a coffee before. I go to her profile. In the few pictures she's put up, she looks a couple of years older than me – or maybe twenty-one, twenty-two. It might be really awkward. Ah fuck it.

I tap a reply.

Hi Serena,

That would be great. Costa at twelve?

x

She replies in seconds.

Sounds perfect! See you then.

My heart flips. *It's not a blind date, it's not a blind date. Stop thinking like that.*

I sit up and go to the bag Dad packed for me. Please let there be something decent.

Jeans – good sign. And my favourite off-the-shoulder grey jumper. I take a hanger from the open wardrobe thing and hang it to make sure the creases fall out.

Dad won't know if I go out at lunchtime tomorrow – he'll assume that I've stayed on college grounds, which is what I usually do because eating in town is so expensive.

There's a knock on the adjoining door.

'Are you decent?' says Dad.

I dive onto the bed and grab my phone.

'Yeah.'

'Don't you ever get bored of having your face in that thing?' he says, sitting in the tub chair by the window.

I sit up and put my phone on the floating shelf.

'What is it?' he says. 'Are you worried about the house?'

'I'm more worried about Mum than the house.'

He hasn't shaved today; his face looks shadowy and tired. Haunted. Even though he said he feels better on the inside.

I just have to blurt it out. I can't keep it in any more.

'Dad?'

'Yeah.'

'Who's Simon Kennedy?'

'What?' He shoots back in the chair. 'Where did you hear that name?'

'I... I...' Deep breath. 'I was looking through Mum's things and I saw a cardboard box and I thought it might have photos in it, but it had a birth certificate with the name Simon Kennedy.'

Dad gets up and starts pacing.

'What is it?' I say. 'Are you mad because I went through your things?'

He kneels on the carpet next to me on the bed.

'No, no,' he says. 'Not at all.' Another deep breath. 'I don't want to overwhelm you while your mum's missing.'

'But I'll just think the worst. I've been worried about it for days.'

He tilts his head to the side, frowning. 'What's the worst thing you thought of?'

'That you were a con artist who's had multiple identities. Or that you were a spy and our whole life is a lie.'

'Wow, you really *have* thought about it.'

'What happened? Were you ever called Simon Kennedy?'

'Yes,' he says. 'But something happened. A friend tried to...'
He stands again. 'It'll sound unbelievable when I say it.'

'Just tell me what happened, Dad.'

'OK.' He sits back in the chair. 'About eighteen years ago, I met up with an old university friend. An extremely dangerous man who... Anyway – he attacked me, drove me to a reservoir and pushed me in. He stole my passport, my mobile phone.'

'What the hell, Dad?'

'Yeah. But there was a dog walker, thank God. Managed to pull me through the driver's side window.'

'Oh my god. Did the police catch him?'

He shakes his head.

'Is the car still there?'

'I don't know.'

'But why didn't the police get him? He tried to kill you!'

'He went abroad. I don't know.' He rubs his face. 'But I had to make sure you and Mum were safe. He came looking for me a few days after it happened. Mum pretended she hadn't heard from me and by the time the police got to our house he'd gone. I told her not to confront him, not to say I was alive.'

'Have you told the police this? Told them that this is who's taken Mum?'

'I don't know that for sure, but yes. I gave them his name straight away. When I told you to go upstairs the first time they came round.'

'What's his name?'

'Alex Buchanan.'

'Do you have a photo of him?'

'That's what I was looking for in that box from the loft, but I couldn't find any.'

'You said he was dangerous,' I say. 'What did he do?'

He stares at me, silent for a moment.

'He hurt a friend of mine from uni. And there are rumours he killed a girl at college two years before that.'

'And you told the police at the time?'

'Of course! We went as a group. Me, Rick, Chloe. But there was no evidence. He'd had a bad childhood, apparently. Had a good solicitor, too, by the sounds of it. That's why I went to meet him the night he tried to kill me. The police hinted that they had DNA evidence from the killer that matched the two girls. I managed to get a glass Alex had been drinking from. He must've seen me take it.'

'Where is he now?'

'If I knew that I'd... That's why I changed my name, that's why your mum and I aren't on social media. But it looks like he finally caught up with us.'

'Is Mum really called Joanna?'

He smiles. 'Yeah.' He barely says the word aloud – he's blinking hard, trying not to cry. 'But she didn't want to draw any attention to us – kept herself to herself, hiding from the world. She's stronger than you think, you know.'

'There's a lot I don't know about both of you.'

Parents always say that they weren't always parents, that they had their own lives before they married, had kids. This has taken that to a whole new level.

'Is that why we moved so much when I was a kid?'

His head shoots up.

'I didn't know you remembered that. You were so young.'

'I don't remember the houses. Just remember starting a new school when everyone already had their friend groups.'

'Except for Hannah.'

I smile at the thought of her being one of the only kids who was nice to me.

'Yeah.'

I've a hundred more questions, but it looks as though he's breaking. I can't picture him being called Simon.

I lie down on the bed. It feels as though my parents aren't

my parents – that I've been switched and landed in someone else's life.

'Do you want some time to yourself?' he says.

'Yes, please.'

He comes closer to me. For a moment, I think he's going to rub my hair like he used to do when I was a kid, but he doesn't. And I want to cry again. I want to be a child, live in that bubble of Mum and Dad, and not have to deal with weird shit like this. I wish I didn't know any of it. I want everything to be back to normal but that's never going to happen.

I need my mum. She'd tell me everything's going to be OK.

When I first started at the high school, she stroked my hair every night when I cried myself to sleep. 'It'll get better soon,' she said. 'Really, it will. You do believe me, don't you?' And I nodded. She was right, in the end, because Hannah made everything OK.

But Mum's not here now. Dad might've lied – she might not be called Joanna. He probably didn't want to overwhelm me with the secrets they've been keeping.

I feel totally disconnected from them. What Dad said was completely outrageous. Why would he want to keep it quiet? If someone had tried to kill me, I'd have run to the police. Shared his photo on social media. Not rested until the fucker was caught.

I get up and check that the door is properly locked. Then drag the ironing board out of the wardrobe and place it under the handle. I'm half-tempted to ask Dad if I can sleep in his room.

This Alex Buchanan got away with attempted murder for nearly twenty years. And Dad is a witness, first-hand. All these years we've been running, and I hadn't even realised.

I lie on my bed but leave the light on.

There's no way I'm going to be able to sleep tonight.

CHAPTER 28
JOANNA

He's untied me from the bedpost. I didn't think he would. I pull up my sleeve; my wrist has a circle of angry red and an open friction wound is weeping. Ignoring the pain of it, I jump off the bed and go straight for the door. I shake it by the handle, but it barely budges. I dart to the window, but there isn't a handle to open it. I can't see outside. There's an opaque film covering the glass from the other side.

'Help!' I cup my hands against the window. 'Help!'

I scream as loud and as high-pitched as I can muster.

I listen at the window.

Nothing. There's no one here. Where the hell am I that I can't hear a thing outside?

I head to the television. It's on standby and there are no buttons to switch it on, back or front. I pull open the drawers of the chest. Empty. No clues as to where this is and who is keeping me here.

'What are you looking for?'

The man's voice makes me jump, though I should've expected it.

'Why am I here?' I shout, looking directly above, at the

camera. 'Why won't you listen when I say you have the wrong person?'

'I've been watching you for a long time, Joanna,' he says. 'I'm not mistaken. Joanna Sawyer, née McNally, born 1981, Sharoe Green Hospital, Preston.'

I stumble back onto the bed.

'And I think you know why you're here. Look at the picture of Rachel on the wall.'

'What?'

'Come on, Joanna. I know you're not stupid. Look at her. Read the article.'

I shuffle right, towards the wall.

MISSING, NOW MURDERED

The body of Rachel Beckwith, 17, has been discovered four months after the teenager disappeared. Rachel, a student at Runsdale College, was last seen at a bus stop on her way to a party. There were several sightings of Rachel that evening and police believe that she was killed on the night she disappeared. Rachel's parents are being comforted by family and request privacy while they come to terms with this, the worst possible outcome.

If you know anything in connection with the murder of Rachel Beckwith, please contact Crimestoppers.

I have never heard of Rachel Beckwith. This was in 1991 and she was from Yorkshire. I've never lived there, and I was only ten in 1991.

'What's this got to do with me?' I say. 'I didn't know her.'

The television flicks on with the YouTube logo, then cuts to an opening sequence.

Stephanie Kendal: Mystery Monday.

A woman appears in front of the camera. She has long dark hair, glasses, and perfect make-up. She looks late twenties, early thirties.

'*Hey, guys. Hello and welcome to my channel. Today, we're going to be looking at three seemingly separate cases of three women in the North of England. The first dating back over twenty years. But before we dive in, here's a message from our sponsor.*'

It's the same woman in a different outfit reading from a script, fawning about how great HelloFresh! is.

'*And now back to the cases. I've heard a lot about each of these, but I haven't thought about doing a video because there isn't much to say other than what's been reported in the media. But, after getting an email several weeks ago, it has been suggested that these cases are linked. I know most of you will groan at this, but they've asked me to keep their identity anonymous.*' She holds her hands up. '*But bear with me. When you hear till the end, you'll know why.*'

It cuts to a blurry picture – an image that's been taken of a physical photograph. It's of a girl aged fourteen or fifteen. She has shoulder-length mousey hair, and she's wearing a white Minnie Mouse jumper, and a stonewash denim skirt. She's sitting on a swing and there are bruises and cuts on her knees, unless that's a trick of the light.

'*This is Sarah-Jane Crosswell, who was only fourteen years old when she was found beaten to death in a country-lane ditch on the outskirts of Halifax in 1990. There were no witnesses, and her murder remains unsolved to this day. Close to where her body was discovered, was a black bicycle that wasn't believed to be Sarah-Jane's.*'

A picture of Rachel Beckwith appears on the screen. It's a different one to the article on the wall. A full colour photo of her sitting next to three friends, all who have their faces blurred. She's holding a green bottle that has a green and black label with a palm tree. It looks like a Castaway.

'This is Rachel Beckwith. She was born in West Yorkshire in nineteen seventy-five. She was described by her family as a happy, kind, and fun girl – a typical teenager. She wanted to study Drama at university before her life was tragically cut short on a night out in 1991. Rachel was last seen at a bus stop on Grove Street – one of the main streets in York. But, after talking to some of her friends, it was revealed to me that she was, in fact, seen at the party she was making her way to.'

There's generic footage of a house party, people pretending to have fun. There are two people outside, obviously actors.

'Rachel was seen with a mystery male standing outside the house of one of her college friends. This man has never been identified and no one has come forward claiming to be him.'

It cuts to a photograph of another woman. She has jet-black hair in a loose ponytail at the top of her head. Her eyes are surrounded by thick black eyeliner and her nose has a pretty diamond stud. Her lips are painted red and she's wearing a fluffy black jumper.

'This is Siobhan O'Hara. Siobhan was twenty-one years old when she was found strangled behind a fish and chip shop in York in 1996. Siobhan was described as a quiet woman, serious, but she had a fantastic sense of humour. She was studying at York University, with hopes of being an English teacher. Sadly, her mother and father passed away within months of each other, in 2009, without seeing Siobhan's killer brought to justice. Just heartbreaking.'

Another picture comes onto the screen.

A woman with big brown eyes and dark straight hair that's decorated with tinsel. She's wearing a white polo neck and she has her arm around someone off-camera.

I know, before Stephanie Kendal says anything, who the woman is.

'This is Natalie Baxter. Natalie was twenty-three years old when she went missing in 2010. Natalie was studying nursing at the University of Central Lancashire when she disappeared at a roadside after her car had broken down. Natalie has been described as extremely bright, very funny, and would do anything for her family. It was reported that she went missing in broad daylight. There has been no sign of Natalie since that day and her body has never been found. Natalie's family is still active in their search for her.'

I rush to the corner and vomit into the bucket.

Oh God.

'There have been suggestions, mainly on Reddit, that these cases are connected. That there has been a serial killer operating in Northern England for over twenty years. His name is Alex Buchanan. A man who hasn't been seen in nearly a decade, and no photograph of him has ever been found. Is he, himself, dead? Or does he walk among us? He's been dubbed The Killer in the Shadows. Every ninety seconds, a person is reported missing in the UK – that's 170,000 per year. Are there more cases connected to Alex Buchanan that we don't know about?'

The YouTube footage stops and is replaced with a black screen.

Three words in large red font appear.

You're next, Joanna.

CHAPTER 29

2005

Last week, I emailed the pub Simon and I went to, after setting up an official-looking email address. I asked if they still had CCTV from the night in question, but they'd wiped it after thirty days. That was the last thing I had to take care of, because breaking in and stealing it wasn't hugely appealing.

I fling down Simon's phone. It's been pretty quiet, this last week. The messages from his girlfriend have tailed off. The words she called him! She's extremely creative. Wonder if she'll keep the baby.

I'm getting restless. Waiting. Even from his watery grave he has this hold over me. There's been nothing on the news about him. There's been barely anything from Chloe, either. I bet she was the one pushing all of this in the first place. For someone who only met me for a few hours, she sure does hate me. She's probably a good judge of character, but you won't hear me saying *that* out loud.

A knock at the door.

'Alex?' It's Angela. 'Can I come in?'

We're still sleeping in separate rooms, but now it's because *she* wants to. She gets hot all the time and, apparently, I snore.

Think it's a hint to lose weight, even though I've only put on seven pounds. She's not said it out loud, but I know that's what she's getting at.

'Yeah.'

I stick Simon's phone under the pillowcase as she comes into my room. She's wearing her ugly pink towelling bath robe and her hair's a complete mess. I've given up trying to suggest that simply brushing her hair will make her look more presentable.

'Didn't you hear the phone ring?' she says.

'No.'

'I just got the strangest phone call. Someone asking for you.'

'Who?'

Fuck. Did someone see me with Simon? Has Chloe tracked me down after all?

'I don't know,' she says. 'A nurse from A&E.'

'And what did that nurse say?'

Spit it the fuck out, woman.

'That your father is in hospital. Had a heart attack and he's in intensive care.'

My whole body relaxes.

'Oh,' I say. 'Is that all?'

'What do you mean?' she says. 'You said your father lives in Australia.'

'It'll be a mistake. They just look at records and put two and two together and come up with the wrong answer.'

'Well, I did tell them they had the wrong Alex Buchanan.'

'What ward did they say he's in?'

'They didn't. Why do you want to know?'

'It doesn't matter, Ang.' I lean across and go to kiss her cheek, in thanks for the call not being about Simon. She jerks back as though I'm about to spit in her face or something. 'What was that?'

She rubs her tummy. You can tell she's pregnant now, not

just bloated from the pasta she's taken to eating at all hours of the day and night.

'I'm sorry. It's just that...' She wiggles her bottom. 'I've been getting pains.'

'Shall we go to the hospital?'

'I don't know. And now I feel like I'm...' She stands up and there's blood on the covers and on her dressing gown. 'Oh God, Alex. What's happening?'

* * *

The maternity ward is in a separate building to the Coronary Care Unit. I told Angela I've gone for some fresh air. They're keeping her in for observation, even though the bleeding stopped a few hours ago.

The notion that the baby's life might end – that it's out of my control – is like nothing I've felt before. It's the first time I've felt that I am being punished: some divine retribution. Maybe, if I don't have any more bad thoughts, my baby will be OK.

I give my name to the receptionist and a nurse leads me to a private room.

'He's tired,' she says, 'but he's been awake for longer today.'

'Is he going to be OK?' I say.

She does the head tilt.

'He has severe heart disease,' she says. 'We're trying to make him comfortable.'

It takes Dad a few moments to recognise me. He's wearing an oxygen mask and takes it off as I sit on the chair next to him. His face is pale, almost grey. It's like the blood's been sucked out of him.

'I didn't think you'd come,' he says in one breath. It takes him a few seconds to recover. 'I didn't think I'd see you again.'

'The nurse said they're keeping you comfortable,' I say. 'Do you need me to get you anything?'

He shakes his head.

'Everything's here now.' He closes his eyes, and I think he's asleep until he says, 'I've been dreaming about your mother. Do you ever dream of her?'

'No.'

'Do you ever think of her?'

'I try not to.'

'It's like... you blame her... that you think it's her fault... that you were doing the world a favour.'

His words are punctuated by shallow breaths.

'I don't know what you mean,' I say.

'Is it because... you blanked it out... Is that what you've been... doing?'

'No.'

'When you're in my... position, you'll... want to confess... Say what you've done... before leaving... facing the punishment on... the other side.'

'I don't believe in that,' I say, and I shouldn't have because it's not *me* lying there, dying. He's probably scared. I would be, too. Although it would probably be a relief to close my eyes and sink into the darkness. The eternal blackness, because that's all there is. Anyone who says otherwise is completely deluded. Just like there's no such thing as karma.

'I did it... because I love you.'

'I don't want to hear it, Dad.'

He seems to have forgotten all the years of Gilly and him fighting – physically and verbally. The times I'd hear them knocking each other around when I was listening from my room. Now he's talking as though he's some sort of saint.

'I didn't ask for you to lie for me,' I say. 'Maybe it would've been better if I'd been arrested, taken to jail. It's both of your fault for making me who I am.'

He's frowning, staring straight at me.

'Who you are?' he says.

'Do you think I could just forget about what happened? Turn into someone normal? I could never be normal. Not after living with you two. It was toxic.'

A tear runs down the side of his face. The first time I've ever seen him cry.

'What do you want me to say?' I keep my voice even. It's not right to shout at a dying man. 'Dad?'

'That you're sorry for what you've done.'

He can't know about *everything*. All he knows is what I did to Gilly. Words mean nothing to me, but they'll mean everything to him. That he hasn't wasted years of his life in prison trying to protect me. I get it. I really do. But he's not accepting any blame for the way things turned out.

'Of course I'm sorry,' I say. 'I think about her all the time. And I am grateful for what you did for me.'

His breathing is getting louder, slower.

'Thank you, son.'

My phone vibrates in my pocket.

'I'm sorry,' I say. 'I have to go. Angela is in the maternity unit. She's pregnant and there have been some complications.'

'Pregnant? Oh, that's wonderful, son.' He closes his eyes. 'Everything will be all right. Don't you worry.'

I get up, go to leave, but linger at the door.

This is the last time I'm going to see him.

'Goodbye, Dad.'

Beep, beep, beep. The sound of the machines connected to his failing heart. The sound of the oxygen, hissing through the mask on the pillow next to his head.

'Bye, son.'

He doesn't pretend we will see each other again, either.

I leg it down the corridors, down in the lift, and out into the cold September air. I read the message Ang sent – *I need you here now* – and I already know what's happened. My baby isn't alive any more.

Everything will be all right, Dad had said.

Fucking lying bastard.

* * *

I'm sitting on a bench outside the hospital grounds. It'll take hours, apparently. It's unbelievable that we – Angela – will have to go through labour, only for... I can't think about it. Angela will never get over this. She's fragile. Always has been. It almost brings tears to my eyes.

I glance up as an ambulance wails past.

This place is surrounded by death, sickness, disease.

My attention is drawn to the pavement opposite. About ten metres away is a figure, staring straight at me. He's almost six foot tall, wearing a dark coat to the knee, and a ridiculous woolly hat with a giant bobble. It's just like the style Simon used to wear.

This man might not be looking at me, though. Perhaps he's just lost a loved one, too.

I stand up; a large cloud of my breath dissipates around me.

He's still there, watching.

'Is everything OK?' I shout across the now-empty road.

There's a woman walking towards me from my right. She's in her late sixties and has a bandage across her eye.

'Alex Buchanan?' he shouts in a light northern accent. 'Is that you?'

The adrenaline is shooting up my arms, down my legs.

The woman passes slowly by.

'No, mate,' I say. 'You must have me confused with someone else.'

I try to keep my legs steady as I walk back towards the entrance.

It's him, I know it is.

Simon's alive.

CHAPTER 30

SCARLETT

In the short time I managed to sleep, I dreamt of Alex Buchanan and Simon Kennedy. In it, Alex crept into the house and dragged my unconscious mother down the stairs and into his car, and drove it into the water at the docklands. My mind had made him look like Mr Jackson, which was ridiculous because he's at least ten years younger than what Alex would be now: the same age as my dad.

'Have you got everything?' says Dad, through the open door between our rooms.

'Yeah.'

He barely spoke during breakfast, didn't refer to what he said last night. I had a million questions, but we have to find Mum first. Questions can come after that. And it was busy anyway, in the hotel restaurant. Most of them were lone people in suits, quietly eating while staring at the subtitles on the news on the silent TV.

I check my messages again as we leave the rooms and head to the lift. It's the first time in ages – years probably – that I haven't had an early morning text from Hannah. Come to think of it, she didn't message me last night, either. Do she and her dad think we're guilty because the police are searching our house? Dad hasn't said if they found anything. Surely, they don't need more than a day to search the place.

Dad drops the key cards into the slot in reception, and we go outside to the car.

'What the hell?' he says.

I'm waiting for him to unlock it. 'What's up?'

'Doesn't matter.'

He bleeps open the doors and I get into the back.

'What is it, Dad?'

'Someone's scratched the side of the car. Drunken yobs, probably.'

'You don't think...?'

'No. There's no way he could know that we're here. And there's no way he'd be able to hold Mum and follow us at the same time.'

'What if he's not working alone?'

'People like him don't have friends.'

Dad doesn't have friends, either, but I don't say anything. I keep checking my phone, worrying, in case the police ring me. In the middle of the night when I couldn't sleep and was coming up with no results from *missing Simon Kennedy* and *car* and *reservoir*, I sent in an anonymous tip on the Crimestoppers website. What if they tracked my phone and called me back?

They probably get thousands of tips every day. It'll take them ages to get to mine. How could Dad not know if his car's been found? Surely that's enough evidence to say that this Alex guy tried to kill him?

But I've just found out about this whole thing. Dad's been dealing with it quietly for years. Always watching, always aware of his surroundings. He said that he took up martial arts after I was born – said he needed a focus. But now I wonder if that was his way of taking control over his situation. He was taught to always be on the lookout for danger before it finds you. And that it's better to run away from it than having to face it head-on. We've lived in four different houses since I was born. I'd always thought it was because of Dad's job, but now I realise he's been trying to keep us safe from the man who tried to kill him. Why isn't he more worried that Alex Buchanan kidnapped Mum? Maybe he's the one putting on a brave front.

'Don't get too caught up in that,' he says, glancing at my phone. 'Especially when you're walking around. You need to be vigilant. I don't think you should even be going to college.'

'But we can't go home, can we? It's always busy at college; there's always someone around. And Hannah's been going to the loos with me at break times.'

My shoulders drop when I see Mr Jackson waiting for me yet again.

'Who's that?' says Dad, seeing that a strange man is staring straight at me.

'My tutor.'

'He looks a bit intense. Is he always like that?'

'No. I guess he's taking his new responsibility seriously.' I glance at Dad as he's scrutinising Jackson. 'He's a bit... touchy-feely.'

'What do you mean?' He unclips his seatbelt. 'Has he touched you?'

'Only on my hand.' I don't know why I'm minimising the way Jackson made me feel. 'What are you doing?'

Dad opens his car door. 'Wait there a sec.'

'No, Dad.' I get out, walk quickly to where he's already started talking to him.

'...and I'd rather Scarlett had a student chaperone with her,' says Dad. 'I don't want her to be alone... even in a classroom environment. I want her to feel safe.'

'OK. Yes,' says Jackson. 'I can organise that.'

'And I mean in class with you, too. Can't be too careful.'

Jackson glances at me, folds his arms.

'Of course,' he says. 'Have you anyone in mind?'

'Er. Hannah Winterson?'

'Hannah's not in today,' he says, a bit too quickly.

'Really?'

I take out my phone. No new messages.

Kai's walking towards the gates, though he hasn't spotted us. He's got his earphones in and is talking into his phone. I try to make eye contact, but he doesn't see me. Dad follows my eye line.

'Kai!' I shout, but he doesn't hear. I intercept him, gesturing for him to free his ears. 'Can you do me a big favour?'

'I think so,' he says. 'How big?'

'Just say you'll be my chaperone for the day, but you don't have to, really. Just while we're in form.'

'Who's that with Jackson?' he says, tweaking his hair.

'It's my dad.'

'No way.' He slides his phone into the pocket of his leather jacket and strides over. He holds out his hand to Dad. 'Kai Raynor,' he says. 'Nice to meet you.' He holds out an arm and puts it around me. 'It would be my honour to chaperone this young lady for the day.'

Dad's still frowning. He must've heard me talking about Kai before, but to be honest it wouldn't surprise me if he hadn't been listening properly.

Dad shakes Kai's hand.

'Yeah. OK,' he says. 'Thanks, Kai. And thank you, Mr Jackson.' He walks towards the car. 'Come and get your bag, Scarlett.' He opens the boot. 'Was that all right? We could make a formal complaint. He looks well shifty.'

'No, it's OK, Dad. I think he's got the message.'

'But what if he does it to another pupil?'

'He might've just been trying to be nice. I'll keep my eye out... see if it was a one-off.'

'OK, well...'

He takes my rucksack out the boot and slams it shut. Jackson has gone inside and Kai's standing on his own, staring at Dad.

'Is your phone charged?' he says. 'Do you need to take a charger?'

'Dad, I'll be fine. Let me know if there's any news.' I hoist my bag onto my shoulder. 'Do you think we'll be allowed back home today?'

'I hope so. I'll text you when I find out. I'll see you out here after college. Remember to keep alert.'

'I will, Dad.'

He smiles a little before getting in the car. He must've waved at Kai, because my friend waves back at him. We link arms as we walk through the gates.

'You've been keeping him a secret,' he says. 'Why didn't you tell me your dad was fit.'

'Kai, you think everyone's fit.'

'True.' We take the steps up to the huge red-brick building that looks ancient compared to the modern blocks built around it. 'So how come I have the privilege of being your bodyguard today? Did you tell your dad Jackson was creeping you out?'

'Yeah. And Hannah's not in today.'

'Charming,' he says, opening the door for me. 'I'm not even first choice.'

'I didn't have much time to think about it to be honest.'

The carpet in the corridor is purple and patchy, but we sit in our spot against the grand staircase.

'Well,' he says, sitting cross-legged. 'I'm glad Hannah's not here. I get you to myself and I can speak without constant—'

'Interruption.'

'Ha!' He raises a palm for a high five. 'I always knew we had that psychic vibe going on.' He pulls out his phone. 'Any news about your mum?'

'No. But the police searched the house yesterday. We had to stay in a hotel.'

'I heard about your house,' he says. 'Mum says there's a thread about your mum on Netsleuths.'

'What the hell is Netsleuths? Don't tell me: sleuths on the net.'

'Well, yeah. Clue's in the name. Basically, wannabe detectives throwing theories around under the cover of dubious nicknames. Mum reckons the kidnapper is posting on there.'

Kai's scrolling through the posts.

'You know this is my life, Kai,' I say. 'It's not for people's entertainment. My mum's missing. We don't know what's happened to her.' I look round at all the people going about as though everything's normal. 'I shouldn't even be here. I should be out there, looking.'

'Shit, Scar,' he says. 'I'm so sorry. God, I'm so self-involved sometimes.'

'At least you're self-aware.'

'True.'

He takes a SodaStream bottle out of his satchel.

'I sneaked out some voddie,' he says. 'Thought it might help – you know, take the edge off, as my mother would say.'

He unscrews the black lid and holds it out to me. I take it and down a few swigs.

'Ugh.'

'Yeah, I know,' he says, taking it back, and pouring a shot into the lid. 'Never been pissed at college before. High school, yeah, obvs.'

The bell sounds and we stand too quickly. We hold on to each other for balance.

My head whooshes and my arms feel totally melted.

'Oh God,' I say, spotting my nemesis heading towards us. 'It's Tilly.'

'Oh, fucking hell,' says Kai. 'I hate that bitch.'

Tilly stops in front of us.

'So sorry to hear about your mum, Scarlett,' she says, smirking. 'It's just awful. Do the police think your dad did it?' She turns to one of her companions. 'I always thought he was dodgy. That's what my dad says.'

'Who's your dad?' says Kai, and I nudge him with my elbow.

'He's a police officer, actually,' she says. 'They've been looking into Scarlett's dad.'

'As if they'd tell you,' says Kai.

'Dad tells me everything,' she says.

'Bullshit,' I say. 'He must know you wouldn't be able to keep your mouth shut.'

She goes to speak, but she can't really. She's already proved my point.

'It really does take the edge off, doesn't it?' I say to Kai.

Kai puts his satchel over his head and across his body.

'I've had worse starts to the day.' He links his arm through mine again and we head towards Room 12. 'Let's go and perv on Jackson,' he says. 'See how he fucking likes it.'

'I do love you, Kai.'

'What was that about Jackson?' shouts Tilly, behind us.

'Get a life, Tilly!' shouts Kai. He leans his head on my shoulder. 'Daddy probably doesn't talk to her at all. Feel a bit sorry for her.'

'I don't.'

And then I remember, again.

Mum.

* * *

It's lunchtime and I'm heading into town, and the effects of the vodka have almost worn off, and now I feel like crying because the numbing effects have gone. Kai didn't take much convincing to abandon his role as my guardian, because he's been at the vodka since second period. Kai doesn't do well with free time. He gets bored with his own company after five minutes.

I check my phone for the hundredth time. Hannah hasn't replied to any of my WhatsApp messages, nor has she returned my phone calls. This is highly unusual. When she's sick, nine times out of ten she sends me a photo of her sad face while lying in bed.

Dad's ringing.

'Hey, Scarlett,' he says. 'Just a quick call to check you're OK.'

'Am fine.'

'Are you sure? You sound a bit...'

'Just tired, that's all. Didn't sleep well.'

'I get it. Well, the police have left – we're free to go back home. I'm going to pop into the police station this afternoon. They have CCTV and they want me to identify Mum.'

'What? When did they get this? Shall I come? I can meet you there.'

'It's OK. You stay at college.' Immediate pang of guilt. 'I want you to have as much normality as possible because we don't know...'

He trails off and I'm glad because I don't want to hear what he was about to say.

'Are you outside?' he says. 'Is Kai still with you?'

Shit. I hate lying to him, especially after us spending so much time together over the last few days. Last week, I'd have told him a little white lie without thinking.

'I'm just popping to the shops outside college.'

Technically it's not a lie. Only the shops in town are over a kilometre away.

'Shall I stay on the line until you get back through the gates?' he says. 'I can't let anything happen to you, Scarlett.'

'Dad, I'm fine. There are loads of students about.'

Again, not totally false.

'OK. I wasn't going to tell you this, but the police have been keeping up a presence – driving by, that sort of thing. Have you seen any police cars?'

One passes by as he says it, and I lock eyes with the officer in the passenger seat.

'Yes,' I say. 'All the time. Don't worry about me, Dad.'

'I'm going to worry when there's someone out there taking women off the streets.'

'Women?' I say. 'Have there been more than Mum?'

'It was just a turn of phrase. Anyway, I'll let you go. I'll pick you up after college. See you later.'

I go to press End, but Dad's already gone.

There's a message from Serena. Half of me hopes she's going to cancel.

I'm here! Sitting near the window. Looking forward to meeting you! X

My stomach cramps: a sick feeling pulses through me. God, I can't get the runs now. How mortifying – going to the toilet in a busy Costa. It always happens when I'm nervous. I try not to think about it. It might go away. They say the gut is linked to emotions, don't they? I wish mine wasn't so in sync with my mind.

I think I see her. I've tried to bury the idea that she might really be some bloke, but rationally, I was the one who contacted her. She's probably relieved *I'm* who I said I was.

As I push open the door, I turn the corners of my mouth up because Hannah says I have a resting bitch face (don't we all?). This place is full – it always is at lunchtime, but it's too expensive for Hannah and me to come every day. The baristas are gracefully weaving between each other behind a counter. I love the smell of fresh coffee, but I'm not keen on the taste unless it has the same amount of milk in. I'll pretend otherwise, though. Being picky isn't a good first impression.

Serena stands and I don't know whether to hug her or shake her hand. She doesn't initiate anything, so I just sit opposite her. There are two hot drinks already on the table.

'Hope you like hot chocolate,' she says, scooping whipped cream into her mouth with a finger. 'I never make them at home.'

'Yeah, I love hot chocolate,' I say, copying her. 'God, that cream's amazing.'

Vodka's still having an effect, then.

I take the chance to look at her while she uses a spoon to skim off the chocolate powder. She's wearing a denim jacket, like me, only hers is black and is covered in circular badges that I can't make out. Her diamond nose stud is twinkling in the reflection of the sun and her shoulder-length curly hair is perfectly styled.

She reaches her hand across the table, and I almost jump when she rests it on mine.

'Sorry,' she says. 'You must be really wary at the moment. Especially of people you haven't met before. How are you doing? Is there any news about your mum?'

'No.' I take a sachet of sweetener from the mini jug on the table and weave it between my fingers – a distraction from her staring at me like I'm the only person here. 'The police searched our house yesterday.'

She raises her eyebrows for a moment. Shit. Will she think me and my dad are murderers? It's what *I* feel people are thinking since the house search.

'That's horrible,' she says. 'Mum said they did that with Natalie's flat. And her boyfriend's flat. They thought he'd murdered her for months. Some people still do.'

'God, I'm sorry, Serena. Must be really hard for your family.'

'You'd think it would get easier with time, but it doesn't. I told you about my grandad. He doesn't live with my gran any more. Natalie looked a lot like Grandad, and I don't think Gran could bear it.' She twirls a curl. 'I know I shouldn't do that.'

'What?'

'Talk about her in the past tense. I can't remember Natalie, really. Just snippets that are memories I've put together from photographs, so they're probably not even my real memories anyway.'

'There's something about your aunt that feels... I don't know. Familiar. It's like on some level I knew I'd experience something like this...' I have no idea what I'm saying. I clear my throat and sit up straight. 'I watched a YouTube video about Natalie,' I say. 'It said she disappeared on a busy road in broad daylight.'

Serena's mid-drink, so she nods.

'Hmm.' She wipes white foam from her top lip. 'I wouldn't call it a busy road. It's one of those country lanes. Grandad puts flowers on a gate near there on the anniversary of her disappearance, and on her birthday.'

'That's heartbreaking.'

'I know. He feels a connection to her there. And there's no telling him that something bad might've happened to her. He still thinks that her life here got too much and she's in a hammock on a beach somewhere, on the other side of the world.'

'Did the police find anything in her car?'

'Her handbag was gone. It had her purse inside, and driving licence, bank cards. They haven't been used since. But her coat and her university books, plus her latest assignment paper was left in the car. Proper old school, printed out.'

'She was at uni?'

'Yeah, but she worked at a bar in Blackpool town centre.

Stag and hen central. That's what the media went with at the time.'

'And she'd finished an assignment?'

'Yeah, that's what I thought. If you're going to run away, why work on something you don't have to?'

'So strange.'

'It is when it happens in real life. You know that now. I've grown up with it. The media appeals on anniversaries, trying to get her name out there. They're not interested unless there's some new information. Mum says some people will know what happened. That if someone dies, they'll no longer feel loyalties to keep a secret. So basically, we're waiting for an unknown person to die and then we'll find out the truth. Or we won't.'

I wonder if I'll talk about Mum in thirteen years' time like Serena talks about Natalie. With a detachment like it never happened and Mum was just a character from my distant past.

'I think my mum was in the wrong place at the wrong time,' I say. 'Dad thinks someone was casing the street in the days before she was kidnapped.'

'Did the police get a number plate?'

'Not from our footage. But they might have from other Ring doorbells. They've not told us. Or rather, Dad's not told me if they have.'

'I hope they find her, Scarlett. I don't want you to go through what we've gone through.'

'Thanks,' I say.

I can't say that I hope so, too. That would be rubbing her face in it.

'Was there blood at the scene?' she says.

'Blood? No, I don't think so. They don't know where my mum was taken. Why?'

She looks behind her, maybe checking people aren't listening. She leans forward and I get a waft of the products on her hair – coconut, mixed with a flowery perfume. I resist the urge to touch her hair.

'They didn't release it to the public,' she says. 'But there was blood on the ground where my auntie's car was found. They have DNA from Natalie and another unknown. It wasn't her boyfriend; that's why he was cleared.'

'Did they have DNA testing from blood back then?'

'It was only thirteen years ago,' she says. 'But I get what you mean. They barely had internet back then.' She smiles and taps her phone. 'And how did people live without these? We know where everyone is, these days.'

'Yeah.' I take out my phone and show her Find My Friends. 'My dad checks where I am all the time since Mum. I don't think he cared before that.'

'Course he did,' she says. 'It's just more apparent now.'

'No.' I stir the almost-cold drink. 'He was never here, really. Even when he was. Always in his office... said he had to work all the time.'

'Did your mum work?'

My head shoots up.

'Sorry, sorry,' she says. 'I didn't mean...' She holds up a hand, loops a finger to rewind. '*Does* your mum work?'

'Yeah,' I say. 'For a homelessness charity.'

'Really? God. Shit things happen to good people, eh?'

'That's what I don't understand. My mum didn't have any enemies, didn't do anything out of the ordinary.'

'You have to get that idea out of your head,' she says, pushing her empty cup away from her. 'You're saying that it's the actions of the victim that make them vulnerable, but it's nothing to do with that. Blame is completely on the person who took her.'

My face flushes. She must think I'm an immature idiot. I feel like one right now.

She taps the table as she stands.

'Let's get out of here,' she says. 'Shall we go for a proper drink?'

'I can't.' I stand and push my chair in. 'Dad has my location, and my tutors are keeping an eye out for me.' Plus, I don't have fake ID.

'Fair enough.' She heads to the door, and I follow out into the daylight that seems a hundred times brighter than before. 'You're more sensible than I am. I'd have switched my location services off.'

'He'd come looking for me if I did that,' I say, laughing.

'Shit, really?' she says. 'That's full on.'

'I mean, only since Mum disappeared. He wouldn't have otherwise. Probably wouldn't have noticed if I was gone for a few days last week.'

She stops outside WHSmith.

'Do you want me to walk you back to college?' she says. 'I don't have to meet my dad until three.'

'No, it's OK,' I say. 'It's a bit out the way. You might get lost on the way back.'

'OK. It's been nice to meet you. We should do this again. Maybe you could come to Blackpool some time.'

'Definitely.'

'Keep in touch.' She hugs me, giving a gentle squeeze and there's that lovely smell again. Shit. I think she heard me sniff her hair so of course my face goes red again. 'Let me know if there's any news about your mum. I keep checking online, just in case. I hope they find her soon.'

'So do I.'

Oh God. It feels as though the blood has left my head. I sway and the tears come. I haven't eaten much today, and I feel vile. Everything's piling on top of me, and I thought this would be a distraction. But all I picture is Mum, bloodied and beaten and lying somewhere, or buried in the middle of nowhere.

Serena guides me to a bench. She rubs my back as the

queasiness grows. She's making it worse. Oh God. I'm going to—

Ugh. All over the pavement.

'Oh God,' I say, wiping my mouth. 'I'm so sorry. It's just all too much.'

A couple of passers-by look at me as though I'm a pathetic piece of shit.

'What are you looking at?' shouts Serena, and they turn around quickly. They don't want any trouble. 'Bloody nosy bastards.'

'I don't think I can get up,' I say, gripping the bench.

'Shall I call your dad?'

'I'll just have a minute. It'll go away soon.'

My face feels ice cold from the inside. I feel like I drank a bottle of vodka – not just a few shots.

'Here.' Serena hands me a cereal bar. 'Eat some of this. It might help settle your stomach.'

'Thanks.' I take a bite but want to spit it straight out because it's like chewing cardboard. Finally, I manage to swallow it. I go to give it back.

'It's OK,' she says. 'You hang on to that.'

'Sorry,' I say. 'As if you'd want it back.'

'I didn't like to say.'

She's still got her arm across my back. It feels as though we've known each other for years. I read that people who've suffered the same traumas often feel a bond that transcends trivialities. But it feels too intense. I don't want to talk about blood, DNA, missing anniversaries. My mum has only just gone missing. I don't want to think about what my life would be like without her in it.

'I feel a bit better now.' I stand to assess my balance. 'Yes. Definitely better. I'll be OK to walk.'

'Are you sure? Do you want me to walk you part of the way?'

'It's OK. Thanks, Serena.'

'I'll ring you tonight,' she says, standing too. 'To make sure you're OK.'

'OK.'

She kisses me on the cheek and stays next to the bench as I walk away. After a hundred metres, I turn and she's still there. She holds up a palm; I wave back. After about five hundred metres, I turn round, and she's gone. My life is becoming more and more surreal. I just want everything to go back to normal.

* * *

Kai and I skipped all afternoon lessons. We've been lying on doubled-up chairs in the Lounge and have basically been napping for hours. Mainly because Kai was so wasted and needed to sober up before home time, and me because I felt like I was going to puke again.

The bell goes for end tutorial, and we walk, arms wrapped round each other, to Room 12. We sit with our heads resting on the desk while Jackson takes the end-of-day register. We mumble when our names are called and rush out before everyone else, in case Jackson pulls us up and smells the vodka still apparent on Kai's breath.

I've a lone extra-strong mint in my denim jacket. I wipe off the fluff.

'Here,' I say to him. 'Have this.'

'But vodka's famously unsmellable.'

'That's not even a word. And *I* can smell it.'

'Mum won't be able to smell it,' he says. 'The house smells of cigarettes even though she smokes outside.'

We've reached the gates.

'I'll be OK from here,' I say. 'You don't want to miss the bus.'

'Are you sure?'

'Yes, yes.' I look at the time on my phone. 'Dad will be here in approximately two minutes. I'll be fine.'

'All right then, Scar.' He holds my shoulders as he gives me two air kisses. 'Text me tonight if you need a chat.'

'Thanks, Kai,' I shout after him. 'Message me when you get back, so I don't worry about you.'

He holds up an arm, points to the sky and gives me a twirl.

I sit on the low stone wall next to the gates. There are some students still huddled around Corsas and Fiestas. The lucky ones whose parents bought them cars. The freedom.

While I'm waiting – Dad's four minutes late – I try Hannah again.

It goes to voicemail.

'Hi, Han,' I say. 'Ring me back. I'm really worried about you. If you don't call me back by five, then I'm coming round.'

She hates people coming round unannounced – or even with two hours' notice. If she doesn't respond, I'll definitely have to go round. It must be serious if she's switched her phone off. I'll ask Dad if we can do a drive-by on the way home.

He's still not here.

My phone beeps. I bring the screen up, expecting it to be a reply from Hannah, but it's a message from a number I don't recognise.

Pete is driving you home.

My heart starts pounding. Where's my dad? And why is Pete picking me up? He and Gran go everywhere together – I don't remember ever being on my own with him.

I try calling Dad, but there's no answer.

A white van stops in front of me. The passenger seat window is tinted. I can't see beyond my own reflection. I turn round to see Mr Jackson, standing at the gate again. He walks slowly towards me.

'Everything OK, Scarlett?'

'I...'

The passenger window slides down. Pete is sitting in the driving seat. He's wearing shades and his grey hair slicked back as though he's just washed it.

'Hey, Scarlett,' he says. 'Your dad asked me to collect you. He's been stuck in town.'

'But town's only up the road.'

He shrugs. 'That's what I've been told. Hop in. Your gran's waiting for you at the house.'

I open the door and get in. It'll be fine. It's only Pete.

'Is he still at the police station?' I clunk in my seatbelt. 'Haven't they let him go?'

He mirror, signal, manoeuvres.

'They did,' he says. 'Several hours ago, according to them.'

'So where is he?'

'I don't know, love.'

He wouldn't just leave me waiting without letting me know. I check my phone again in case I've missed a message, a call or even an email.

Nothing.

I try ringing him.

'If he's driving,' says Pete, 'he probably won't answer.'

'Where will he be driving to?'

'No idea. Your dad'll be all right, try not to worry.'

I glance at the back of his van. I've always wanted to know what he keeps in here.

There are piles of boxes, a tool box, and about twenty bottles of mineral water.

'You get thirsty a lot?' I say.

'Got them from a friend,' he says. 'No questions asked.'

'Right.'

Hardly jewellery or expensive electronics.

'So...' I begin, but I don't know what to say.

'You're dying to ask, aren't you?' he says.

I know what he thinks I'm thinking, but he's wrong.

Well, he's right, now.

'Yeah,' I say.

'I didn't hurt anyone,' he says. 'It was corporate crime. Fraud. Went bankrupt and didn't declare all my accounts.'

'Ah, OK.'

'What did you think?'

I shrug, pretending to be cool.

'Murder, manslaughter. Armed robbery maybe.'

'Wow, Scarlett,' he says. 'Some imagination you've got there. Can you really picture me murdering someone?'

'No one *looks* like a murderer.'

'True,' he says. 'This is very true.'

CHAPTER 31

2005

Sometimes, I feel as though he's watching me from a distance, waiting to come out from the shadows just like he did at the hospital three months ago. I've stayed this long for Angela. Losing the baby has broken her, but I'm losing the will.

No one's been looking at the house, or following me on the street, and after weeks of me checking over my shoulder and peering out the curtains, I finally got more cameras installed covering front and back gardens, the hallway and the rear door. Apart from a few local cats and a hedgehog, there's been nothing suspicious.

Angela's still in bed. She's always in bed.

It's been months and there's nothing I can say or do to make things better for her, but I've never been good at that. What could I possibly do or say to make it better, anyway? She can barely look at me. I'm a constant reminder of what she lost.

We called him Joshua and planted a tree for him at the children's cemetery, which is only a twenty-minute walk away. Angela doesn't like to go there too often. She says she still feels him inside her, which is a bit creepy if you ask me.

I visit him every week. Take him a flower, or a teddy, or

something I think he'd like. Now it's almost Christmas, I've been buying little toy cars for him – a collection I've put in a beautiful glass bowl.

There you go. I've finally found my sentimental side.

Simon's baby will be due soon. I wonder if it'll be a boy or a girl. I kept track of his girlfriend on the internet for a while, but after Joshua died, I couldn't face the imminent onslaught of baby pictures.

Saying that, if Simon's still alive, he won't miss the birth of his child. I'll have to get over myself and keep watch. Then I'll find him. He made a terrible mistake confronting me at the hospital. I almost killed him once; what makes him think I won't come back to finish the job?

I head out of my home office, suitcase packed, and leave it on the landing.

I tap on her door.

'Ang, are you awake?'

'Hmm.'

Inside, the air is stale, sweet like death, but she's still clinging on. Permanently medicated. I don't know what the doctor's prescribed her, but it knocks her out twenty-four seven. It's like her body is slowly shutting down and she's letting it happen.

'I'm going away, remember? To see Penny before Christmas.' I sit on the bed next to her. 'Your aunt's coming round to keep an eye on you. OK?'

'Hmm.' She has no concept of what day, week, or month it is.

She's lying on her side, cuddling a yellow cellular baby blanket, stroking the silky hem.

'Ang?' I say, trying to keep my tone light. 'Can you hear me? I'm going away.'

I stand and head to the door.

'Alex,' she says. I turn around. She's now lying on her back, staring at the ceiling. 'I know what you are.'

'Excuse me?'

'Simon said.'

I walk back over and stand beside her, feeling as though I'm eight feet tall. She's so fragile, it wouldn't take much to break her.

'What do you mean Simon said? You didn't even meet Simon.'

Her eyes close. The woman's delirious. What if Simon spoke to her the night Joshua died? Told her everything I'd done? Would she believe it?

She probably would.

Underneath the surface of pretence, it's like we hate each other. Is this what marriage is really like? That my mother and father were an extreme example of normal?

I reach a hand down to stroke her cheek. She still has such a beautiful face. I run my fingers down her neck. It's like she wants me to end it all for her.

But it doesn't work like that. Not any more.

* * *

It's always better to pay a little extra for the airport lounge; you don't need to have a first-class ticket, these days. I'd say it cuts out the riff-raff, but it's too cheap to do that. Wankers in football kits, showing off pale limbs, is not a good look, especially in winter. Not that they give a shit. They've been allowed out for a week. They're making the most of it with all-you-can-drink Stella Artois.

I've been pondering what Angela said before I left. Now I think about it, she probably didn't even say the name Simon. It was my brain making connections where there were none. I texted Angela's aunt, and Angela's actually out of bed.

Is six months a reasonable amount of time to serve divorce papers? I gave the solicitor the old spiel, last week, about us drifting apart, and that Angela couldn't look at me without remembering the baby. If we separated for a year, it would make it easier and cheaper. Doubt she'd miss me, if she actually noticed I was gone.

I have a one-way ticket and enough funds to last me a few months. I'm starting with Nice, where the French go to holiday.

I'm jerked from behind as a woman and her friend sit in the booth behind me. They're wittering on about some promotion.

'Cheers, my darling,' says the one furthest away.

My money's on Prosecco. Everyone's drinking it these days.

'Thank you, honey!' It feels like she says it right in my ear. 'We are going to get absolutely mental this weekend and I don't want to remember one second.'

Fucking hell. She means business.

'So,' one of them says, after their second drink, 'if you met a stranger on holiday and they suggested you each murder your other halves, would you do it?'

'Jesus,' says the other. 'Not getting on with Ollie, then? Hope you kept the receipt for his Christmas present.'

'I'd totally do it. Totally.'

I'll wait until they're a few more glasses in.

Might as well join them. But first, I'll take the opportunity to take a look at who I'm listening to. I head to the bar, trusting the rest of the clientele not to nick off with my carry-on.

'Two double vodka and Cokes,' I say to the smiley bar man – obviously just started his shift. 'So I don't have to keep getting up.'

'Sure thing,' he says. 'Most people take three at a time.' He places the two glasses on the counter. 'If we don't get too busy, I can keep you topped up. No need for you to get up, sir.'

'That's very kind of you.'

I take out Simon's credit card – they haven't got those stupid chip and PIN machines installed here yet – and hand it to him. I sign the slip; I've perfected Simon's signature, not that anyone really checks.

I regret getting two drinks as I pass the women's table. The one right behind me is the most beautiful woman I've ever seen. Massive curly red hair, and a sprinkle of freckles on the top of her nose and cheeks. Her lips are painted coral and for a second, I forget that she can see me staring at her.

She catches my eye and I give her a small nod. Don't want to look too keen.

I wait long enough to hear where they're going: Nice.

Of course. It's fate.

And what could be better than meeting someone on holiday. Away from home. No one would know what happened to her for days, weeks, months.

And by then I'll be long gone.

CHAPTER 32

JOANNA

There are footsteps on the floor upstairs. People are talking but I can't make out what they're saying. I stand up on the bed, my legs wobbling.

'Hello?' I yell. 'Can you hear me?'

One of them says something; the other laughs.

I jump off the bed to try to find something to bang the ceiling with. The curtain pole won't budge without me using a screwdriver and the bedposts aren't coming loose.

I take out the top drawer from the chest and stand back on the bed. I hold it above me with both hands and jump. It hits the ceiling – not as loud as I'd like, but I keep banging until their voices quieten.

'Hello?' I shout. 'I'm locked in here. Help me, please!'

There's knocking on the floor above.

'Help me!' I shout again. 'Please, help me!'

'Hello?' It's a woman's voice. 'Are you OK?'

'No. No. Can you let me out?'

I'm waiting for my captor to barge through the door or to blast the high-pitched sound through the speaker.

He mustn't be here. Please let him be out.

'Please be quick. He'll be back soon.'

I jump off the bed and press my ear to the door. I can't hear anything.

I slide to the floor, exhausted. I've been existing on adrenaline and I've crashed. This woman might be part of all this, but I have to take a gamble and trust her. It might be my only chance of escaping this room.

There's banging in the distance.

I stand and pound my fists on the door, even though I can barely think. It's like the blood has drained from my brain.

'I'm in here!'

I'm still pounding when I hear another door burst open, slamming against a wall.

'In here!'

'Stand clear,' she says. 'I'm going to try to break it down.'

'OK.' I lean against the windowsill and wrap my arms around my body, trying to still the shivers. It could be anyone behind that door.

The door wobbles as she hits it once. After the second time, there is only the lock keeping it together. She smashes it into pieces.

She climbs over the broken door; she looks as shocked as I am.

I collapse into a pathetic heap onto the floor, but I know I have to summon the energy to escape.

'Didn't know I had that in me,' she gasps as she drops the fire extinguisher. 'Shit. Sorry.' She wipes her hands on her smart black trousers. 'Are you OK?'

'Thank you so much.' I burst into shocked, relieved tears. 'Thank you, thank you. We need to get out of here. He'll be back any minute.' She takes hold of my hand and pulls me up. She wipes my tears away and wraps her arms around me. I must smell awful but I hug her back.

'Oh my god,' she says. 'You're shaking.' She gazes in fascinated horror around the room. 'Why does it look like a bedroom in here?'

'I don't know,' I say, trying to hurry her through the door, away from the terror that's been my life in this room. 'I think it was a message to say he'd been watching – that he knew intimate details about my life.'

'Jesus Christ,' she says as she looks around again. 'What a psychopath.' Her shoulders shake with a shiver. 'Come on. Let's get you out of here.'

She steps back and I follow, trembling, as she leaves the room. She looks into a small kitchen, then a room with monitors, keyboards and black-out blinds to keep out the daylight.

'Jeez,' she says. 'What the hell?'

'What is this place?' I say, trying to push her out of the door. 'Is it an apartment block? Are we close to town? My family will be looking for me.'

'A small office block,' she says, 'on the outskirts of Preston. We just moved in today. How long have you been locked in here? Who the hell would do this to you? Are you hurt? Do you need an ambulance?'

'I don't know. I haven't seen his face. And I'm fine, I think. My wrist is starting to heal.'

She holds up my hand to look at it.

'Oh, love,' she says. 'We have a first aid kit upstairs.'

As we finally reach the front door, she picks up something off a desk. 'Is this yours?' she says, holding up a mobile phone.

'Yes,' I say.

She passes it to me.

'The battery's dead. I need to let my family know I'm OK.' I open the door, checking left and right. It's clear. 'We need to leave now,' I say, panic rising in my voice. 'He's watching my every move.'

'I won't let anything bad happen to you,' she replies soothingly. 'OK? We can phone the police from upstairs. Come on.'

She takes me by the hand and pulls me into a corridor with a stairwell. I follow her upstairs. We run along another corridor and stop at a door that we go inside. She locks and bolts it. By the window is a man sitting at a laptop. He can't be much older than Scarlett. He stands, pushing his glasses to the bridge of his nose.

'What's going on?' he says, standing. 'Are you OK?'

'My name's Joanna,' I say. 'Someone kidnapped me. I've been here for days.'

'Oh my god,' he says, grabbing his phone off the desk. 'I've heard about you on the news. I'll call the police.'

'Thank you,' I say, feeling my knees tremble. 'Thank you.'

There's a bang from downstairs.

'Oh no,' I say, gripping the woman's arm. 'That's him, I know it.'

She lets me cling to her as she closes the internal blinds and turns off the light.

'Everyone,' she whispers, pointing to a desk against the wall under the window, 'under here.'

I get underneath and press myself against the wall.

We're all quiet as we listen to him downstairs. He's shouting but I can't make out what he's saying.

'He's going to come up here,' I whisper. 'He has cameras everywhere in that place.'

'Who is it?' asks the young lad, his arms are around his knees. 'Did he hurt you?'

'No. I don't know,' I say. 'I think he's a serial killer. He showed me videos about women who were murdered... said I was going to be next.'

'Holy shit.'

'Shh.' The woman in the suit puts a finger on her lips, and mouths, 'He's coming.'

I cover my mouth with both hands. Oh God. Would he dare grab me in front of these two? A look passes between them.

They look petrified; the lad is shaking. Her hand reaches mine. She squeezes it tight.

I close my eyes as I wait for him to bang on the door.

She strokes the side of my hand with her thumb.

He's thumping the doors along the corridor, trying the handles.

'Joanna!' he shouts. 'I know you're here, Joanna.'

He gets to this one. He's only a few feet away from us.

The bolts are drawn; the door's locked.

He runs along the corridor and into the stairwell. He's going up another level.

He's shouting now. Calling out to the empty offices upstairs.

'Where are you, Joanna? I know you're here somewhere.' Glass smashes. There's banging as though he's trying to kick in a door. 'And if I can't find you, I'm coming after Scarlett.'

CHAPTER 33

SCARLETT

Pete's theory is wrong. Dad isn't home when we pull up outside, and Gran is standing at the window. She runs towards me when I walk into the living room.

'Thank God you're OK,' she says. 'I was driving myself mad with worry.'

'I'm not that late.'

'Only because I sent Pete up to the college to get you. I've been checking your dad has been on time collecting you since your mother disappeared, and it's lucky I did.'

'But Pete said Dad asked him to get me.'

'Sorry, love,' says Pete. 'That's what Rhona told me to tell you, so you didn't panic on the way home.'

'He's probably still at the police station,' I say.

'I've rung and checked,' says Gran. 'He left over an hour ago.'

'That's if they're telling the truth,' says Pete.

'Why would they lie about that?' I'm standing at the window. Halfway down the street is a black BMW with a man and a woman sitting inside. 'How long has that car been there?'

Pete stands next to me, rests his hands on the sill and peers out.

'I don't know,' he says. 'We only got here half an hour ago before I went to pick you up. Have a look, Rhona – did you notice that car when we arrived?'

'Should we look so obviously?' she says. 'If they're watching the house then we don't want them to know that we know.'

'Why?'

'I don't know.' She pulls the curtain around the curve of the window. 'Shall I take them a cup of tea, then? Let them know we're onto them?'

'That's an even worse idea, Rhona.'

Next door's door opens. Mr Shepherd's lingering on his front step.

'Well, that doesn't surprise me,' says Gran. 'Even *he's* noticed.'

'Shh,' says Pete. 'He'll have heard you. Wait there.'

He does a little jog out the living room and out the front door.

'Oh my god,' says Gran. 'He's talking to him.'

She presses her ear to the window.

I sit on the sofa. 'What are they saying?'

'I can't hear,' she says. 'Now they're both walking towards the car. I don't know what they think they're doing – they're in their sixties, for goodness' sake.'

She comes away from the window and picks up some print-outs of A4 on the coffee table.

'What are those?' I say.

'Pete's been doing some research into this "Audio Tech" company.' She puts on her glasses. 'It was formed at the beginning of this year and registered to a man called Richard Burfield.'

'What's the address?'

'It's a solicitor's firm in London, but that's not unusual. Pete looked it up online. Apparently, their premises are on an industrial estate just off the M6.'

'Shall we go there? See if that's where Mum's being kept?'

'They'll be long gone by now, Scarlett. They ran off with half a million pounds. They won't be sitting there waiting to be caught, will they? They'll be in the Bahamas or something. Anyway, those people weren't the ones who were conned.'

'Did Pete manage to trace this "Bob" that Dad was talking about?'

'No. Pete seems to think he doesn't exist.' She gets up and hovers by the window again.

'You think Dad made it up?'

'That's not what I meant,' she says. 'They're coming back.'

The Shepherds' door opens and closes; Pete walks back into the living room, his face red and sweaty from the ten metre jog.

'They said they're just keeping an eye on the house. Said that James – your dad – was only released a few minutes ago.'

'Oh,' says Gran. 'How strange.'

'Just a miscommunication.'

'Well?' says Gran.

'Well, what?' says Pete.

'Do they want a cup of tea or not?'

* * *

It's been two hours since Dad was released, but he isn't home. Gran and Pete are still downstairs, and the doorbell has just sounded. I hover on the landing and see two people dressed in suits walk through the front door.

Should I go down? Will they think I'm just some stupid kid?

I walk slowly downstairs, hearing nothing but murmuring coming from the living room.

'Is there any news?' I say. They're standing – a man and a woman – in the middle of the living room, and Gran and Pete are sitting on the settee. 'About Mum or Dad?'

'What's that about your dad?' the woman says. 'Sorry. I'm Detective Sergeant Ellie Gable and this is Detective Sergeant Mo Chowdhury.'

'He hasn't come home from the police station yet,' says Gran. 'But I'm sure it's nothing to worry about.'

'OK,' says Ellie Gable. 'Well, we were wanting to speak to him again after a new development at our end.'

'Do you know who took Mum?' I say.

Why don't they just say why they're here?

'Not yet.' She gives me a smile that says they're nowhere near finding her. 'Has your dad mentioned any names to you? He gave us a list, but it was small.'

'Alex Buchanan?' I say, and the detectives exchange a look. 'Did Dad give you that name?'

'It's a name we've come across before,' says Mo Chowdhury.

'Have you tracked him down?' I say. 'Dad thinks he's got Mum and then he's going to come after me. I can't find him online.'

'It's best you don't try,' says Gable. 'Just leave the detective work to us, Scarlett.'

I feel about ten years old. How mortifying.

'No need to talk to her like that, love,' says Pete. 'We can't just sit around doing nothing.' He's been doing his own investigating, so I think he felt the sting of her words, too. 'What about this Alex fella, then? Have you talked to him?'

'We haven't, I'm afraid,' says Gable.

'Are you even doing your job properly?' says Pete.

Gran's eyes widen. She folds her arms, probably trying to stop herself putting a hand across Pete's mouth. I've never seen someone be so cheeky to police officers before, but he'll be used to dealing with them.

'I can assure you we are,' says Gable.

'So where is he, then?'

Ellie Gable rolls her eyes slightly at her colleague.

How rude. It's like we're an inconvenience. Maybe she expected us to be huddled together in a corner sobbing and subdued. Not bombarding them with questions.

'Alex Buchanan,' says Mo Chowdhury, 'hasn't been seen since 2005. There has been no evidence of his existence, no proof of life, since then.'

'So, he's dead?' I say. 'He can't be.'

'We're doing our best,' he says. 'We have a number of leads.'

'Did my dad mention the name Simon Kennedy?' I say, feeling silly again, because of course he would've mentioned it.

Ellie Gable's expression changes.

'Where did you hear that name?'

Shit. He didn't.

'I...' Gran and Pete are looking at me, too. I can't be the only one Dad confided in about this. It's too big of a thing. It's not as if it's a crime, changing his name. And it was only because the police didn't do their job and arrest Alex Buchanan when he tried to kill Dad years ago.

One of their phones is ringing. It's Mo's. He takes it out of his pocket.

'DS Chowdhury,' he says. He listens for a couple of seconds. 'Right. OK.'

He ends the call.

'Thanks for your help,' he says. 'DS Gable and I will keep you informed with any updates.'

They walk out the living room, down the hall, and out the front door.

'Yeah,' says Pete. 'Course they will.'

I check my phone as I walk upstairs to my room. I've been looking every ten minutes, to see if there's a missed call from Mum.

Something's different.

The messages I sent this morning have been read.

I press to call her but it goes straight to voicemail. Either the battery's died, or someone's switched it off.

CHAPTER 34

JOANNA

After sitting under the desk for over an hour, I think he's left the building. The woman – I still don't know her name because we've been silent – crawls out. I'm cradling my mobile in my hands. I press the power button and it switches on with only three per cent battery.

'We need to ring the police again,' I say, remaining on the floor, my feet going numb. 'They should've been here by now.'

'Of course.' She holds out a hand to me, helping me out. 'Max will phone again, won't you, Max?'

'Yeah,' he says, ducking out and standing. 'Sure thing.'

'Why are you being so calm?' I say. 'That man's crazy. He could kill us all.'

'It's OK,' she says. 'He thinks this place is empty.' She walks towards the only two desks with computers, opens a drawer and takes out some clothes. 'There's a shower in the back room.' She hands me tracksuit bottoms and a T-shirt. 'You can borrow these – they're clean. It's my running gear. For when I get the chance.' She smiles and points to the door at the other side of the room. 'So you'll be all fresh when the police arrive.'

Max is tapping on his keyboard.

'Are you going to call them back?' I say.

He spins around on his chair and waves his mobile.

'Just about to.' He smiles. He mustn't be more than eighteen or nineteen. 'They said they were on their way.'

'There's a towel in there,' she says.

'OK,' I say, walking towards the door. I stop and turn round. 'What did you say your name was?'

'It's Holly.' She sits at her desk, her back to me. 'See you in a few minutes.'

I continue my way to the bathroom.

Keep calm, breathe.

I open the door and close it as casually as I can.

Shit. There's no lock.

The room has a toilet, sink and a shower cubicle but no window.

I flick on the shower and undress. I need to scrub myself clean after days of grime and sweat have coated my skin. I scrub my scalp with the shampoo.

I get out and wrap myself in the giant white towel. I dab my wrist dry – it's beginning to scab but it's still tender.

She said her name is Holly. Is she the same Holly who emailed me?

I put on the trousers and T-shirt and bundle my clothes in a ball. I carry them under my arm as I open the door and walk back towards them, my legs shaking, arms trembling. I'm trying to appear calm, but I can't manage a smile when they both turn around.

Holly stands and pulls out a chair.

'Come and sit here, Joanna,' she says.

I'm still holding my dirty clothes as I sit on the office chair she's holding.

'Do I know you?' I say. 'Did you email me on Sunday night?'

She takes my clothes and puts them in a drawer.

'You really think it was a serial killer who was keeping you?' she says. 'That he was going to murder you?'

'It's what he made me think,' I say. 'I should write all of it down in case I forget their names.' I look to Max. 'Do you have a pen and paper?'

'I don't think you're going to need those,' says Holly.

She walks round to the other side of the desk and sits in front of a screen. She taps on the keyboard. Max turns to me – he's only a few feet away – and smiles, his lips pressed together.

'Show her, Max,' says Holly.

Max uses his mouse to navigate to a file on his screen. He clicks it and photographs of five people appear. Holly stands and grabs a pen. She leans across and points to each as she says, 'Sarah-Jane Crosswell, Rachel Beckwith, Siobhan O'Hara, Simon Kennedy, and Natalie Baxter.'

I stand and look closely at the screen.

'I've never seen any of these people before,' I say.

'We thought you'd say that.' Holly sits down and taps the pen on her lip. 'It seems as though you know less than we thought.'

'You think the same person killed them all?' I say.

'Oh yes,' she says. 'We're almost certain of it. There's no evidence, though. That's why the police can't arrest him.' She stands again, looks out the window. 'Though it's been a hell of a search to find him, I can tell you.'

'What's his name?' I say. 'Why do you think it's anything to do with me?'

I'm trying to avoid looking at Natalie Baxter's face on the screen. It feels as though her eyes are following me.

'His name is Alex Buchanan,' she says.

'I don't know anyone called Alex Buchanan,' I say.

'Oh, Joanna, Joanna,' she says. 'I'm sorry to tell you, but you do. Max, if you could do the honours.'

Her eyes don't leave my face. She wants to see my reaction.

There's a photograph on the screen but I don't want to look at it.

'It took us a while to get a picture of him,' she says. 'Turns out he doesn't like having his photo taken. This' – she stands and taps the screen with her pen again – 'is Alex Buchanan.'

I look at the screen, at a photograph of a newlywed couple. The woman is very young, early twenties. She's beautiful and has white-blonde hair. The man next to her I don't have to look at for longer than a second, because staring back at me is a picture of my husband.

CHAPTER 35

2005

I didn't think it was possible to fall in love so quickly. Not just pretend love like it was with Angela. OK, I realise I'm talking about her in the past tense, even though it's only been a couple of days since I last saw her. I'll stay away for a few months while our solicitors deal with everything. She'll be relieved we're getting divorced because I don't think she even likes me, let alone loves me.

I head out of my apartment, which is only a few minutes' walk from the beach. I'm wearing shorts, a white T-shirt, and a navy blazer; the weather here is mild for December. I'm a little early, but it'll give me time to get the perfect table overlooking the sea.

'*Bonjour, monsieur,*' says the waiter.

'*Bonjour.*'

'Would you like to see the menu?'

It's happened a lot since I've been here. My French accent must be terrible.

'Yes, please,' I say. 'I'm expecting a companion. She should be here any minute.'

I can't be Alex any more. I know that. I toyed with the idea of telling her *I* was called Simon Kennedy, but that might get me into trouble further down the line. It's best if I never mention his name again.

'Hello,' she says.

Her beautiful red hair is flowing in the gentle breeze. She's wearing an amber-coloured dress under a gold cotton wrap that grazes her beautiful shoulders.

Fuck. What's happening to me?

Such soppy sappy thoughts.

I stand and take her hand, kiss her on both cheeks.

'How very continental,' she says, pulling out a chair.

Shit. Should've pulled it out for her.

'Would you like a drink?' says the waiter.

The service here is excellent; I road tested it yesterday afternoon.

'A bottle of Corona for me,' I say.

'I'll have the same, please,' she says.

She has impeccable manners, which is such an underrated quality.

'Is your friend still asleep?' I say.

'I don't think she's gone to bed yet,' she says. 'She met a man called Jean last night and has been out ever since.'

'Aren't you worried about her?' I say.

'Nah. She's been replying to my texts.'

'Ah,' I say.

You and I both know that you shouldn't rely on texted replies as proof of life, but I don't put that worry in her head.

'I'm sure she'll be fine,' I say.

The waiter places our beers on the table, along with a small bowl of olives. Bet they're going to charge a small fortune for those.

'So,' she says, placing her elbow on the table and resting her chin on her hand. 'What have you got planned for the rest of your trip?'

'I might head over to Cannes, maybe travel to Italy.'

'Aren't you going home for Christmas?'

'No one to be home for. I had the idea of heading to Paris to see in the New Year,' I say. 'You should join me.'

She throws her head back as she laughs. Such a graceful, smooth neck. Her delicate gold necklace shimmers on her skin.

'Yeah, I wish.' She runs a finger down the condensation of the bottle. 'I'll have used up all my leave by the end of the year.'

'Joanna!'

There's a screeching voice behind me. I turn around.

Oh God, it's her annoying friend.

'Amy!' Joanna stands and runs to her. 'Where have you been?'

'I told you,' says Amy. 'I was with Jean. He cooked me pancakes this morning.'

Jesus. This woman is classless.

Why are these two people friends?

'So, who's this?' Amy lifts her sunglasses to reveal that she hadn't just been drinking last night. Her pupils are so wide, her eyes look black. 'I recognise you.'

'He was on our flight,' says Joanna. 'Remember?'

'Ah right. Yeah.' Amy plonks herself down on the spare chair. 'Josh? Jack?'

'It's James.'

I hold my hand out and she shakes it. Cold, clammy hands.

'Nice to meet you, James.'

James was the first name that came to my lips when I introduced myself to Joanna. It was in our top three names for a boy. Mine and Angela's, that is.

Amy looks around. 'Any chance I could grab one of those?'

'Here,' I say, passing her my beer. 'Have mine.'

'God, thanks.' She puts it to her lips and glugs down almost half. 'I'll get out your hair. Just need the key from Jo.'

'You've got a key,' says Joanna, smiling. 'Remember? They gave us two.'

She's a lot more patient than I am. This Amy is such an annoying flake.

'Oh yeah. Sorry, Jo.' She drinks the rest of my beer. 'I'll head on back. Think I'll sleep for a week.' She stands as unsteadily as she sat. She kisses Joanna on the cheek. 'See you later, Jo-Jo.'

We both watch as Amy tries to carry herself normally.

'Should we walk her back?' I say. 'Make sure she gets there OK?'

'She'll be fine,' says Joanna. 'Our hotel is only a few hundred metres from here.'

'Mine too,' I say.

'Do you want to get another drink here?' she says. 'Or do you want to go somewhere else? We went to this fantastic little restaurant near the harbour yesterday. It does the best *moules et frites*.'

My plan isn't going to plan. Amy ruined it anyway.

But you know me. Always up for winging it.

I should loosen up a little.

I signal for the bill.

'That sounds perfect,' I say. 'The fresh air has made me really hungry.'

The waiter places the receipt with my change. They didn't charge for the olives.

I really should try to be a little less suspicious of everyone.

CHAPTER 36
SCARLETT

The police left nearly an hour ago and Dad's phone is ringing out. They obviously haven't looked hard enough for this Alex Buchanan if he hasn't been seen in years. If *I* had gone to the police and said someone tried to kill me, and they didn't do anything about it, I'd totally lose faith in them. Did they think Dad was making it up? They don't seem to believe that he has anything to do with my mum's disappearance, but they're not going to tell us everything they have. Buchanan probably is dead. If he thought he'd killed my dad years ago, he's not going to hang around, waiting to be caught.

My phone pings with a text. It's from Hannah.

I'm OK. Been really ill.

She must've been near unconscious for her to not reply to me until now. It's been over twenty-hour hours. *I'm coming round,* I fire back.

I grab my charger – my phone's on five per cent – and head downstairs. Sky News is blaring from the living room. When I open the door, I see Gran and Pete are sitting side-by-side with their eyes closed. They must be exhausted. Gran will barely be sleeping at night. I tiptoe through to the dining area to grab a pen and paper from the drawer.

I scribble a quick note to Gran and Pete and lean it against the TV screen. They're still fast asleep and Gran has started snoring lightly. I linger to look at her, almost jealous of her dreams. I'm so tired I don't know how I'm still able to walk. But I head outside, closing the front door gently.

The car is still there, a few metres up from the house. The man is reading a newspaper – which makes him about fifty, I guess – and the woman is on her phone. They both look up as I walk past. The man frowns; a small smile's on his lips.

'Where are you going, Scarlett?' he says.

My instinct is to run away. Did Pete actually say these two were police, or just that they're watching the house?

'Only round the corner,' I say. 'My gran knows where I'm going.'

Well, she will do when she wakes and reads the note.

'Do you want us to drive you round?' he says.

'No, thanks.' I point to some random house on the right. 'It's only round the corner.'

'Well, OK. We're here if you need us. It's going to be getting dark soon.'

I have a feeling they're going to be watching me all the way to Hannah's but I suppose that's not a terrible thing. Definitely police. They wouldn't be chatting to me if they were about to kidnap me, would they?

As I have a final glance before I turn the corner, I literally bump into Mr Shepherd.

'Oh,' I say. 'I'm sorry.'

It takes him a moment to register it's me, his eyes narrowing behind his thick glasses. This close, I can see flecks of grey at the roots of his shiny black hair.

'It's you!' he says, standing back slightly. 'Should you be going out alone?'

'I'm OK,' I say, sounding as unsure as I feel. 'Not going far.'

'Right, OK.' He does a one-eighty of his surroundings. 'Shall I walk with you?'

'No, no. It's fine.' I start walking away. 'Bye, now.'

'Wait, wait.' He pulls out a leaflet from his inside pocket and hands it to me. 'Have a read of this,' he says. 'It might offer some comfort.'

'Thank you,' I say, smiling and nodding. 'Will do.'

I walk a few paces before checking he's not following. I've never encountered as many people in two minutes of leaving the house before.

It's not far to Hannah's, so I resist putting in my earpods. As well as having barely any battery, it wouldn't be safe. I glance at the leaflet Mr Shepherd gave me as I approach a bin. The banner at the top states: *The Family of World Peace and Unification.*

Right, OK. Not something I was expecting, but it kind of explains a lot. Instead of binning it, I fold it and stick it in my top pocket. Don't need any more bad luck.

Hannah eventually answers the door after I knocked three times and shouted through the letterbox.

'Shit, Han,' I say. 'You look awful.'

'Yeah, thanks, Scar,' she says. She stands aside and beckons me in.

'Where's your dad?' I say, following her up the stairs.

'Hmm,' she says. 'Came in at one in the morning, and then left at eight. I reckon he's got himself a new girlfriend.'

'Really? That doesn't sound like him.'

Hannah pushes open her bedroom door and gets straight into bed, pulling the covers up to her chin.

'Doesn't he worry about you being alone in the house?' I say, sitting next to her.

'He's been ringing me every hour. He's scared about his job. And with Mum not being reliable with money...' She pats the contraption sitting on her bedside cabinet. 'He put a landline upstairs. Says he can't trust me to keep my phone charged. Ha!' She plucks a tissue, wipes her nose, and throws it behind her. 'Any news about your mum? I'm sorry I've been out of it – I've never felt this horrendous before.'

'A lot's happened, actually,' I say. I hold up my phone. 'Mum's read my recent messages. I don't know if it's actually her, though. But the police might be able to trace the phone as it's been powered on.'

Hannah opens her mouth, but closes it quickly. She tilts her head to the side.

'I hope she comes home soon, Scar.'

She says it as though she's humouring me. But hope is what's keeping me going. I have to believe Mum's coming home because the alternative is just too horrendous to think about. And no news is good news. That's what Gran keeps saying. Mum's belongings haven't been found yet. It's like she vanished off the planet.

'Dad said someone tried to kill him,' I say.

Hannah sits up. 'What the...? When? Today?'

'About twenty years ago.' I'm still in my jacket, and I'm clinging to my phone charger. I plug it into my phone and put it into one of Hannah's spare sockets behind her bedside table. 'One of his friends. He tried to drown Dad in a reservoir.' I tap the name into Google, but there are hundreds, thousands of Simon Kennedys out there. Narrowing the search to Preston brings up a Companies House listing, but there's no photo attached to it.

'What?' she repeats. 'And he told the police, right?'

'He said he did. But this guy still hasn't been caught. It's like he's vanished, too.' I pause. 'Dad changed his name so this man wouldn't find us.'

'No way.'

'His real name is Simon Kennedy.'

'I can't believe it.'

'No,' I say. 'It sounds...'

'And you think this guy has something to do with your mum?'

'I gave the police his name and they didn't seem interested.'

'But if this man tried to kill your dad, why would he come back and do this and attract the attention of the police?'

'I don't know, Han.'

'Something's not adding up here,' she says.

'I reported it online the other day. Gave the two names and the location of the reservoir, but I've not heard anything back, which isn't surprising as I didn't leave my details.'

'So it really is anonymous, then?'

I nod. Hannah grabs her iPad from under the covers and I shift round next to her.

'Let's do some digging,' she says, as if my life is some sort of Netflix documentary.

She presses the Safari icon and types in *Simon Kennedy*, *car*, and *reservoir*. Unlike yesterday, there are five results at the top, all posted within the last couple of hours.

I have a sharp intake of breath.

Will Simon Kennedy's family finally get closure?
Could the Milton Keynes Missing Man Mystery be Solved After Eighteen Years?

'Eh?' says Hannah, resting her chin on her hand. 'So they must've acted on your tip-off.'

'My dad was from Milton Keynes?'

Hannah clicks onto one of the YouTube video links.

Is this where Dad is now – is it the reason he didn't collect me from college? Am I about to see my father on screen with his real family instead of being here with me?

Hannah presses play.

A reporter is standing on a footpath. Behind him is a large reservoir within lush green hills. There's a police tent next to the water, and a car that's covered in mud – the windows are the same colour as the body, like a giant toy car that's been battered and bashed. Is this Dad's old car? He begins his report.

'The mystery of missing Milton Keynes man and father of one may finally have been solved. Simon Kennedy, who was aged 30 at the time, went missing almost twenty years ago. His family has been searching for him ever since, but that search might now have come to an end.

'It is thought that the remains found in this car are that of him, Simon Kennedy. It was discovered this morning, submerged here in Langdale Reservoir, after police received a tip-off. A post-mortem will take place in the next few days to try to discover what happened that day, eighteen years ago and some hundred and fifty miles from his home in Milton Keynes. Police are appealing for witnesses who might have seen any activity around this area in 2005.'

'They must be wrong,' I say. 'My dad isn't dead. Why would they announce it was him before taking a sample of DNA?'

Hannah clicks on another video – a short one posted only an hour ago...

The voiceover accompanies footage panning round the rescued car.

'Police have confirmed that the remains found today in Langdale Reservoir are those of Simon Kennedy, who was identified using dental records. A further post-mortem will be conducted over the next few days to try to establish cause of death. The investigation continues.'

'Shit, Scar,' says Hannah. 'Whoever your dad is, it's obviously not Simon Kennedy.'

It's like the blood has drained from my head, my chest, and emptied into my feet. I sway, stars in front of my eyes.

I stand, grabbing the side of the bed until I can focus. 'I have to get home.'

'Do you want me to come with you?' says Hannah.

'No, no. Thanks. I'll text you later.' I bend down to hug her. 'I'm in a bloody nightmare.'

'Scarlett,' she shouts after me as I head out the room. 'Are you sure...?'

Her words fade as I race down the stairs. When I get to the hall, the front door opens. It's Hannah's dad.

'Hello, Scarlett,' he says. 'How are you bearing up? Any news?'

I shake my head. I can't tell him about Dad – I wouldn't know *what* to tell him about Dad.

He glances at my shoes and coat. 'Are you coming or going? Will you be staying for tea?'

I side step past him out the door.

'Sorry,' I shout as I run down the path. 'I need to go home.'

CHAPTER 37

10TH JULY 2010

'Daddy, Mummy's sleeping on the sofa.'

Kids are so much more interesting when they start talking. And it turns out that my father was right after all: everything *is* going to be OK.

Now, I wouldn't go as far as to say that fatherhood has completely changed me, but when Scarlett was born some part of me was altered. It scared me that I was responsible for this little thing, this part of me. I wasn't being punished, after all. I sometimes think of Angela, of what she's doing now. We haven't seen each other since the day I left. When I went to collect the rest of my things, she was at her aunt's house. Or that's what she said. It was all very amicable, really. I think she lives with that bloke Harry who was my best man at our wedding. They have a Labradoodle or something. Good for Harry. He always had a thing for Angela. Amazing what you can tell from a Facebook profile. I can never have one myself, of course. Joanna posts all the time on there, though. She loves it.

'Mummy was up late last night, Scarlett,' I say, rolling out of bed. 'And I bet you woke her up early this morning, didn't you?'

'Probably,' she says, one of her new favourite words.

She's sitting cross-legged at the end of the bed, her beautiful red hair messy, the early morning sunlight casting a halo of light on her curls.

'Won't be a sec,' I say. 'Wait there.'

I have to close the door to the bathroom because I've gained a mini stalker, following me everywhere.

I piss, flush, and wash my hands, pausing to look in the mirror. The grey hairs are getting more frequent, but they don't make me look distinguished; they make me look ancient.

Old.

Double the age of Rachel Beckwith. I could be her father, now.

My reflection blurs and I'm taken back to that night. The chilly air and the cigarette smoke mixed with her breath – one of her final breaths. I should've counted them. I should've relished those last moments, because I didn't know if I could do it. But once I started, I had to finish. It would've been her word against mine of course, but I couldn't take the risk. Didn't want to waste my life in prison like my father did. A product of a hundred mistakes made in the past.

I think of Rachel as my first, but of course she wasn't.

A knock on the bathroom door.

'Hurry up, Daddy. I starving.'

'Coming.'

No. I have to suppress this darkness. Scarlett has given me that reason. I need to keep her face in my mind whenever my thoughts turn to the past. I'm James now. I'm so far removed from Alex Buchanan. He's a stranger to me. A child that left tiny fragments of memories in my brain. Compartmentalised. Most of the time.

'What have I told you about sitting at the top of the stairs?' I say, coming out of the bathroom.

'I can't remember, Daddy,' she says, reaching up for my hand.

I take hold of her hand and match her step. First foot down, second foot down. It takes us twice as long as it would do on my own, but it's Saturday so I don't mind.

Saturdays are my favourite day of the week, because I hate my job, and consequently Sunday afternoons are a mixture of dread and trying to forget about Monday. Why did I end up working in such a shitty place? I'm so much better than that. I need to be where the money is. Get us an even bigger house. All that money is just sitting in my account – the one I haven't told Joanna about yet because I've yet to think of a reason why I have it. She's one person I can't lie to. She sees straight through me.

Finally, we reach the bottom and I open the door to the living room.

'Mummy, Mummy!' says Scarlett. 'You're awake.'

And she is. She's standing at the mirror in the living room. Saturdays are her favourite day of the week, too, and she doesn't want to waste it. Works hard, plays hard and boy does she. Earns more than me, too, but I don't mind.

'Hey,' I say, kissing the back of her neck as she decides whether to put her hair up or leave it down.

'God, I'm so hungover,' she says. 'You should've seen Amy last night. Couldn't get her away from the karaoke... made me have a go. Forced me.'

'"Reach For the Stars"?'

'It was either that or—'

'Céline Dion.'

A flashback to mine and Angela's wedding that I push to the side.

'Yeah. Céline's only ever a good idea after five Southern Comforts.'

I pick up Scarlett and place her on the sofa. I grab her favourite blanket and make a big show of lifting it in the air and covering her. I love her little giggle. It never fails to make me smile. I flick on the television to a repeat of *Teletubbies*, though at almost four years old, she's growing out of it.

'Are you sure you don't want me to drive you there?' I ask Joanna.

'No, it's OK, love,' she says. 'I'll be setting back after Scarlett's bath time.' She kisses me quickly on the lips. 'But thanks.'

She heads to the hall to put on her boots and comes back in wearing her bright yellow jacket. She bends to kiss an engrossed Scarlett goodbye.

'See you later, Lettie Lou,' she whispers.

'Bye-bye, Mummy.'

She grabs the car keys from the bowl.

'See you later, lovelies! I'm escaping while I can!'

I hear her humming as she walks to the car. She's been looking forward to this Manchester shopping trip with Amy for weeks. God knows why – I mean, it's shopping. But it makes her happy.

'Right, Miss Scarlett,' I say. 'Would you like Coco Pops or Rice Krispies?'

'Pop-Tarts!' she says.

I wander into the kitchen and open the cupboards.

'Do Pop-Tarts still exist?'

I grab the packet. It seems they do. I stick two in the toaster and tiptoe into the living room. Scarlett's captivated by the television and squeals when I pop up behind her.

'Boo!'

She giggles. 'Naughty Daddy.'

I crawl round and kneel at her little feet.

'What do you reckon to a trip to Blackpool?' I say.

'I reckon,' she says. 'Reckon yes.'

I don't think she knows what 'reckon' means, and the way she says it, I don't think I do, either.

'We can go up the Tower and play on the arcades.'

She jumps again when she hears the toaster pop. Her eyes widen and she clenches her fists, holding them above her head.

'Pop-Tarts and Tower,' she says. 'Good Daddy!'

I stand and walk to the kitchen.

Yes. Blackpool.

That'll blow the cobwebs away.

CHAPTER 38
2023

I'm sitting in my car in the middle of bloody nowhere and there's no sign of them. Fucking Holly. Who'd have thought Simon's fiancée had it in her to orchestrate such an elaborate fucking scheme. Bitch. Though I bet she wasn't the one to come up with Audio Tech. That has Chloe's name written all over it: a way to take my money as well as my wife.

The text from Holly the morning Joanna went missing was simple.

> You took someone I love, now I have someone you love. Confess and she'll go free.

It's been a nightmare trying to cover my murky tracks.

I select a number in my phone. I haven't spoken to her in years. She might not have the same number.

'Hello?' I say. 'Ang?'

'Who is this?' Her voice sounds different, deeper.

'It's Alex,' I say, the name sounding alien to me.

'Oh.' There's a barking dog in the background. 'Alex. Gosh. It's been a while. How are you?'

'Good, good.' Bad, very bad. 'Just a quick call, but I don't suppose anyone's showed up at yours, asking about me?'

'Oh,' she says again, surprised. 'Yes. About five years ago I think it was. This woman approached me as I was leaving work. Bit older than me, tall, dark hair.'

That'd be Chloe, then.

'This is so strange that you're phoning to ask about this after so long. Why do you think she approached me? Is it someone you know?'

'No, well not really. I'm being stalked by this woman and she's causing trouble with my family.'

'Oh, Alex. That's awful. Is everything OK?'

It's hard not to soften at her concern. She was always such a kind, sensitive person.

'What did she say, Ang?' I say. 'I'm sorry to be so blunt, but we're having a bit of bother with her at the moment. Do you remember what she said?'

'Funnily enough, yes I do. Because it was so strange, you see. I told my dad and Harry about it and they found it hilarious.'

'Go on.' Tick tock, tick tock.

'She asked if I knew where you were, but of course I didn't. She said you were a very dangerous man and I couldn't help but laugh. I think I offended her – you should've seen her face. I told her you couldn't be that dangerous because you were...'

'I was what,' I say, pressing. I haven't got all bloody day.

'You were so boring,' she says. 'All you ever did was play video games in the attic room while you were pretending to work.'

'Oh.'

'Sorry, Alex,' she says. 'Have I upset you?'

'No, no. Not at all.' I've been called worse things, I suppose.

'Hang on,' she says. 'A car's just pulled up outside.' I hear her footsteps. 'I think it's a police car. God, I hope Harry's not had an accident. He's always driving too fast. I keep telling him to be careful.'

'Don't...' I start, but I can't let her hear my alarm. They might be there for something completely unrelated.

'Don't what?' she says.

'It's OK.' I wipe the sweat from my top lip. 'It's been lovely to chat to you, Ang. We should meet for a catch up some time.'

'Sure,' she says, knowing as well as I do that will never happen. 'Bye, Alex.'

Shit. The police are there because of me, I can sense it.

I select Pete's contact. He answers after ten rings – what the fuck, Pete?

'Is everything OK there?' I say. 'Scarlett OK?'

'Er, yes, yes everything's fine.'

'You didn't tell Scarlett where I was?'

'No, no.'

'Do you think she still believes that Joanna is with another man?'

'No,' he says, his voice echoing. He must've gone into the downstairs bathroom. 'The police came round earlier, which of course didn't make sense because I told Scarlett you were still at the police station.'

'Shit.'

'Yeah. And she mentioned someone called Simon Kennedy and another name – Alex something. Do you know these people?'

I should've got rid of those papers years ago – why the hell didn't I just leave them in the loft? I'm surprised the police didn't find them, but a pile of burned papers in the garden would have gained more attention. I made it even worse by telling Scarlett that story. I only have myself to blame if she repeats it. Too close to the truth. Caught off guard. It was painful lying to my little girl. I wish I could say I'd never lie to her again, but I don't like where this whole situation is going.

'No,' I say. Too little too late. He probably doesn't believe me, but he's hardly the most honest person in the world.

'*Pete, Pete.*' It's Rhona in the background. '*Scarlett's not in her room.*'

I turn the key in the ignition.

'What?' I say. 'Pete?'

'It's OK, James,' he says. 'It's OK. She left us a note. She's popped round to Hannah's.'

I can hear a touch of guilt mixed with relief in his voice. What the hell were they doing that they didn't notice Scarlett leaving the house? She could be anywhere.

'I'm coming home,' I say.

I never should have left.

CHAPTER 39

JOANNA

'You know,' says Holly, still sitting in the chair opposite me, 'he's had several different aliases. Where did you two meet?'

'I'd have thought you would already know that,' I say, trying to sound fearless, but I'm feeling anything but.

'Oh, come on, Joanna,' she says. 'Humour us.'

'Nice,' I say. 'In France.'

'Everyone knows where Nice is,' says Max, speaking for the first time in ages.

'Because Simon's credit cards were used there,' she says. 'Your husband told me Simon had run off with another woman, though when he paid me a visit he said his name was Johnny.'

'Why are you so interested in my husband?' I say, looking to each of them. 'Who's Simon?'

Holly stands, reaches down next to her, and picks up a large holdall. She takes out a small wallet and flings across photographs. 'See. Simon was my fiancé. We lived together. We were expecting a child. And I read his credit card statements that came to our house. Your husband travelled across Europe. I thought it was Simon with his new girlfriend. I was in pieces. I thought, *How could he rub it in my face?* He knew I'd see the transactions.'

I pick up the photos of a smiling couple, holding glasses of champagne, her with her diamond ring to the camera with a mock shocked face.

'The police thought he'd just run off,' she says, still standing. 'They said that people do that all the time – that there was proof of life and Simon didn't want to be contacted. Probably just a phone call, no real investigation. It was only when Chloe paid me a visit a few months later that it clicked. She really hates your husband, you know. It was her idea to decorate the room like that.'

'Mum,' says Max. 'There's a new video on YouTube about Dad.'

'Mum?' I say. 'So, you're mother and son?'

'I think the lack of sleep has made you rather slow today,' says Holly. There is such venom in her voice – as though I was the one who did this to her. 'This morning,' she continues, 'Simon's car was found in a reservoir in Cheshire. Can you imagine that? That he was there in his car for all these years? Can you?' She pushes the office chair on its wheels with such force that it bashes against the wall and falls on its side. 'Which is why we had to take this all a step further. Because Rick was doing a rather shit job of getting anything out of you. Too fucking soft. I should've known. He tracked Alex years ago, when he was sitting outside the hospital, but Rick let him out of his sight.'

'Rick? Who's Rick?'

'Did you know Alex was married before? He left her after their baby died. He used to leave little toys at the grave. There was a sizeable collection, you know. He hadn't visited for ages. Until last year, that is. But I digress.'

Holly walks round the two desks to Max's computer. She clicks onto a file and brings up one of the girls' pictures. She grabs the top of the monitor and rotates it forcefully so it's facing me.

'Rachel,' she says. 'Do you remember Rachel? I didn't meet her personally, but Rick knew her. Rick and Chloe know your husband murdered her. Rick has spent most of his life with people looking at him, thinking he's a murderer. Do you know how much that destroyed his life? Do you have any idea how many lives your husband has ruined?'

'But...' I say, the word barely audible. 'How do you know my husband did all of this?'

'Chloe said that Alex – that's your husband's real name by the way – was the last person seen with Rachel. She said that Simon told her Alex left the flat they shared at university for a brief window just down the road from where Siobhan O'Hara was killed. And, after looking up his movements after that, it appears that he lived in the Blackpool area when Natalie Baxter went missing. And poor Sarah-Jane Crosswell. She went to the same school as your husband, but she was found on the side of the road after being battered to death with a rock. She was four-teen years old! Now, don't tell me that they are all coincidences. Four different women and girls, in the areas your husband happened to be.'

'He can't have done it,' I say. 'He can't. He wouldn't hurt anyone. This is all circumstantial. The police would've arrested him if it were true.'

'They didn't know where he was,' says Holly. 'But we managed to track him down. We believe that the DNA from the scene of the Siobhan O'Hara murder, and on the car of the Natalie Baxter disappearance, will be that of your husband.'

'What? What DNA?'

'We need you to ring your husband and ask him to come and join us.'

I stand, my legs wobbly.

'I just need to go to the bathroom.'

'Hey—' says Max, leaping forward, trying to grab me.

'Leave her,' says Holly. 'There isn't anywhere for her to go.'

I'm almost crawling to the door. When I get there, I shut myself in, and slide to the floor.

My hair is starting to frizz; the roots are beginning to show.

If I didn't have Scarlett, I would have descended into darkness. Escaped with alcohol, drugs, whatever I could get my hands on until I could forget completely.

Scarlett.

I need to be here for my beautiful daughter.

My daughter who has the same red hair as me, that I've been trying to disguise for years. I always thought I was the reason we had to keep a low profile. But what Holly says James has done is a million times worse. He let me think it was my fault we had to move every few years.

Who abandons their wife when she's just lost a child? But that's not the worst of the things they say he's done.

I turn on the tap and splash my face with freezing cold water, yet the shock of it doesn't take away the images of those women and girls from my mind. Young, vibrant, their lives ahead of them.

I've been living with a stranger. And, if Holly's right, I married a serial killer.

CHAPTER 40
SCARLETT

When I reach the house, my gran is almost in tears.

'What's happened?' I say. 'Have they found Mum?'

'Scarlett,' she says. 'We were so worried about you. I felt terrible. Your dad's on his way. He was searching for your mum. He shouldn't be too long.'

'Oh God.'

She blinks, confused by my words.

'Dad...' I start. 'Dad's not who he says he is.'

'What?'

I head up the stairs.

'What do you mean, Scarlett?'

She calls for Pete. He's probably in on it, too. Is everyone in on this? Do Mum, Gran, everyone know that my dad's real name isn't James?

Why would my dad lie to me? What would be the point of him saying he was Simon Kennedy? I grab the cardboard box from underneath his bed. I swipe the cobwebs away and tip the contents onto the floor.

The passport. Yes, it's definitely my dad's photo. The birth certificate is a certified copy, issued the same year as the pass-port: 2006. One year after Simon Kennedy disappeared.

Inside a buff folder is a bundle of statements to an address in Yorkshire. A loan for twenty thousand pounds, cleared out of the account, maxed out of its overdraft. Another, a loan for fifteen thousand pounds, maxed overdraft. A mortgage letter – an offer of three hundred thousand pounds. A quick total in my head of all these accounts is nearly half a million. What the actual fuck?

I bundle the papers back into the box, squashing them down.

My hands are shaking.

Dad is a bloody con artist. He never was Simon Kennedy.

But how would he know that Simon Kennedy wouldn't be coming back? Unless he didn't know. Identity fraud happens all the time.

But the overwhelming feeling of dread, of absolute fear, won't go away.

There's only one way Dad would know Simon Kennedy wouldn't report this fraud.

If he was the man who put him there, in that car.

I carry the box downstairs. I need help. I can't do this on my own. Gran and Pete will know what to do.

As I reach the bottom step, the front door slams open.

It's Dad, his face set, his frame suddenly much bulkier and stronger than I'd ever realised before.

'You need to come with me, Scarlett,' he says. 'Now.'

'I'm not going anywhere with you.' I walk backwards, until I reach the living room door. I push through it; the television's still blaring. But Gran and Pete are gone. 'Gran! Pete!' I run into the kitchen, but they're not there either. 'Where are they?' I say to him, my dad. If he actually *is* my father. 'What did you do with them?'

'Don't be ridiculous, Scarlett,' he says, storming towards me.

'I haven't done anything to them. They've probably nipped out for food.'

'But they wouldn't do that without telling me.' I'm against the hall wall. I'm shaking all over; my legs are about to collapse. I never thought I would ever be afraid of my dad. 'Please,' I say. 'Just let me speak to them.'

'What's got into you, Scarlett?' he says. I don't believe the fake concern on his face. 'What the hell has happened?'

'I watched the news,' I say, still gripping hold of the cardboard box. 'You're not Simon Kennedy. Simon Kennedy's dead. They found his body in the reservoir you told me about. Who are you really? What have you done?'

Dad spins around, punches the wall with such force it makes me jump.

'What have *you* done, Scarlett?' He says it quietly, with such composure that sends my body trembling even more. Calculated calmness. 'Listen,' he says. 'I can explain. The whole thing's been a misunderstanding. I can explain in the car on the way to your mum.'

'What?'

'I found her,' he says, almost pleading with his hands. 'This is what I've been doing since the police released me. Do you think they'd let me go if they thought I would lie about such significant things?'

'Maybe they didn't know.'

He gives a hollow laugh.

'You think...' he starts. 'You think you've uncovered this big mystery when they have hundreds of officers on the case? You think that I could really do anything to hurt anyone? Have I ever, ever hurt you? Or your mum? I love you both; I just want you both home, safe, where you belong.'

'No,' I whisper in shame, before recovering myself. 'But they didn't know where he was. Only you knew that he would never come back.'

He looks at his watch.

'Listen. We have to move now or they're going to harm your mother.'

He knows what to say, doesn't he? A con artist who can lie without conscience.

But he's still my dad. Mum said I used to idolise him when I was little. Used to follow him round. But this can't be the same person, can it?

'Are you and Mum my real parents?' I say. 'Because now I don't know. I'm the only one with this red hair. Mum has dark hair, you have dark hair, Gran used to have dark hair. It's genetically impossible, isn't it?'

'Now you're being silly, Scarlett. Of course you're our daughter.' Dad's phone starts to ring. 'It's your mum.'

He holds his phone up to prove it before walking to the front door and closes it as he speaks. If it was Mum, he would've let me talk to her. I don't believe it's her at all. I will never believe anything he says again.

CHAPTER 41

2023

'Now you're being silly, Scarlett,' I say. 'Of course you're our daughter.'

Jesus Christ. My life is going to shit. Why the fuck is this happening now?

It's Joanna's phone again; I hold it up to my daughter.

'It's your mum.'

I press answer and wait until I'm outside.

'Hello.'

'Now come on, Alex,' says Holly. 'You can put a stop to all of this. You've had days to make this stop, yet you've been ignoring me. Aren't you worried that you'll never see your daughter or your wife again?'

'There's no way you can get to my daughter.'

In the distance, headlights flash.

'Did you see that?' she says. 'They're armed, and they're not sentimental. Pretty dangerous combination, don't you think?'

I run back into the house.

'You have to come with me, Scarlett. Now!'

She's sitting on the hallway floor. Her face is blotchy and red. Her eyelids swollen. My beautiful little girl is broken.

'Come on, Scar,' I say. 'There are dangerous people close by. They've threatened to hurt you, to hurt your mum. We have to go.'

'I can't believe anything you say.'

Her bottom lip is sticking out, trembling. She's trying not to cry.

'You don't have to believe me. I can drop you off at Hannah's, make sure they call the police. OK?'

'Alex!' Holly's shouting from my phone. 'You need to come here.'

'Let me talk to my wife,' I growl, standing at the front door as Pete walks into the hallway.

'Pete,' I say, grabbing his arm before he heads outside. 'There's a car over there. They're threatening to take Scarlett. Can you call the police? I have to go and get Jo.'

He nods his head, trying to compute the information I've just bombarded him with.

'Bolt the doors,' I say. 'Front and back.'

'OK, OK,' he says, giving a brief glance up the road where the car flashes its headlights again. 'I've got this.'

'Alex!'

'I'm here,' I say. 'Please, can I talk to Joanna?'

There are a few seconds of rustling.

'James? Is that you?'

'Jo. Oh my god, Joanna.' I get into my car. 'Are you OK – have they hurt you?'

'No, they've not hurt me. They've been saying that you killed these women. She says she wants you to confess and then she'll let me go.'

'Who says?'

'Holly. And her son, Max, and someone called Rick. Holly says she was engaged to someone called Simon Kennedy.'

I cover the microphone. 'Fuck!' I bash the steering wheel. 'Fuck, fuck, fuck!'

Deep breath.

'OK,' I say. 'Tell me where you are.'

'Not so fast, Alex.'

It's that bitch Holly again.

'What?' I start the engine. 'Just tell me where you are.'

'And when you get here, you're going to confess,' she says. 'Because we have our eyes on Scarlett. And that won't end as neatly.'

* * *

I pull up to an industrial unit that houses only a couple of businesses. There's a light on, up on the second floor. I pull open the communal door, run up the stairs two at a time, and follow the light. I come to a door with the sign: 'Audio Tech'.

I try the door, but it's locked.

There's movement from the other side.

'Hello, Alex,' says Holly, opening the door. Why the fuck is she wearing a suit? 'So nice of you to join us.'

A young lad is sitting next to my wife. Jesus, he's the spitting image of Simon. Standing on the other side of the room are two blokes dressed in black.

'Are those your heavies?' I say, trying to keep my voice light, but looking for any other exit except the door Holly just locked again.

'You don't recognise them?'

I narrow my eyes, but my sight isn't what it used to be.

'It's Rachel's ex-boyfriend, Rick, and your college friend Phil.'

'Ah, Phil. Warhammer Phil. How's it going?' He doesn't react. 'Look, I think there's been a misunderstanding here.' I hold up my hands as I walk slowly towards my wife. 'Let's put all of this behind us and I won't tell the police you *unlawfully* kidnapped my wife.' I kneel down at her feet. 'Are you OK?'

She shakes her head. She looks exhausted, terrified. She bends down close to my head.

'They know about Natalie Baxter,' she breathes.

I stroke her hair, but she flinches. What have they told her about me?

'It's OK,' I say. 'It'll be OK.'

'That's enough of the soppy reunions,' says Holly. 'The police are on their way.'

'You've no proof that I did anything.'

'Your wife definitely knows something about Natalie Baxter. Her reaction was somewhat telling. And there's unknown DNA at the scene where Natalie was last seen. I'm sure the police would be able to match it with yours.' She looks at Joanna. 'Or hers. Were you in all of this together?'

'No!' shouts Joanna. 'It was—'

'Fine!' I interrupt. 'I'll talk to the police, admit everything. But you have to let Joanna go. She's nothing to do with any of this.'

They have nothing. I know they have nothing.

Otherwise, the police would have arrested me. Bunch of shitty vigilantes taking the law into their own grubby hands.

'Are you going to confess to stealing my money?' I say. 'Because I take it you're behind this sham company, Audio Tech.'

'I wouldn't call it stealing,' she says. 'You obtained it fraudulently, using Simon's name. It'll have to be repaid.'

'Yeah, as if you're going to pay the loans back to the bank.'

She doesn't say anything.

'Rick,' she calls across the room. 'Drive Joanna back home, will you, there's a love.'

There are sirens in the distance.

About bloody time.

Pete must've called them, told them to trace my phone.

I take my wife's hand.

There must be at least seven cars outside; the blue lights are beaming into the room.

Heavy footsteps are on the stairs. Figures wearing black line the corridor – peering through the interior windows.

The door is forced open, and I stand aside.

But they come straight towards me.

Within seconds I'm on the floor, hands behind my back. Two other officers grab the boy and Holly. I crane my neck to the side. Even while being handcuffed, she's watching me with a smug smirk on her face.

'Alex Buchanan, I'm arresting you for the murder of Simon Kennedy...'

I close my eyes to drown out her words as they try to pull me up from the ground.

The last person I see before they drag me away is Joanna. One of the loves of my life.

I'm going to do what my father did for me. Joanna doesn't have to worry any more.

They bundle me into the back of a reinforced police van and slam the doors closed.

I close my eyes again as the van starts moving.

I'm so fucking tired.

CHAPTER 42

JOANNA

I'm staring at the noticeboard but I'm not taking anything in. I'm sitting in the reception of the police station, waiting for Pete to pick me up. They've given me a grey tracksuit to wear because they took my clothes – and the gym wear Holly leant me – as evidence.

My husband is in the same building, but I'm not allowed to talk to him. The detective, Ellie Gable, couldn't tell me what evidence they have against him, but they wouldn't arrest him for nothing.

The door opens and a gust of cold wind bites my ankles.

'Mum!' Scarlett rushes towards me, hugging my waist.

'Oh, Scarlett.' I wrap my arms around her, stroke her hair. I feel complete again; my missing part has returned to me. 'I'm so sorry.'

She pulls away from me.

'It's not your fault, Mum.' She sits down next to me. 'Where's Dad?'

She's looking at the floor. She looks exhausted. Her eyes are surrounded by shadows.

'He's...' I start. 'They...'

'I know he's not really called James,' she says. 'He's not called Simon, either.'

'Simon?'

'I found some documents. Dad stole hundreds of thousands of pounds pretending to be Simon Kennedy.'

'Oh, Scarlett. How did you find that out?'

'I was trying to find you,' she says, tears dropping from her cheeks into her hair. 'Dad was acting really weird. You don't seem surprised.'

I put my arm around her shoulders and pull her towards me.

'Did you never suspect he wasn't who he said he was?' she says.

'A lot's happened over the years, Scarlett. I became a shadow of myself. Hiding from the world.'

'What were you hiding from?'

She's looking at me with such trust. Her big brown eyes so innocent.

'Do you think Dad did what they say he did?' she says, not waiting for an answer.

'I don't know, love,' I say, because I can't tell her what I really think. 'We'll have to see if he's charged.'

'My Jo-Jo!' My mum bursts into the room and I stand to hug her. 'I've been worried sick; I can't believe it. I thought I'd lost you, my darling girl.'

'It's good see you, Mum.'

'Come on,' she says. 'Let's get you home.'

CHAPTER 43

2023

They're bluffing, I know it. They have nothing on me. She's sitting in front of me now, so bloody smug.

'OK. Let's run through this timeline,' she says. 'Your mum was murdered by your father in 1989, then you went to stay with your grandparents in Yorkshire. You went to Runsdale College in 1991 and to York University in 1993. You married your first wife in 2002 and divorced in 2006. In 2010, you were with your second wife and lived in the Manchester area.'

'Bloody hell,' I say. '*This is Your Life*, is it?'

'I'm summarising,' she says. 'Do you confirm these details are correct?'

'No comment.'

She rubs a temple. It looks like she's been awake for days. It's not a good look.

'Detective Gable,' says my solicitor, a charming young man from Warrington. 'If you have no evidence to tie my client to the charges listed, then I suggest you release him immediately.'

'You might suggest it, but I'm getting there.' She slides a piece of paper towards me. 'Can you confirm that this is you in this image. For the tape, I am showing Mr Buchanan a photograph of a passport in the name of Simon Kennedy.'

'No comment.'

'I think you knew you'd get away with obtaining funds by deception because you knew that Simon Kennedy was dead.'

'No comment.'

So, she only *thinks* that. She has no evidence whatsoever.

The door opens. Someone wants a word with DS Gable.

She pauses the tape.

I tap my fingers on the table. A trait I've inherited from my father. It does relieve the stress, somewhat.

'What's going on?' I say.

'I'll go and find out,' my solicitor says.

For fuck's sake, I'm telling him his fucking job. I've no chance with this one.

He comes back a few minutes later.

'The DNA found on the bodies of Rachel Beckwith and Siobhan O'Hara is a match. Plus DNA on the door handle of Natalie Baxter's car.' He's not looking at me now. He picked the wrong side to bat for. 'They're going to charge you, I'm afraid.'

'If I tell them where Natalie's remains are,' I say, 'will they do a deal?'

He shakes his head, shrugs. 'I seriously doubt it,' he says, 'but it would be the decent thing to do.'

CHAPTER 44
SCARLETT

I've been in my bed with the curtains closed since my dad was charged a week ago. I can't use my phone because I keep getting hateful messages, and I can't go on social media because the story's been shared hundreds of thousands of times. There are headlines like *Serial Killer Used Two Identities to Cover His Tracks*, and *Hiding in Suburbia: The Multiple Murderer Who Hid in Plain Sight*.

I don't know how I'm going to get over this. I can't compute that these crimes are anything to do with my father. It doesn't make sense at all.

There's a tap on my door.

'Scarlett, love.'

'Come in, Mum.'

She opens the door and places a tray with a sandwich and a glass of water on the end of my bed.

'For when you're hungry, love.' She lingers at the door. 'There are some visitors for you. Are you up to seeing them?'

'Is it Hannah and Kai?'

She smiles.

When I heard the news about Dad, I thought no one would

want to talk to me again. That I was tainted by what he'd done – that they'd think I inherited a broken gene. But they've been amazing, calling me every day on the landline that Pete installed in my room, because I couldn't trust myself not to Google everything if I had possession of my phone.

'Yes, please,' I say.

She leaves my door open, and hollers for them. It's like a stampede up the stairs.

'Oh my god, Scar!' Kai's the first one in. His hair's in a quiff and he has a new piercing in his nose. He flops onto my bed, lying on his side. 'You look amazing, considering what you've been through, hun.'

'I've brought you some cupcakes,' says Hannah. She puts the box on my bedside table before giving me a hug. I wouldn't have got through this past week without her. 'You look like shit, Scar.'

'Hannah!' Kai's offended on my behalf. 'It's because she hasn't seen daylight for a week.' He gets up and opens the curtains – the sunlight pulses into my eyes. 'How are you doing, Scar? Have you changed your mind about coming back to college?'

'No,' I say, sitting up a bit. 'Mum said it's best if we get away for a while. Apparently, there's a cottage in Yorkshire that's in the family – my great-grandmother left it to me.'

'Fuck off,' says Kai. 'You own a fucking house? When's the party?'

I smile a little. I can't bring myself to laugh. When I catch myself, I see those missing posters, the picture of Simon Kennedy. Serena sitting in front of me in Costa when it was my dad who... God, I can't even bring myself to think it. I've tried a hundred times to compose a message to her, but no words are enough.

'When we're settled,' I say.

'At least there won't be a trial,' says Hannah, twirling on my swivel chair. 'Can't believe he confessed, but then, he had no choice with the DNA.'

'Hannah!' Kai and I say it at the same time.

'Just saying...' She looks out the window. 'And those people that kidnapped your mum. Hope they get found guilty. Can't believe all that's happened. Dad said you're going to need years of therapy to get over it.'

'Jesus, Hannah,' says Kai. 'You can think things without saying them, you know.' He rests a hand on my leg. 'Though, to be fair, my mum suggested the same. Only *her* kind of therapy involves shitloads of booze.'

Mum's at my door again.

'Thanks for visiting, you two,' she says. 'I think Scarlett could do with her rest.'

They both kiss me on the cheek before heading out the door.

I know they'll be talking about me when they leave, but that's OK.

'Are you ready to come downstairs?' says Mum, after the front door shuts. 'Maybe we can watch a film, take our minds off things.'

She hands me my fluffy dressing gown and I go to the bathroom to splash water on my face. When I look in the mirror, I see parts of my face that belong to him – my eyes, my lips. I hope to God that's where the resemblance ends.

EPILOGUE

I'm sitting here after bagging a seat by the window, but it's only because Jason Tranter has no visitors today. This is his usual place. Always the best for Jason. He doesn't like me. In fact, most of them don't like me. The only one I get along with is that psychopath Donnie Kay. He says he actually prefers being inside to being 'out there'. He's the only one who loves talking about what he did, but I let my mind drift off when he starts going on about it. Sick bastard.

They're ten minutes late. They're meant to be on time. It's strict like that in here. We only have fifty minutes left, and if they don't make it, it'll be four weeks till the next visit.

Frank Sebold is in the corner chatting with his wife. He's been here the longest and he's about seventy-odd. Can't imagine that. Not that I have to. Three life sentences mean I'm never going to see the stars again. Not unless it's through the bars of my window. Shit. There's too much time to think in here.

Some nights they come to me in my dreams, and they're together, laughing and pointing at me. I have days when the gravitas of what happened consumes me—

They're here. Thank fuck for that. Can't be wallowing in all that shit. Bad things happen to good people all the time; I'm sure I'll get over it eventually. Maybe get myself another degree, turn to God. Who knows.

It's the first time I've seen Scarlett since the worst day of my life, and I want to rush to her and wrap my arms around her. But she's not looking at me; her head's down. She looks taller; her shoulders are an inch higher than my wife's. Joanna's smiling at me and I can't tell if she means it.

Neither of them hug me.

'It's so good to see you both,' I say. 'How's college going, Scarlett? Nearly exam time?'

'I told you, James,' says Joanna. 'Scarlett hasn't been to college since...'

She still hasn't referred to me as Alex, even though she knows. Everyone knows. But I get it. Keep things separate.

'Sorry,' I say. 'I remember, now. So how's everything at home?'

Joanna's frowning; she's about to cry.

'That's what I'm— we're here to talk about,' she says. She shuffles in the plastic chair.

She turns to Scarlett and nods to the refreshments table in the corner. 'Will you get us a drink, love? Maybe some biscuits?'

'What's happened, Jo?' I say.

'I just need to make sure... that before we move, that you're not going to...' She's talking so quietly. 'To tell anyone what I did.'

'You mean if you divorce me and meet someone else that I'm not going to blab in revenge?'

Her mouth drops open; her cheeks flush.

'I...'

'I know that will happen, Jo. But you're my daughter's mother. I will always love you. That's why you have to live your life, look after Scarlett.'

'I didn't think you'd understand. I don't know if I can live with myself after what I did.'

'You have to, for Scarlett. I did the worst part of it. That's all you need to remember.'

'But I think about that night, every day.'

'I know.'

Her eyes drift to the window, to the outside and I know she's reliving it.

* * *

It was the day Joanna had gone shopping in Manchester with Amy – 10ᵗʰ July 2010. Scarlett was almost four years old, and we'd not long returned home from our day trip to Blackpool.

It had just gone seven when my mobile rang. Scarlett was in the bath, squirting ducks with a water pistol, and I was sitting on the toilet seat.

'Hey, Jo!' I said. 'You having a good time?'

Breathing down the line. Sniffs and faint sobs.

'Joanna? Are you there?' I got up and went to the landing. 'Joanna?'

'Oh no,' she said.

'Joanna, answer me. What the hell has happened?'

'I was so tired, James. I didn't see her.'

'Didn't see who?'

'I don't know. She was on the road. I didn't see her. Only closed my eyes for a little bit, seconds.'

'Where are you, Joanna?'

She was only a few minutes' drive from home, and I didn't know what I was going to find because she'd been hysterical on the phone. I drove down the short country lane that ran alongside the main road. What the hell was she doing driving down there?

I saw her car parked next to another – an old red Fiesta – and pulled up behind it.

'Wait there a sec, honey,' I said, opening my door. 'I'm just going to fetch Mummy. Her car broke down.'

'Joanna?' I shouted.

I heard her crying. She was sitting next to a woman who was lying still on the ground. A handbag's contents spilled out on the road.

'She's dead, James,' she said as I crouched down next to her. 'I can't bring her back.'

'Shit.' I stood. Wandered into the road. 'Fuck!' There was no one around. The nearest farmhouse was over a mile away, but it was still daylight. 'Did anyone pass you? Did anyone see you?'

She shook her head.

'I don't know. I think I passed someone at the junction. I can't remember. They're going to recognise me, aren't they?'

'Fuck.'

'I'm so sorry, James. They're going to send me to prison. They're going to take me away from Scarlett. Away from you.'

She cried into her coat. Her bright yellow coat that could be seen from a hundred feet away – her bright red hair that people always remembered her for.

Fucking hell.

I grabbed her by the shoulders.

'Listen,' I said. 'You have to pull it together. For Scarlett. OK?' I took her hands and pulled her up gently. 'Do you understand? Joanna?'

She nodded, wiping her nose on her sleeve.

'The keys are in the ignition of my car,' I said. 'You need to drive Scarlett home, then get rid of these clothes. OK?'

She nodded again.

'For Scarlett,' I said, directing her. I opened the car door, placed her inside and pulled across the seatbelt. 'Joanna!'

She looked up at me, her eyes wide with shock, panic.

'It's only a few minutes. You have to do this. I'll drive your car home, OK?'

'What are you going—'

'Don't ask me that, Joanna. And don't mention this to anyone. If we get through tonight, then everything will be OK. Right?'

'Yes. Everything will be OK.' She turned on the ignition. 'Her name's Natalie Baxter. She's so young.'

'Natalie Baxter,' said Scarlett from the back seat. 'Natalie Baxter! Natalie Baxter's asleep on the road.'

Joanna turned around slowly.

'You're here, my baby,' she said. 'I'll get you home safe, sweetheart.'

'You sure you can do it?' I said.

'I can do it.'

I watched as she slowly navigated out of view and hoped to God that she managed it.

I walked towards the woman lying on the ground. You wouldn't have known she was dead to look at her, except for the trickle of blood that ran out of her right ear. Like Simon.

I had another look around, scanning the landscape, the farmhouse. All clear.

I dragged her by the feet into the field for as long as I could, for ten minutes, until I came to a small mound. It was a well that had long since dried up. I pulled her feet down first, then pushed her shoulders until I heard the crack of bones at the bottom. I scooped dirt with my hands, digging deep into the mud and threw it down the hole.

My heart was racing and I was breathless by the time I got back to the road. I pulled my sleeve over my hand and wiped the door handle of the Fiesta that Jo must've pulled open.

I got into the driver's seat of Jo's car. Thank God her keys were still in the ignition. I drove without headlights until I reached the main road.

As long as we got through the night without a knock on the door, everything would be OK.

How wrong I was. It took thirteen years for that knock at the door. Poor Scarlett doesn't realise she saw the dead body of Natalie Baxter all those years ago from her little car seat.

* * *

Scarlett comes back and places two plastic cups of orange squash on the table, one in front of her mother, the other in front of me.

It's a small act that warms my heart. There must be one in there somewhere.

'Thanks so much, Scarlett,' I say, reaching over to touch her hand, but she swipes it away.

She glances up at me and the hatred in her eyes actually pierces my chest.

It's a feeling my father must've felt every time I looked at him. Every prison visit my scorn towards him was palpable between us.

What Scarlett doesn't realise is that without me, she wouldn't have a mother on the outside, either. And there's no way she can ever know that.

They're going to move somewhere else, probably change their names. Become other people. Forget about me.

It turns out karma is real.

And it's a fucking bitch.

A LETTER FROM ELISABETH CARPENTER

I want to say a huge thank you for choosing to read *The Family on Smith Street*. If you want to keep up to date with all my latest releases, just sign up at the following link. Your email address will never be shared and you can unsubscribe at any time.

www.bookouture.com/elisabeth-carpenter

I love exploring reasons that make people act the way they do, and the lengths they'd go to, to protect the people they love. In contrast, I like to inject a little love and humour into my books. Where there is shadow, there is light, and I hope this adds an all-important human element to my work.

Thank you again for reading my book. I hope you enjoyed it and, if you did, I would be very grateful if you could write a review. I'd love to hear what you think, and it makes such a difference helping new readers to discover one of my books for the first time.

I love hearing from my readers – you can get in touch on my Facebook page, through Twitter, or my website.

Best wishes,

Elisabeth

KEEP IN TOUCH WITH ELISABETH CARPENTER

elisabethcarpenter.co.uk

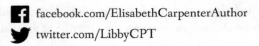 facebook.com/ElisabethCarpenterAuthor
twitter.com/LibbyCPT

ACKNOWLEDGEMENTS

Thank you so much to my agent, Caroline Hardman. Thank you to the team at Hardman & Swainson, the best literary agency in the world!

Thank you to Susannah Hamilton, my wonderful editor, whose notes and suggestions have been invaluable. Thank you to the wonderful team at Bookouture – it's the start of a fabulous adventure!

Thank you to my family and friends for your constant support. Thank you to Sam Carrington, Caroline England, and Carolyn Gillis for always being there.

Thank you to my readers – I hope you enjoy this one!